The Grand Passion

She had no idea how it happened. She'd concentrated so intently on her plot for revenge—on every step in the carefully mapped route toward his seduction—that she hadn't noticed that she herself was being seduced. It was only when she lay trembling in his arms after he'd kissed her that the awareness burst on her like a sharp blow to the face: she loved him.

Until that moment it had seemed so certain that the game was hers. At every crucial crossroad, when he could have chosen a path away from her, she'd won. It had seemed so easy. Too easy. Why hadn't she seen it before? Lotherwood was too clever to be taken in by a woman playing a game. He was not fooled by pretense. It was her *real* feeling that had taken him in!

Elizabeth Mansfield
The Grand Passion

A JOVE BOOK

THE GRAND PASSION

A Jove Book / published by arrangement with
the author

PRINTING HISTORY
Jove edition / June 1986

ISBN: 0-515-08697-5

Jove Books are published by The Berkley Publishing Group,
200 Madison Avenue, New York, N.Y. 10016.
The words "A JOVE BOOK" and the "J" with sunburst
are trademarks belonging to Jove Publications, Inc.

PRINTED IN THE UNITED STATES OF AMERICA

❧ *Prologue* ❧

Matthew John Lotherwood, the Marquis of Bradbourne, had no interest in having his fortune told. From his place near the doorway of his aunt's enormous ballroom, he eyed with amused disdain the long line of guests who stood waiting like gullible sheep to hear the gypsy woman (hired by his aunt, Lady Wetherfield, for the occasion) read their fortunes in their palms, on cards, or in her crystal ball. Throughout the many hours of the ball's duration, a steady stream of the most *haute* of London's *ton* had been waiting in that line. "Mooncalves and cods-heads the lot of them," Lotherwood said to a crony standing nearby, and they both, laughing, turned and made their way through the crowd to the buffet.

Lady Wetherfield's annual ball was always a squeeze. Even the most jaded of partygoers was eager to accept an invitation to one of her galas, for she could always be counted on to provide something more than dancing and a supper of lobster cakes and champagne. She invariably added a distinctive touch—a group of Turkish dancers in native dress, perhaps, or a troupe of acrobatic jugglers. The *ton* agreed that no one was better than Letitia Wetherfield at surprising her guests with some sort of original, enjoyable entertainment. This year was no exception. In fact, it was beginning to look as if her special surprise this evening—the fortune-telling gypsy woman —might turn out to be one of her greatest successes.

Lady Wetherfield had installed her gypsy (a certain

Madame Zyto) on the balcony overlooking the ballroom, under a colorful tent-top of green and gold striped duck cloth, expecting to attract some mild interest from the older females who did not dance. She didn't dream, however, that almost every one of her one hundred and fifty guests would wish for a reading. Getting a glimpse into one's future was proving to be a most popular diversion.

Lotherwood, finding the crowd around the buffet too dense, gave up the struggle and turned away from the food. He leaned against one of the ballroom's fluted pillars and amused himself by studying the faces of the guests waiting to see the gypsy. The women were eager and impatient, but the men consistently pretended to indifference. It was farcical to him to note that, while they were undeterred by a wait of almost an hour, the men scoffed loudly and disparagingly as they stood in line, not one of them admitting to feeling even the least bit of credulity in the efficacy of fortune-telling in general or this gypsy in particular. But he couldn't fail to notice that, when they sat down at the gypsy's table, despite their previous pretense of scorn for this whole activity, they all paid fascinated attention to every look on the gypsy's face and every word she uttered. And when they left her company and climbed down the stairs again, they were either vociferously elated or noticeably dejected by what they'd heard.

"Ain't you going to hear what she has to say, Matt?" came a voice at his elbow. He turned to find his friend, Lord Kelsey, at his side. Randolph Kelsey, overdressed as usual in a striped satin waistcoat and sporting the highest shirtpoints in the room, was observing the gypsy through his quizzing glass. "You ought to go up there before too long, you know. The queue'll only get longer once supper's over."

"Not I," Lotherwood answered with a shrug. "I've nothing much to learn about my future, now that I'm leg-shackled."

Lord Kelsey laughed. "You're right. As a betrothed man, your future is too disgustingly clear."

Lotherwood sighed in rueful agreement. It *was* too disgustingly clear. He'd held back from wedlock for as long as he could, but finally, at thirty-two, he could postpone it no longer. For all these years he'd been contentedly living the life of the Compleat Corinthian—young, strong, and wealthy, he'd concentrated his energies on nothing more than sports and amusements. Like others of his set, he'd not permitted

himself to become involved in anything serious. Every subject—war, politics, the national economy, even marital
love—was to be taken lightly and made the object only of wit-
ticisms. Sport was the primary interest of the true Corinthian,
but even in this he did not become emotionally involved.
Whether he won or lost the game, the Corinthian greeted the
result with equal imperturbability. The playing was all.

Lotherwood was one of the fortunate ones who excelled at
everything he tried, but his reputation as a sportsman was particularly enviable in horsemanship. When it came to horses,
whatever the sport (riding, handling the ribbons, riding to the
hounds), there was hardly an honor he hadn't won. But lately
he'd begun to find the excitement of the chase wearing thin.
He was in his thirties now; he had begun to realize that it was
time to put aside these boyish pursuits and turn his attention
to more mature concerns.

He'd already taken the first step toward his future by
becoming betrothed. His betrothal was completely in keeping
with Corinthian tradition: the girl he'd chosen was as pretty,
well-bred, lighthearted, and accomplished as anyone on the
Marriage Mart, and, most important, one did not have to lose
one's head over her. No true Sporting Gentleman would allow
himself to be shattered by love. In love, as in sport, one kept
one's head.

His friend Dolph Kelsey was certainly in the right of it,
Lotherwood realized as he stood watching the fortune-teller
do her work. His future *was* disgustingly clear. No gypsy
would have trouble guessing it, for it promised to be a completely predictable existence: quiet years on his Essex estates
dealing with the business of the lands, raising a brood of
children, and settling down each evening at his hearth with an
unexceptional wife. What could a gypsy tell him about his
future that he didn't already know?

The two gentleman continued to observe the gypsy at her
work. The woman was undoubtedly talented, Lotherwood
thought as he watched. She was a withered old crone, but her
long, gnarled fingers showed a youthful agility as they flipped
through her cards or lingered lovingly on her crystal ball.
Madame Zyto sat behind a round, draped table like a queen
holding a series of private audiences, dispensing futures, dark
or bright, with a dignified, awesome disinterest. There was an
exotic witchery in the almost skeletal shape of her cheeks and

the blackness of her eyes. "Why don't you go up there, Dolph?" Lotherwood suggested suddenly. "You'll probably be vastly entertained."

"I already have. She told me I'm soon to be wed, to a girl of much sweetness. Did you ever hear the like? There ain't a girl in all of our acquaintance whom I could describe as one of 'much sweetness.' Can you?"

Lotherwood shook his head. "Not one, with the exception of the lovely young chit who's hurrying toward us right now."

Dolph turned and peered at the approaching figure through his glass. "Oh, your Viola! Well, I can't count *her,* now that you've staked your claim."

And indeed the young lady approaching did have an aspect of charming sweetness. Viola Lovell was slightly under average height, with a figure that was both slim and softly rounded. She wore a rose-colored gown that shed a glow upon a complexion unmarred by the slightest imperfection, although at the moment the additional glow was not needed. The girl was pink with excitement, and her bronze-gold curls bounced as she hurried toward them. "Oh, Matt," she cried as she drew near, "it was simply amazing! The gypsy woman knew *everything about me!* It was quite uncanny. She must be *bewitched!*"

"Really, Vi?" Dolph asked curiously. "What did she tell you?"

"She knew my age to the month, and that I had a married sister who is with child. And she said that I excelled at the pianoforte and that I would be wed this summer! Is that not remarkable?"

Lotherwood tucked her arm in his and patted her hand soothingly. "Don't excite yourself, my dear. I see nothing very remarkable in that. Every young woman of education excels at the pianoforte, does she not? And as for your being wed in summer, since our banns were announced this very week in *The Times,* it is hardly surprising that the gypsy foretold the wedding."

"But she could not have known who I was, could she? There are at least one hundred and fifty people here."

Lord Kelsey smiled down at her indulgently and took her other arm. "But Miss Bubblehead, don't you know that almost every one of the hundred and fifty are babbling about your betrothal? The gypsy's bound to have heard something of it.''

The gentlemen, as if in accordance with a prearranged plan, turned to lead her toward the buffet tables. But Viola hung back. "Oh, pooh! I don't believe she can have known me,'' she insisted. "There's something otherworldly about the woman, really there is. Matt, please, you *must* go up to hear what she says to you! I shall *die* of curiosity if you don't.''

Lotherwood, having been frustrated earlier in his attempt to get to the buffet, was by this time much more interested in his aunt's famous lobster cakes than in bothering about a wizened old fortune-teller. "Anyone in the room can tell you my fortune, if you're so curious,'' he told his betrothed. "Ask Dolph, here. Tell her, Dolph. Make a prediction that I shall settle down in Essex with a charming wife and become a docile and respectable husband—''

"*Please*, Matt!'' Viola implored. "Perhaps she'll foresee that we shall travel abroad! Would *that* convince you that she has mystical powers?''

"Since there's hardly a couple of our acquaintance who does *not* travel abroad on their wedding trip, I would be more impressed with her powers if she'd foresee *no* sea voyage in my future," Lotherwood teased. But Viola's eyes were looking up into his with such beseeching charm that he had to surrender.

He left his betrothed in Kelsey's care and joined the queue waiting for the gypsy with the good sportsmanship of a Corinthian who'd lost a contest. But the line moved very slowly, and by the time Lotherwood was seated at the table on the balcony, his usually easygoing nature had been pushed to its limits. Moreover, the way Madame Zyto cocked her head and fixed a glittering eye on him did nothing to assuage his irritation. "Get on with it, woman,'' he muttered. "I've already waited over an hour. I want to get to the buffet before the lobster's gone.''

"Ye're an 'andsome vun, ain't ye, ye gamecock?'' the crone chortled in brazen rudeness, studying his face carefully. Her accent was made of a strange combination of cockney and Romany, yet the words were clear and distinct and the voice free of the hoarseness of old age. "The ladies mus' tumble ower each-other for a smile from ye. Dark 'air, thick lips, poverful chin. Just the sort o' looks ve females itch for.''

Lotherwood raised his brows, both disgusted and amused. "I thought you were to tell the *future*, ma'am," he reminded her pointedly.

"Oh, I see yer future right enough." She passed her hands lightly over her crystal ball but barely looked at it. "Ye're t' be married . . . right soon."

"Yes, so you said to my betrothed. You told her summer."

"Did I? Per'aps so." She shuffled her worn but still colorful cards. "*Your* vedding vill be sooner."

"Oh?" Lotherwood gave a snorting laugh. "How can I possibly be wed before my bride?"

The gypsy woman smiled back, revealing two horrid black teeth. "Because, m' lord, yer betrothed ain't going t' *be* yer bride."

"Indeed?"

"Ah, yes, indeed, indeed. Yer bride'll be somevun else entire."

"You don't say!" He leaned forward and placed his elbows on her table. "Can you see in this crystal ball of yours just who that bride will be?"

The gypsy woman nodded. With a jangle of her bracelets she passed her hands over her ball again and peered within. "I can see 'er plain as a pack-saddle. Tall, she is, vith short, dark 'air." She looked up and cackled loudly. "You can see 'er, too, if ye've a mind."

"I? How can I see her? I thought no one could see into your crystal ball but yourself."

"Not in the ball. Down there, below."

"What?" Lotherwood found himself enthralled despite himself. "Do you mean she's *here?*"

The gypsy woman, smiling an enigmatic smile, lifted her hand. With a long, misshapen, beringed finger she led his eye over the railing and down below to where a group of ladies sat on divans beside the dance floor. Lotherwood rose from his chair and leaned over the banister. Among the seated dowagers was a young woman with thick, dark, cropped curls. At that moment she turned her head and looked up, meeting his eyes. Lotherwood felt a peculiar shock; it seemed as if an inner clock that always beat within his chest suddenly stopped working. The feeling was only momentary, but he couldn't imagine what had brought it on. Was it the eyes looking up at him? He was loathe to admit to himself that those eyes had a mesmerizing effect on him, but they were certainly remarkable—a strangely light blue. "*That* one?" he asked the gypsy in amazement. "The one with the ice-blue eyes who's staring at me?"

"Yes. Indeed, indeed. That vun."

The girl below, noting Lotherwood's stare, raised her eyebrows in cold disdain and turned away. The look was a decided set-down, but Lotherwood continued to peer at her. "How can you make such a ridiculous statement?" he demanded of the gypsy. "I'm not even acquainted with that creature."

"No?" Madame Zyto shrugged her thin shoulders under her fringed, rose-embroidered shawl. "Then ye soon vill be."

Lotherwood, annoyed with himself for falling under the gypsy's spell, turned and looked at her with one eyebrow cocked disapprovingly. "I think, ma'am, that I shall tell my aunt, Lady Wetherfield, that you are a fraud."

The gypsy woman's eyes glowed as they traveled over him from head to toe. "Ye've a good leg, too, ye 'ave. Muscled as fine as a Romany stallion."

"An *incorrigible* fraud." He withdrew a gold coin from his pocket and threw it on the table. "But entertaining, I'll grant you that."

She picked up the coin, bit it, and grinned a black-toothed grin at him. "I thank ye, m'lord. Yer aunt, she know'd I be entertaining. But I varned 'er I tell the truth if I see it plain. I seen it plain just now. The girl vith the ice-blue eyes'll be yer bride."

Lotherwood glanced over the railing and down to the women on the divans. The dark-haired girl was not looking up this time.

The gypsy was suddenly standing beside him. "Aye, m'lord, she's the vun. Yer true bride. Me crystal ball don't lie."

Lotherwood stared at the gypsy woman for a moment in wonder; she seemed so utterly sincere. Then he threw back his head and guffawed. "I almost wish it didn't!" he said when the paroxysm had passed. He continued to chuckle as he walked away, shaking his head and muttering, "My true bride! Indeed, indeed!"

After the last carriage had rolled away down the street, and the lights in the Wetherfield house had darkened, a gypsy wagon rolled up to the back door. The gypsy woman, huddled in her fringed shawl, came hurrying out of the house. Just as she stepped into the street, a cloaked figure emerged from the shadows of the shrubbery. "Madame Zyto? Over here," came a lady's voice.

The gypsy woman told someone in the wagon to wait and went quickly to where the lady in the cloak was standing.

"You did well," the lady said.

With a nod of agreement, the gypsy put out her hand. The lady—a dark-haired girl with ice-blue eyes—wordlessly handed the gypsy woman a bag of coins and disappeared into the shadows.

❧ One ❧

It was almost exactly six months earlier—and hundreds of miles north of London—that Jeremy Beringer paid a call on Tess Brownlow, the girl with the ice-blue eyes. He hesitated in the doorway and glanced across the room at Tess with an expression that was half laughing and half sheepish. His hands were hidden behind his back, his hat was askew, and the tightly curled blond locks of hair that were uncovered by his hat were wet with droplets of melted snow. "May I come in?" he asked with unaccustomed diffidence.

Tess Brownlow, who was negligently lounging in an armchair near the fire with her stockinged feet toasting on the hearth, had been only a moment before staring glumly into the flames. But at the sight of Jeremy Beringer her mood brightened at once. She was always glad to see him. His round, open face exuded cheerfulness, and his eyes held a glow when he looked at her that they held for no one else. Although he had a wide circle of intimates in Todmorden, none of them were as close to him as she. It was a closeness that came from having grown up together and having shared a lifetime of youthful experiences. It was only lately (since the day two months ago when he'd first offered for her) that a tension had sprung up between them. Their friendship had been strained by his declaration of love . . . love that she could not requite. Nevertheless, she now grinned up at him with unalloyed delight. "You gudgeon, Jeremy Beringer! Did you do it *again?* I don't see why you insist on stealing in without Mercliff seeing you. Why do you so dislike being properly announced?''

The young man stepped into the sitting room, closed the door quietly behind him, and grinned back at her. "One, because it's a challenge to find new ways to thwart your mother's stuffy butler. Two, because it's fun. And three, because I love to catch you unawares, as you are now, with your shoes off.''

Tess immediately sat up and reached for her slippers. "You're incorrigible! Still behaving exactly as you did when you were twelve.''

Jeremy ignored the mild rebuke and crossed the room. With a ceremonious bow, he removed from behind his back the beribboned nosegay he'd been hiding and tossed it into her lap. Then he unceremoniously ruffled her dark, short-cropped curls, planted a kiss on her nose, and dropped down on the hearth before her. He took her slippers from her hands and proceeded to put them on for her. "I *don't* behave exactly in the same way," he corrected. "At twelve, I stole over for a game of spillikins. At fourteen it was, if memory serves, silverloo. Now I have a quite different purpose in mind.''

Tess knew very well what his purpose was. He was going to offer for her again. She'd just endured a violent argument with her mother on the subject. "He's going to ask you *just once more,*" her mother had warned, "so if you have a grain of feeling, you'll have him.''

But Tess had strenuously objected. She and her mother never could see eye to eye on the subject of love and marriage. Mama considered her some sort of misfit for having reached the advanced age of twenty-three without ever having experienced what Mama liked to call the Grand Passion. "Freakish, that's what you are!" Mama always reminded her. "I've never heard of anyone who's refused to fall in love by your age!''

But Tess didn't see how she could make herself fall in love. She would certainly do so if she could. She would especially like to feel the Grand Passion for Jeremy. There was no one in the world more gentle, more congenial, more suitable for her to love. But her feelings for him were no stronger than sisterly. Shouldn't she wait, she'd asked her mother, until she found someone toward whom her feelings were stronger?

Mama had groaned with exasperation. "If you searched for *years,* you'd not find a better man for you than Jeremy. Come to your senses, my girl. You're not such a great beauty, you know, that you can expect to pick and choose. You're more than a shade too tall for most men, and your eyes are decidedly piercing. What's more, you're rapidly approaching the age of spinsterhood. So you may as well fall in love at once, or you'll be too late!"

Tess had been saucy enough to laugh. "That's an amusing speech, coming from you, Mama," she'd responded. "You're the one who always likes to prose on and on about the Grand Passion. Should I not wait for the man who can inspire the Grand Passion in me?"

"No, you should not!" her mother had retorted. "You can't wait forever for something that may not occur! Perhaps you're the sort who will *never* feel it. By the age of three-and-twenty any other girl would have fallen in love a half-dozen times! I don't understand you at all, Teresa Brownlow, not at all. How can you be so cruel? Everyone knows the boy has loved you since he was in short coats! We've prayed all these years, Lydia Beringer and I, that you would have him. It's a match made in heaven! Listen to me, Tess. Lydia tells me that Jeremy means to make you another offer this evening, but it is for the last time! Even Jeremy cannot be expected to withstand rejection forever. You've often told me that he's as dear to you as a brother. Then *take him!* If you have any heart in you, love will come later. I've heard that is often the case."

Tess had fixed her "decidedly piercing" eyes on her mother's face. "But what if it should turn out *not* to be the case?" she'd asked pointedly.

Her mother had thrown up her hands in impatience. "Then you will be no worse off than the majority of wives! Do you think *my* life was ecstatic with your father? I may have thought of him as my Grand Passion at first, but I soon learned what a mistake I'd made. Nevertheless, I made the best of it."

"I'm sorry, Mama, but I don't wish to have to say, one day, that I'd 'made the best' of my life."

It was then that Mama had said those vituperative words that still rang in Tess's ears. "Don't think yourself so high above the rest of the world, my girl!" she'd warned in a voice quavering with angry tears. "You are merely a woman, and

women must marry if they are to live any proper sort of life."
She'd pulled a handkerchief from her sleeve and sniffed into it
furiously. "I sometimes think you've no feminine feelings at
all! I hate to admit such a thing about my very own and only
child, but the truth is, Tess Brownlow, that you're *cold!* I've
always suspected it. As cold as your father!"

Jeremy's voice cut into her reverie. "Did you hear me,
Tess? I said I have a different purpose in mind tonight from
the intentions I used to have when we were children. Don't
you want to know what it is?"

"I've already been informed about your purpose," she
answered dryly.

"Oh?" He paused in his attempt to button the strap of her
right shoe. "Who informed you?"

She picked up the little bouquet he'd dropped in her lap.
"Lady Beringer told my mother, and Mama, of course, told
me."

Jeremy frowned in annoyance. "I ought to wring my
mother's neck," he muttered, returning his attention to the
shoe. "I suppose there's no point now in making my little
speech."

Tess merely shrugged and put her nose to the blooms.
"Mmmmm . . ." She sighed, breathing in their fragrance.
"These are a delight. I don't know how you always manage to
find flowers to bring to me, no matter what the season."

"Love makes me resourceful," he responded promptly,
successfully buttoning the little strap. "If you marry me, I'll
always manage to surround you with blossoms."

She stared at him for a moment, a fond warmth toward him
welling up in her throat. *Why not?* she thought suddenly. *He
really is such a dear. And Mama would be so happy. Lady
Beringer would be happy. Jeremy would be happy. In fact,
everyone in Todmorden would be happy!* With her heart
beating rather wildly at this impetuous decision, she buried her
face in the nosegay and murmured, "That will be lovely."

"Irises in April," he went on heedlessly, "armfuls of tea
roses in June, and in July the most glorious white—" He
seemed suddenly to turn to stone. Her left shoe slid from his
grasp unnoticed, while his eyes flew up to her face. "*What* did
you say?" he gasped at last.

"I said," she repeated, smiling at him tenderly, "that it will
be lovely to be always surrounded by blossoms."

Jeremy blinked. His smile faded, and as the import of her remark dawned on him, his cheeks whitened and his Adam's apple bobbed up and down. "Are you saying that . . . that you'll—?"

She nodded at him, her eyes misty.

"Oh, my *Lord!* You're not shamming it, are you?" His expression of disbelief was slowly replaced by one of utter joy. "Do you really mean to *have* me?"

"Jeremy, you looby," she teased, "can't you comprehend a *yes* when you hear it?"

With a cry of triumph, he jumped up and seized her in his arms. Lifting her high off the floor, he swung her round and round, shouting all the while, "Tess, Tess, my darling! My *love!* I can't *believe* it!"

Tess, bereft of breath, leaned a cheek on his hair. "Put me down, you idiot!" she managed to gasp.

"No, I'm *never* going to put you down! I'm going to whirl you round like this until . . . oh, until our wedding day!"

"But you must put me down, my darling, at least for a little while. There are things we must do."

"Do?" He set her on her feet and kissed her breathlessly. "What must we do?"

"We must find my other slipper, for one thing," she laughed, holding him off.

"Yes, I suppose we must." In a blissful daze he wandered back to the hearth, picked up the neglected shoe, and knelt before her to put it on. "Though I don't understand why we must put this on right now."

She looked down and gently stroked his soft, tightly curled hair. He was so sweet and lovable that something inside her seemed to open up . . . to uncurl like the petals of a blossom. *See, Mama?* a voice inside her whispered. *I'm not cold at all!*

He was looking up at her quizzically. "Well? Are you going to tell me?"

"Tell you what?"

"Tell me why are you so concerned about putting on this dashed shoe!"

"Because, my dear," she murmured, kneeling to help him button the little strap, "it would be quite shocking for me to be only half-shod when we go."

"Go?"

"Yes, go." She kissed him quickly, then drew him to the

door. "We must go and tell the news to our respective mothers."

Abruptly he paused in the doorway. "I say, Tess," he mumbled, his face clouding over, "they haven't tried to . . . I mean, you weren't *coerced* into accepting me, were you?"

She put a hand to his cheek in a gesture of reassurance. "When have you ever known me to be coerced into anything?"

"That's right," he said, smiling in relief. "Too mulish by half." He took her two hands in his. "Tess, you don't know how happy you've made me tonight."

"Yes, I do, my love. Because I'm happy, too." And, surprisingly, she did feel happy . . . quite astonishingly happy, considering that only a half hour before she'd had no intention in the world of marrying him.

They proceeded hand in hand down the corridor toward her mother's dressing room, Tess inwardly marveling at her amazing about-face. If he hadn't brought her those unseasonal flowers—

The flowers! She suddenly stopped in her tracks. "Oh, wait just a moment, Jeremy. I've forgotten my nosegay."

She ran back to the sitting room and picked up her bouquet, but instead of hurrying out again, she found herself staring at the blossoms in fascination. Could the course of a life turn on such a little thing as this? she wondered.

After a few moment's hesitation, however, she turned and went purposefully to the door. Yes, it was true that the decision she'd made was impetuous, but she was not having second thoughts. Not at all. She was sure her decision, for all its abruptness, was a good one. If what she felt for Jeremy was not a Grand Passion, it was surely the next best thing. Surely. Wasn't it?

❧ Two ❧

By midnight the passengers who'd gathered at the Bull and Mouth Inn in St. Martins-le-Grand began to grumble. They were bound for Manchester on the night mail, and they'd just been told that their departure would be delayed for another half hour. Since this was the second half-hour delay, and since the weather was decidedly nasty, it was not surprising that the news was greeted with curses and groans. However, it was apparent that standing about in the courtyard in the icy rain would bring them no solace, so six of them (five men and an elderly lady) betook themselves inside to the taproom to warm their innards with mulled ale. Only two passengers, both middle-aged men, remained outdoors. They huddled under the balcony that edged the second story, watching glumly as the postboys splashed about in the downpour loading the baggage atop the stage.

The rain seemed to turn to sleet before their eyes. Most of the windows of the coaching inn were dark by this time of night, but enough light spilled from the taproom windows to show them that the road was getting slick. Though the two travelers were unknown to each other, they exchanged worried glances. Then, as if each could read the other's mind, they both peered up at the dark sky and shook their heads. Everything that surrounded them—the entire surface of the earth— was turning glassy. The wooden gateposts of the courtyard took on a sheen as if they'd suddenly turned to polished silver,

15

the cobbles of the roadway began to reflect back the faint light from the taproom windows, the branches of the spindly trees in the corners of the yard began to glisten, and, most depressing of all to the two travelers, the twigs tinkled every time the wind blew, the brittle sound evoking a feeling of imminent danger.

One of the pair, a portly gentleman with a tall hat and a woolen muffler wound tightly round his neck and over his chin, tested the roadway with his boot and shook his head. "I shouldn't like to be coachman on a night like this," he muttered aloud, keeping his eyes fixed on the postboys so that he wouldn't seem to be addressing his remark to someone to whom he hadn't been introduced.

The other man was not troubled by such niceties of manners. "Think ye they'll call it off?" he asked, facing the portly gentleman with blunt directness.

"Call it off?" He threw his fellow traveler a doleful glance. "Not bloody likely. Not the mail."

The other man frowned. "Are ye thinkin' that per'aps they should?"

"The stage will depart whether I think they should or not," the portly gentleman responded. "The only question is whether they should depart with us or without us. If I hadn't sent my solemn promise to be in Manchester by Friday to examine a sick uncle, I would certainly think twice about going."

"Oh? Ye're a doctor, are ye?"

"Yes, I am. Permit me to introduce myself. Josiah Pomfrett, at your service."

The other man took the proffered hand eagerly. "I'm William Tothill. Honored to make yer acquaintance, sir. I mysel' am on my way to Leeds. On business, y' know. Lookin' at property t' establish a cotton mill. There's a land agent expectin' me, but the appointment ain't so urgent that I should endanger m' life—"

At that moment a covered high-perch phaeton wheeled into the courtyard at breakneck speed and skidded to a halt beside the mail. One of the postboys ran to grasp the horses' halters, and another hurried round the side to let down the steps. But before he could reach the door, it flew open. A young man leaped to the ground, a portmanteau in one hand and an enormous bouquet of flowers wrapped in layers of tissue-thin paper in the other. "We made it!" he shouted happily at the driver of the phaeton. "Thanks, Algy, old fellow!"

The driver, Algy, grinned down at him in triumph. "Told you so!" he shouted through the wind. Flourishing his hat at his friend, he signaled the postboys to step aside. Then, without a moment's pause, he wheeled his horses about and departed. The young man who'd alighted lifted his flowers in a grateful salute to his friend, waving them at Algy until the phaeton disappeared from view. Then he handed his portmanteau to one of the boys and, at last becoming aware of his surroundings, took belated notice of the sleet that was drizzling on his face, accumulating on his hatbrim, and dribbling down into the collar of his greatcoat. He tossed his untied muffler round his neck and looked about him. It was only then that he saw the two men who were watching him from under the balcony. Acknowledging their presence with a friendly salute, he loped over to join them. Once under the sheltering roof, he grinned at them with engaging self-mockery. "I was certain I'd missed it," he confided cheerfully.

"Me an' Dr. Pomfrett 'ere was just sayin' as 'ow per'aps the stage shouldn't depart a-tall in this weather," Mr. Tothill offered.

"What? Not depart?" The young man's cheerful expression changed at once. "Oh, no," he exclaimed in alarm, "that couldn't happen, could it?"

"No, I don't think it could," Dr. Pomfrett said. "Although I'm convinced that the mail coach *should* be detained, I know it won't be. The company has a reputation to uphold. The mail must go out in all weather."

"Thank goodness for that." The young man sighed, relieved.

Dr. Pomfrett studied the young man with shrewd, medically trained eyes. The fellow was well dressed and bore himself with the casual nonchalance of the very rich. However, his face had a pleasant openness about it; there was no sign in it of the smugness, snobbishness, or self-satisfaction that one often noticed in the countenances of members of the upper classes. The boy had too round a face to be considered handsome in the classic sense, but Dr. Pomfrett thought his bright blue eyes, full mouth, and cheerful aspect were most appealing. Excitement and happy anticipation seemed to emanate from every part of the young man's body. Ice or no ice, this young fellow was delighted to be going on this journey.

The doctor, being by nature perfectly suited to his profession (the sort who believes himself born to be a comforter and protector of humankind), felt it incumbent upon him to protect the young man from behaving rashly. No one, he was convinced, should board the stage unless there was a dire necessity for him to do so. "I shouldn't be so quick to give thanks if I were you," he said reprovingly. "The ice is accumulating so rapidly that a person of sense ought to think twice about going. There'll be another stage departing tomorrow, after all. Mr. Tothill was just saying that his appointment in the north is not so urgent as to risk danger. By the way, may I take the liberty of making the introductions? This, sir, is Mr. Tothill, and I am Dr. Pomfrett."

The young man said he was Jeremy Beringer, and they shook hands all around. But despite the cordiality of his greeting, young Mr. Beringer showed no intention of heeding the doctor's warning. "If the stage departs," he declared as soon as the introductions were made, "I shall be on it. Mr. Tothill's appointment may not be urgent, but mine is. I came to London for the express purpose of getting these flowers from a friend who has a magnificent greenhouse, and I want to get them back before they wilt. You see, I'm to be married tomorrow in Todmorden, and *that* appointment I don't intend to miss."

"Your bride-to-be might take it amiss if you appeared at the ceremony on crutches or with your arm in a sling," the doctor countered, "which is just what may happen if the stage slides into a ditch."

"Humbug!" Jeremy Beringer declared blithely, his smile taking the sting out of his blunt dismissal of the good doctor's advice. "These drivers know very well how to go on. I don't believe a little ice on the roads will matter."

Dr. Pomfrett shrugged. "I hope you're right, since I shall be on the stage with you despite my misgivings. I've given my word that I'll be in Manchester myself on the morrow."

"Then I'm goin' as well," Mr. Tothill said, chortling like a boy at the prospect of adventure. "If the two o' ye are game, why, then, I ain't the man t' turn tail. What I say is, let's go inside an' drink on our resolve. A bit o' spirits won't sit ill on such a night as this. Any road, I reckon we're in fer a long, cold journey.''

Ten minutes later the coachman announced that the stage was ready for boarding. Six of the passengers, including the doctor and his newfound companions, took places inside, while the other three climbed up on top to the seats behind the coachman's box. There, with only the minor protection provided to their backs by the pile of baggage, they would ride for sixteen hours completely exposed to wind and weather. ''I don't envy that trio,'' Mr. Tothilll remarked as he watched through the window while they climbed up. ''They'll be chilled through.''

''And they'll come down with inflammation of the lungs before the week is out, no doubt,'' the doctor muttered. ''Damned fools!'' He looked at the four men and one woman who were squeezed in with him in the carriage. ''We're *all* of us damned fools!''

The other passengers ignored the doctor's grumbling and tried to settle themselves comfortably in the space meant for four. Mr. Tothill and Jeremy Beringer took the window seats on one side, with Dr. Pomfrett between them. Opposite Jeremy Beringer sat a gentleman with a neatly pressed coat and expertly tied cravat. Beside him was a bald, bespectacled, elderly man who seemed to be made of nothing but skin and bones. His wife, also somewhat frail, occupied the window seat opposite Mr. Tothill. No sooner was she seated than she removed some knitting needles and a half-finished shawl from her oversize reticule and began to knit.

While the others occupied themselves with finding comfortable positions, Mr. Tothill kept his nose pressed to the window. ''I say!'' he exclaimed after a moment. ''Wut's the to-do now?''

Out in the courtyard the coachman was engaged in an altercation with two gentlemen who'd ridden up on horseback. One was dressed in evening clothes and an opera cape, while the other, also undoubtedly a dandy, was costumed as a *coachman!* Tothill couldn't believe his eyes. There was no doubt the fellow was in coachman's livery, but it was the most elegant coachman's livery Mr. Tothill had ever seen. The man wore a greatcoat woven in a huge houndstooth pattern. The coat sported at least a dozen capes and as many large pearl

buttons which gleamed in the dark. His superbly cut boots
were so highly polished that they, too, gleamed. Even the pro-
saic Mr. Tothill could see that the shine of the boots could
have been achieved only with the aid of an expert valet.
"Wut's a gentleman doin' rigged out like a coachman?" he
wondered aloud.

The doctor, wedged in between Tothill and Jeremy Ber-
inger, shifted round and peered out over Tothill's shoulder.
"It looks as if . . . as if he's handing the coachman a *bribe!*
Look at that! *Damme* if he isn't!"

At this, Jeremy lifted himself up and peered out the window
over the backs of the other two. "Oh, he must be an FHC
man," he said calmly.

"FHC man?" The doctor looked over his shoulder at
Jeremy, his brows raised. "What's that?"

"A member of the Four-in-Hand Club. Most exclusive club
in town. Very *haute ton*. But even a dukedom won't get you in
unless you can handle the reins like a master. Only the most
superb horsemen can be FHC men."

"Yes, but what does your FHC man want with our
coachman?" the doctor persisted. "A fellow like that, rich
and titled, can't wish to ride on the stage, can he? He probably
has all sorts of private carriages—each of them a hundred
times more comfortable than this—and his own horses stabled
in every coaching inn from here to Scotland."

"An' why's 'e rigged out like a bloomin' popinjay?" Mr.
Tothill put in. "If it wasn't fer 'is boots an' those dandified
buttons, I'd take 'im fer a driver."

Jeremy Beringer laughed. "Yes, many of them love to deck
themselves out like coachmen. There's nothing they like better
than driving a stage."

"Are you suggesting, Mr. Beringer," the doctor asked, appalled, "that this fellow is bribing our coachman to let him
drive *this* vehicle?"

"It certainly seems so." Jeremy peered out through the
sleet-coated window to corroborate his theory. "Yes, indeed.
There goes our coachman now, making off to the taproom,
I've no doubt. And here comes the FHC man, making ready
to climb up on the box. Why, he looks somewhat familiar!
I've seen him at Brooke's, I believe. I think his name's Lotherwood."

Dr. Pomfrett reddened in fury. "Of all the . . . ! What consummate effrontery! We must stop him at *once!*"

"But why, doctor?" his young companion asked. "Why do you want to stop him?"

The doctor looked from Jeremy's serene face to those of the other passengers. "Are you all mad? This man proposing to drive us to Manchester is an *amateur!* Are you all intending to put your lives in the hands of a man who thinks driving a stagecoach is a *game?*"

"Mercy me!" the elderly woman murmured, blinking at the doctor in mild alarm but not ceasing her knitting. "Are you saying our lives are at risk?"

"That is *exactly* what I'm saying!"

Jeremy Beringer laughed again. "I mean no disrespect, Dr. Pomfrett, but that's rubbish. We are now in the hands of one of the best drivers in the kingdom. I understood your concern for our safety before, but I assure you that you are now in the very best of hands. The man is *FHC!* Believe me, there are none better at handling horses."

Tothill, at least, was won over. "Makes good sense t' me," he said with a shrug.

The doctor looked at the others. "And the rest of you? Does it make good sense to the rest of you?"

"I've heard of the FHC. Top-notch club," said the neatly dressed gentleman sitting across from Jeremy.

"I'm satisfied," said the bald old man. He turned to his wife with courtly concern. "Are you, m' dear?" he asked her.

"Yes, dear," she answered placidly, continuing to knit in serene indifference to her surroundings. "I am if you are."

"So none of you intends to do anything about this?" the doctor demanded in disbelief.

"I don't know what *you're* going to do, my friend," Jeremy Beringer said, "but I intend to get some sleep." With that he slid back to his seat at the opposite window, laid his bouquet carefully in his lap, stretched his legs out as far as they could go, leaned back, put his hands behind his head, and shut his eyes.

At that moment the carriage began to move. The doctor leaned forward nervously and watched from Tothill's window as the stage was maneuvered smoothly over the icy cobbles of the courtyard. Despite the condition of the roadway, the substitute coachman turned the vehicle onto the thoroughfare without so much as a jolt. The skill with which this feat was accomplished impressed Tothill. "A pretty good beginnin', you'll 'ave t'admit," he said to the doctor.

Dr. Pomfrett, somewhat mollified, sat back in his seat. "I suppose so," he grunted, withdrawing a crushed copy of the London *Times* from his pocket. The manner in which he unfolded it and barricaded himself behind it indicated to any interested spectator that not another word would be heard from him.

Thus the occupants of the stage fell silent. The only sounds were the clatter of the horses' hooves on icy cobbles and the squeak of the coach as it rocked along. The journey northward had commenced.

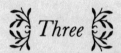

Three

It was sleeting in Todmorden with the same grim determination as in London, so Lady Catherine Brownlow and her daughter Tess sat down to dinner without any expectation of being interrupted by callers. But just as they were about to rise from the dinner table, Mercliff appeared in the dining room doorway to announce that Lady Beringer had arrived.

Lady Brownlow's eyebrows rose. "Tonight? In this dreadful weather? Is anything amiss?"

"I'm sure I couldn't say, my lady," Mercliff muttered, unable to hide a slight shrug at the strange ways of the gentry. "She is waiting in the sitting room."

But Lady Beringer pattered into the dining room just behind him. "I am *not* waiting in the sitting room," she declared eagerly. "I couldn't, shouldn't, and wouldn't wait to show you what I found!"

The unexpected visitor was obviously excited—a condition that had afflicted her the moment she'd learned that Tess was to be her daughter-in-law and that hadn't left her since. She still wore her sleet-spattered cloak and hood, and she carried a loosely wrapped package in her arms with the care and delicacy with which one would carry a baby.

"Good heavens, Lydia, what is so urgent that it takes you out on such a night?" Lady Brownlow asked, getting out of her chair.

"Don't be so pawky," the tiny but spirited Lady Beringer

berated her friend. "It takes a mere three minutes to drive over. One would think I'd come from abroad!"

"But the sleet! Give Mercliff your cloak before you catch your death."

"Never mind my cloak. I found the headdress I told you of, my dear. My grandmother's wedding headdress! Come at once to the sitting room and let us try it on the dear girl! Come, come, Tess, don't dawdle. Wait till you see it!"

Lady Brownlow and Tess dutifully followed Lady Beringer to the sitting room and watched in fascination as she unwrapped her parcel. The headdress proved to be breathtaking. It was a delicate coronet of gold wrought into a circlet of flowers with a beautiful lace veil attached to the back. The two mothers sat Tess down upon the sofa, and as Lady Beringer set the coronet on her head, Lady Brownlow arranged the veil carefully over her shoulders. Then they both stepped back and examined the girl intently.

"Oh, she looks *lovely!*" Lydia Beringer breathed.

"Yes, she does," Lady Brownlow agreed, studying her daughter critically, "although I wish she hadn't cut her hair in that boyish style."

"Oh, Kate, what a hum!" Lady Beringer said, outraged. "You told me yourself that you found the style charming."

"Yes, it *is* charming when she wears a riding habit. But it's a bit informal for a wedding costume, isn't it?"

"Informal or not," Tess informed her mother with a twinkle of amusement, "it will have to do. I can't grow much more by the day after tomorrow."

"Be still, you clunch," her mother ordered. "We are not seeking your opinions. You are only the bride."

"Come, Tess," Lydia Beringer urged. "Take a look at yourself in the mirror there. What do you think of it?"

"I don't know why I should bother to look," Tess said, nevertheless getting up and crossing to an ornate mirror that hung on the south wall between the room's two windows. "As Mama has pointed out, I'm only the bride."

The two mothers followed her across the room, and all three stared into the mirror with fascination. Kate Brownlow would not say so aloud, but she could see at once that Tess made a beautiful bride. Her dark hair and the gold coronet complemented each other, and the antique white veil seemed to emphasize the qualities that made the girl beautiful. Kate did not always find her daughter's looks to be satisfactory. The girl's eyes were sometimes too startlingly light, her chin was too strong, and her mouth too wide. But now, with her face surrounded by the mist of veiling and her hair curling over the gold circlet, she looked positively delectable.

"Perfect!" Lady Beringer murmured. "It couldn't be more perfect."

"Do you think perhaps . . ." Lady Brownlow cocked her head to the left and squinted at the vision in the mirror. ". . . a few plumes? To make it a bit more modish?"

Lydia Beringer cocked her head to the right. "Perhaps. I'm not certain," she said dubiously.

"I have some splendid ones on my blue bonnet. Wait just a moment. I'll get them." And Lady Brownlow hurried from the room.

Lady Beringer and Tess sat down near the fire to wait. Tess removed the headdress and laid it in her lap. "I've been wondering, Lady Lydia," she said without looking at her companion, "if you've ever had any misgivings about . . . about your son's choice of a wife."

"Misgivings?" Lydia Beringer looked over at Tess in surprise. "How can you ask something so silly? For me, as for your mother, this is a dream come true!"

"I know you both have dreamed of it since we were children. To cement your lifelong friendship. To join the two estates. To ensure the proper breeding of your grandchildren. I understand all that. But the truth is that I . . . I may not be the best wife for Jeremy."

"Tess!" Lady Beringer leaned forward, peering at her future daughter-in-law in sudden concern. She was a tiny woman, given to quick movements and abrupt gestures, and the feeling of alarm that Tess's words had given her made her shake her head nervously, causing the long gray-blond tresses that hung down over her ears in corkscrew curls to tremble. "What makes you say such a thing?"

Tess fingered the lace veiling absently. "For one thing, Mama thinks that I'm cold.'"

"Teresa Brownlow! That's not *so!*" Lady Beringer declared, her curls trembling even more. "She *couldn't!*"

"She could and she does. She said it to me just the other day. 'The truth is, Tess Brownlow, that you're cold. As cold as your father!' Those were her very words."

Lady Beringer, horrified, made one of her hasty gestures with her hands. "No! Oh, *no!* If she said those words, she surely didn't *mean* them. I *assure* you, Tess, my love—"

"Even if she didn't mean them, I keep wondering if they're true." Tess turned her eyes to a large portrait of her father which had hung over the mantel for as long as she could remember. "Look at him," she said with a sigh. "I *am* quite like him, am I not?"

Lord Brownlow, strikingly tall and handsome in his magisterial robes, glowered down at them from the wall. But Tess didn't mind the forbidding expression; she was quite accustomed to it. In her childhood she used to spend hours studying the face of the father who'd died when she was in her infancy. By now she was quite comfortable with that glower. In fact, she couldn't imagine her father with any other expression. She wondered if her father had ever laughed. Strange ... her mother rarely spoke about him. But Tess had always suspected that Hubert Maximus Morden, Lord Brownlow, was a cold fish. The artist who'd painted him hadn't even tried to disguise the icy disdain with which he seemed to view the world.

Lady Beringer was also gazing up at the portrait. "No, you're not like him at all," she stated flatly, emphasizing her point with a swing of both her hands and a shake of her head. "You have some of his physical qualities, of course—long limbs, greater-than-average height, strong chin, that darker than dark hair, and lighter than light eyes. In those things you are your father's daughter. But in your nature I believe you are quite yourself."

Tess hoped her mother-in-law-to-be was right. She didn't want to be like her father. She'd always believed—at least until her mother had made that cruel accusation—that she was a woman capable of performing daring deeds for the good of mankind. She wanted very much to believe that she'd been set down on the earth to accomplish something worthwhile ... something beyond the mere propagation of the species. There were times in her life when things happened that set her pulses racing and her spirits aflame. "I *am* capable of strong feelings, am I not?" she muttered, half to herself.

"Of *course* you are!" Lady Beringer cried with sincere vehemence. "Of course you are! Why, everyone remembers the time when your mother's bailiff attempted to oust the

Olneys from their tenancy just because Jem Olney was suspected of poaching, and you immediately and quite violently asserted yourself on their behalf. I'll never forget how you stamped your foot and said that they'd be turned out over your immobile corpse! 'Shall we permit a family with six children to be thrown out on the road just because they might have dined on an illegal pheasant?' you declared in ringing tones. Oh, how we all cheered you that day! You were simply wonderful! And you should see yourself when you argue parliamentary matters with your Uncle Charles. You can be positively passionate at such times."

Tess flicked a quick glance at Lady Beringer's face and then looked away. Being passionate on parliamentary matters was one thing, but being passionate in marriage was quite another. It was with matters of love that Tess was most concerned at the moment. Was Mama right that most normal girls had experienced the Grand Passion by their mid-twenties? Was something wrong with her?

But this was not a question that was proper to put to Lady Beringer. She'd said too much already. Besides, it was clear that her mother and Jeremy's were both too elated by the prospect of their marriage to admit the existence of any sort of impediment. She had best drop the subject. Perhaps Mama was right; perhaps she would learn to feel more deeply for Jeremy after a while.

Fortunately, Lady Brownlow returned at that moment and ended any possibility of the continuation of the conversation. Lady Beringer turned her attention to the plumes with such concentration that Tess almost believed she'd forgotten the exchange completely. Lydia Beringer probably didn't take anything Tess had said at all seriously. It was the headdress she was serious about.

The two mothers led Tess to the sofa and replaced the coronet on her head. With rapt concentration they held the plumes against the coronet, turning them this way and that. "Well? What do you think?" Kate Brownlow asked her friend.

"I don't know. They may be modish, but I think fresh flowers woven in amid the gold would be prettier."

"Fresh flowers?" Kate snorted. "Where do you propose we find fresh flowers in the dead of winter?"

"We shall have them," Lydia Beringer said smugly.

"Jeremy's bringing an armload back with him from London. I think he'd prefer flowers on the headdress to the plumes, don't you, Tess, dearest?" She perched on the sofa beside Tess and gave her hand a comforting squeeze. "Oh, I shall feel so much better about things when Jeremy's back. And so will you, my love," she added sotto voce. "When Jeremy returns, you'll feel better about *everything*."

☙ *Four* ❧

As the London–Manchester stagecoach rocked monotonously on through the night, the passengers, one by one, succumbed to sleep. Even Dr. Pomfrett, lulled by the rocking and the sound of the sleet drumming away on the roof, eventually dropped off. Only the old woman remained awake, her fingers busily at work on her knitting despite the darkness of the coach. When Dr. Pomfrett next opened his eyes, five hours had passed.

The good doctor peered about him nervously. Something had wakened him, but he wasn't sure what it was. Perhaps it was the dawn, which had just sent its first gray rays into the black sky. After a moment, however, he realized that something more dramatic than the dawn had jarred him awake—it was the rocking of the coach. Instead of the soothing cradlelike motion that had put him to sleep, the rocking had become violent. *Good God,* he thought, *the driver's picked up speed! Much too much speed!*

Though he could feel his stomach constrict in alarm, he didn't wish to wake the others and make a fool of himself again. Carefully he leaned over the sleeping Mr. Tothill and lowered the window. Ignoring the sting of the icy wind on his face, he stuck his head out the window. The coachman could be heard through the wind, singing a drinking song at the top of his voice. *Was the fellow drunk?* Dr. Pomfrett wondered. "I say," he shouted, "slow down!"

When there was no response, he repeated his order. But the singing continued, and the carriage proceeded on its way at what seemed to the doctor breakneck speed. "Does anyone up there hear me?" he shouted at the top of his voice. "Tell the coachman to rein in!"

The singing stopped. "Who's tha' yellin' down there?" The speaker's enunciation was slurred and his tongue thick with drink.

"I'm Dr. Pomfrett. And I insist that you slow this vehicle down!"

"Dr. Pomfrett, eh? A surgeon, are you?"

"I don't see what that has to do with—"

"You don't, eh? Then le' me explain. You're tellin' me how t' drive, are y' not? Well, doctor, how would y' like it if I came into your surg'ry an' tol' you how t' remove your patient's diseased spleen?"

"Damn it, man, the roadway's covered with *ice!* I don't have to be an expert driver to see that you're being reckless!"

One of the passengers seated above poked his head out over the little railing. His hat was tied onto his head with his muffler, and his nose and cheeks were red as beets from the cold. But his expression was surprisingly cheerful; he'd evidently become inured to sitting out in the cold. *He must be numb,* the doctor thought.

The passenger looked down at the doctor with a grin. "Don' take on so, m' good man," he advised. " 'Is lordship, 'ere . . .' e's done remarkable well so far, ain't 'e?" He waved his gloved hand over the side. Clutched in it was a bottle of spirits. " 'Ere. Catch this! A dram o' rum'll calm y' down."

The doctor made no attempt to catch the bottle, which fell to the ground with a crash. Several voices from above groaned at the sound. "Blast 'im," someone cursed weepily, " 's broken. All spilt."

"Good heavens, are you *all* drunk up there?" the doctor asked.

" 'Ow else're we t' keep warm?" someone responded.

"Lucky fer us 'is lordship supplied us wi' drink!" shouted another. "I couldn't elsewise 'ave survived the night."

"Coachman!" Dr. Pomfrett barked angrily. "I demand that you slow down at once! As a doctor, I know how drink impairs one's perceptions. You are putting us all in danger."

"Take a damper!" the unseen coachman flung back.

"Nothin's wrong wi' my perceptions. Watch how I take tha' curve ahead, and y'll see how m' percep—oh, my *God!*"

The exclamation made the doctor's blood run cold. He looked ahead to see a farm wagon coming toward them. It was so close that a collision was unavoidable. The turn in the road had kept it out of sight until the last moment. The mail was moving too quickly to stop in time. Before anyone had time to draw another breath, the horses of both vehicles reared. As if in a dream, the doctor saw the wagon's front end rise up and then fall back with a crash. The stagecoach, meanwhile, swayed dizzily from left to right and back again and then tipped over to the doctor's right. The sway threw the doctor back into the coach, causing his head to strike the window frame. It was a shatteringly painful blow, and he knew no more.

His next sensation was of a dash of icy water on his face. He opened his eyes to find Tothill bending over him. "Doctor? Can ye open y'r eyes?"

"Tothill? Wha—?"

"Thank God ye've come to, Doctor Pomfrett. If ye can stand, we've need of ye."

With Mr. Tothill's help, Dr. Pomfrett rose gingerly. His head ached painfully, but his thoughts were clear; therefore concussion was unlikely. His methodical medical mind quickly diagnosed his own condition. Cranial bruise in the dorsal area, not serious. Pelvic bone jarred but not broken. "I'm all right," he told Tothill brusquely and looked about him.

He saw that he was standing in the middle of the road before a scene of chaotic destruction. The morning light, though gray and dismal, revealed the wreckage of the mail coach in hideous detail. The vehicle was lying on its side, the underside completely caved in. It was apparent from the flotsam in the road and the condition of the carriage that it had been dragged on its side for some distance—so far, in fact, that the overturned farm wagon was almost out of sight down the road. The gentleman in the coachman's greatcoat and the man with the hat tied to his head were standing on the wreckage, tossing aside shattered pieces of wood with urgent intensity. The doctor wondered with a chill at his heart if anyone was trapped within.

At his right he could see the neatly dressed gentleman, now looking decidedly disheveled, seated on a portmanteau and

holding his head in a pair of bloody hands. Behind him in the
roadway lay a dead horse. The other horses were all gone.
Tothill noticed the direction of the doctor's gaze. "We put the
poor animal out o' its misery," he explained. "The others ran
off."

Dr. Pomfrett now became aware of a soft, female wailing.
In answer to his questioning look, Tothill took his arm. "It's
'er 'usband. 'E's just layin' on 'is back, unconscious. Will ye
come an' take a look at 'im?"

For the next half hour Dr. Pomfrett had no time to think.
Almost everyone on the coach had sustained some sort of injury, it seemed, and no one but the doctor was capable of
treating the wounds. But the doctor had no idea where his
medical bag was buried, and he could offer only the most
rudimentary assistance. Mr. Tothill felt that the elderly man
was the most seriously injured, but the doctor found that it
wasn't so. The old man had fainted, but when he was brought
round the doctor found nothing more serious in his condition
than a sprained wrist and a large swelling on his bald head. His
wife, on the other hand, who was sitting on the ground beside
her husband and weeping softly, had not noticed a severe
laceration on her own cheek. It had probably been made by
one of her knitting needles. She still clutched the needles
tightly in her hands, but she didn't seem to be aware that the
shawl she'd been knitting was hanging from them in shreds.
Long strands of yarn stretched from her lap to someplace
under the wreckage.

The doctor, unaccountably moved by the destroyed knitting, knelt beside her and gently wrested the needles from her
fingers. He bound her bloody cheek with a large handkerchief;
it was all he could do for her now. Perhaps it was fortunate
that the confusion of her mind muffled the shock of the accident for her. With an almost-silent sigh, he got to his feet and
turned his attention to the other victims. One of the outside
passengers had dislocated a shoulder; another, who had fallen
from the box into the ditch on his face, had so much blood
pouring from his nose that the doctor had the greatest difficulty in staunching it. And the neatly dressed gentleman, completely dazed, had suffered a torn ear and a broken arm. The
doctor patched up these wounds as best he could under these
straitened circumstances. It was not until he'd done all he

could that he suddenly realized he'd seen nothing of Jeremy Beringer.

It was then that the nobleman-turned-coachman tapped him on the shoulder. Dr. Pomfrett turned to face a tall, dark-eyed man whose face was ashen and whose eyes were agonized with guilt. A trail of blood trickled down his face from under his high hat. "You've been injured," the doctor said flatly. "Take off that hat and let me look—"

"Never mind that. Will you come with me, please?" The thick drunkenness of his voice was no longer in evidence. The accident had completely sobered him. The doctor followed him round the wreckage to what had been the carriage roof. A small opening had been gouged out of it. Mr. Tothill and the man with the hat tied to his head were kneeling before it, staring inside with looks of horror on their faces, but when they heard footsteps they rose quickly to their feet and stepped aside.

The coachman got down on hands and knees and crept inside the hole. Dr. Pomfrett followed. There, surrounded by wreckage, Mr. Jeremy Beringer lay prone, a bouquet of blossoms, miraculously almost unblemished, sheltered in the crook of one twisted arm.

Dr. Pomfrett's heart froze for a moment in his chest. It was many seconds before he was able to expel his breath. "Shall I turn him over?" the coachman asked in a whisper, a flicker of hope mixed with the despair in his voice.

The doctor shook his head. He didn't need to turn the fellow over to learn the truth. He knew at once that the young man would never attend his wedding in Todmorden. Jeremy Beringer was dead.

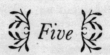

Five

The sleety rain had ended and the sky was actually showing patches of blue by late afternoon of Tess's wedding day, giving both the mother and the mother-in-law of the bride cause for optimism. Although the groom had not yet arrived from London, no one in either the Beringer or Brownlow household was particularly worried. It was to be expected that the dreadful weather of the previous twenty-four hours would have delayed the stage. Everyone agreed that Jeremy would surely return in plenty of time for the wedding.

Meanwhile, arrangements for the ceremony were swiftly proceeding. Lady Brownlow had already made several forays down to the kitchen to supervise the preparation of an elaborate dinner for thirty guests. The butler was busily at work in the library (where the vicar would be conducting the brief service), turning it into a miniature chapel by clearing out all the more massive pieces of furniture and setting the chairs into formal rows facing the fireplace before which the vicar and the betrothed couple would stand. All the housemaids were frenziedly dusting and polishing every chandelier, banister, and windowsill in the house, while Lady Beringer, who'd come over at the crack of dawn to assist in the preparations, was directing the footmen in the placement and hanging of a number of festoons and swags which she'd brought with her to decorate the doorways and stairs-rails.

Tess had been ordered by her mother to remain in her room

to rest. She'd tried to comply with her mother's wishes, but the bustle from below made her nervous, and she'd spent the past several hours pacing from the window to the dressing-room door and back again. This banishment to her bedroom, she realized, was no way to keep her mind from dwelling on her doubts.

The sound of a carriage rolling up the drive sent her flying to the window. She recognized the crest at once. It was her cousin Julia, who was to stand as her matron of honor. Julia and her husband, Sir Edward Quimby, had come all the way from London for the ceremony and had, astonishingly, arrived early! Tess flew out of her room and down the stairs to greet them. "Julia, my dearest!" she cried and flung her arms about the still-cloaked new arrival. "I've never been so glad to see anyone in all my life!"

Before Julia had a chance to respond to this effusive greeting, the entryway became thronged with people, each one with a specific and different purpose in mind. Kate and Lydia emerged from their respective activities to greet the new arrivals, the footmen from London came in from the coach to hand over the baggage to the resident footmen, Sir Edward gave instructions to his coachman regarding the stabling of the horses, and Mercliff moved about in the throng, smoothly directing the footmen to their destinations, ordering the maids to set out tea in the morning room, sending the Londoners' servants below stairs for a warm libation, and collecting from the guests all the cloaks, hats, gloves, shawls, and galoe shoes that travel in this weather required.

In the midst of all the excitement, Lydia Beringer (having overheard Julia telling her aunt that they'd covered the miles between London and Todmorden in less than fifteen hours) managed to inquire of Sir Edward how it was that they'd made the trip from London in such good time. "Why, the London stage was supposed to have left at ten last night," she told him, suddenly worried.

"We left a bit earlier than that," the calm, bespectacled Edward reassured her. "And besides, a private carriage can always make better time than the stage. I'm certain that the mail coach was forced to make stops along the way. The ice and sleet were as dreadful as I've ever seen. I wanted to stop a dozen times, but Julia wouldn't hear of it. She was determined to have a few hours of private conversation with her cousin before the other guests arrived to clutter up the premises."

"Really, Julia," Lady Brownlow said in disapproval, "if your husband wished to stop during the journey, you should have obeyed him."

Julia and her cousin exchanged a quick look of amusement. "I know the marriage service states that a wife must honor and obey her husband, Aunt Kate, but not necessarily his every little whim. Edward doesn't expect me to acquiesce in everything he says."

"Much good it would do me if I did," Edward said, laughing.

"In any case," his wife added, "he knew how much I wanted to have some time alone with Tess, so he let me have my way."

But an hour was to pass before Julia and Tess could extricate themselves from the others for a few precious moments of intimacy. Even after they'd all had tea and Edward had excused himself and gone up to his room for a nap, Kate Brownlow seemed unwilling to permit the two young women to have some time to themselves. "I don't see what you two have to whisper about that we can't hear," she said querulously.

"Come now, Kate," Lady Lydia said, rising from the tea table and making for the door, "you know how it is with young girls. We behaved in the very same way when we were young."

"We most certainly did not! We never would have hinted to our elders that we wished to dispense with their company!"

Except for a mischievous twinkle in her eye, Julia looked repentant. "I didn't mean to suggest that we didn't wish to have your company, Aunt Kate," she began.

"Of course you did," Kate Brownlow snapped, swishing to the door with a great unheaval of skirts and a nose decidedly out of joint, "but since I must return to the kitchen and see what Cook's done with the grouse filets, I take no umbrage. I shall say, however, that in my day a young woman showed greater respect for her elders. I don't know what's come over young women these days. I blame that dreadful Caro Lamb and her ilk. All those cropped curls and that wild behavior and the flouting of the authority of parents and husbands . . . ! Who *knows* where it will end!"

The young women restrained their laughter at the diatribe

until Kate had slammed the door behind her. When their laughter died down, they finally had the chance to examine each other intently. Each felt a curiosity, born of strong affection, to see what changes the past several months had wrought in the other. Having grown up in the same neighborhood, they'd been like sisters until Julia's marriage separated them. Julia was the elder by three years but now seemed even older. A comfortably plump and pleasant-faced young matron, Julia's natural warmth was now a little disguised by a slight touch of London sophistication. She sported a stylishly simple coiffure (long, dusky-blond hair pulled back from her face and tucked tightly into a bun at the top of her head) and a traveling dress of lavender ducapes trimmed with purple velvet that put Tess's country dress of gray worsted decidedly in the shade. "Julia Quimby," Tess exclaimed admiringly, "you've acquired town-bronze! I never thought it of you!"

"Oh, pooh! In town I am almost a mouse," Julia protested.

"Really? To me, my dear, you're looking complete to a shade."

"Am I indeed?" Julia's brow wrinkled. "But you're looking very pale. I thought brides were supposed to have a glow about them. Is anything wrong?"

"I'm not sure. Oh, Julia, I'm so glad you've come! I've wanted so much to have a chance to talk to you."

"Then there *is* something wrong." Julia rose from her chair at the table and perched beside Tess on the love seat. "Are they *forcing* you to wed, Tess? Is that it?"

"No, not at all. Marrying Jeremy was completely my own decision. It's just that I'm not certain that my feelings are sufficiently . . ." She paused, searching for a coherent way to describe the muddle of her feelings.

"Sufficiently what?" Julia prodded.

"Sufficiently . . . strong."

Julia frowned. "Are you saying that you don't *love* Jeremy?"

"I'm saying that I don't know if I love him *enough.*"

"I'm not sure I understand. Love is love, isn't it?"

Tess fixed her eyes on her cousin's face. "Is it, Julia? There are degrees, are there not?"

"Now I'm sure I *don't* understand. Degrees?"

"It's a bit difficult to understand, I suppose," Tess said, running her fingers through her short, troublesome curls.

"Let me see if I can explain. There is friendly love . . . that's one degree. And sisterly love, which is perhaps a higher degree. And wifely love . . . that must be an even higher degree, wouldn't you say?"

"I suppose so. Although I should not have thought of them as differences in degree but in kind."

"In kind? Now *I* don't understand."

"Friendly love and sisterly love are not lower degrees of love. They are different *kinds* of love."

"Yes, I suppose that's so. Then do you think one should marry if one doesn't feel the *wifely* kind?"

Julia, as fond of her cousin as she was of anyone in the world, was suddenly troubled. She took her cousin's hands in hers. "Tess, my love, I'm not sure I know what you mean by wifely love. But my instinct tells me to answer the question with a decided no."

"No?" Tess's eyes flew to her cousin's face. "Are you certain? Love is not the only basis for a sound marriage, is it?"

"I can't think of any other that works half so well."

The young women stared at each other for a moment with worried eyes. Julia wondered if she was saying the right thing. She'd come from London so happily, to be the matron of honor at the nuptials of her favorite cousin, who was also her best friend. She knew Jeremy, too, and was very fond of him. What right had she to give such negative advice? Even the fact that she was older than Tess and had more experience (if one could call being married all of eleven months sufficient experience) did not give her the right to speak on the subject of wedlock with the authority of a seasoned veteran.

She got up and went to the fireplace. Leaning on the mantel, she stared down into the flames and sighed. Tess had never asked her advice before. When they were young and played together, Tess had been the leader. Despite the fact that Julia was older, it had been Tess who originated their adventures and who decided what to do. It was actually rather flattering that Tess now looked to her for guidance; therefore she would not refrain from giving it. "Tess, I don't know if I'm qualified to advise you. But I've learned a little in the course of my less-than-one-year marriage, so I must warn you that it's difficult enough to establish a household with a strange man when one is in love with him. Without love, I shudder to think—"

"*Strange man?* Jeremy is no stranger to me, Julia. I've

known him all my life. And you cannot pretend that your Edward was a stranger to you."

Julia turned from her contemplation of the flames and smiled a wry smile at her cousin. "Believe me, my dear, all men are strange, no matter how well one thinks one knows them beforehand." Her smile widened as she noted the surprise in Tess's face. "Let me tell you how it is," she went on, warming to her subject. "One meets a perfectly charming man, has a perfectly delightful courtship, and goes into marriage with the highest expectations of a lifetime of contentment. And then, ha! The husband suddenly turns pompous when once you found him merely serious. He suddenly becomes jealous when before marriage he was merely protective. He suddenly becomes demanding—expecting you to wait on him hand and foot—when before marriage he was always jumping at your beck and call and fulfilling your every whim."

Tess burst out laughing. "Julia, you humbug! Do you expect me to believe all that? You cannot be speaking of Edward!"

"Of *course* I'm speaking of Edward," Julia declared firmly.

"I don't credit a word of it. You and Edward appear to be the most complacently contended couple in the world."

"Is that how we appear? Complacent?" Julia made a face of mock horror. "How dreadful! I shall take steps to change that image as soon as I return to London. I shall glare at him in public whenever I can, and I'll order him to ogle all the pretty young ladies we see. That should improve matters considerably, don't you agree?"

"As if Edward Quimby would ever ogle anyone but you!" Tess snorted. "He hasn't looked at another female since the day your friend Letty Wetherfield introduced you."

"Nevertheless, my dear," Julia assured her quite seriously, "despite our appearance of complacency, we have both learned, Edward and I, that marriage is not easy. Even if my description of the strangeness of husbands sounded like a humorous untruth, you must not interpret those slight exaggerations as real lies. Everything I said to you has more than a germ of truth. Believe me, if I didn't love Edward, I should be quite revolted with him by this time."

Tess's expression also turned serious. "Are you advising me

not to marry Jeremy? Because if you are, I'm afraid that it is too late. I couldn't withdraw now. I wish we could have talked about this a month ago. A month ago I could have taken such advice, for I'd not yet given him any encouragement. But now that I've agreed to wed him, it would be cruel to renege. He is the dearest, sweetest young man I've ever known, and he has cared for me since we were children. I couldn't bear to hurt him so."

"If you care so much for his feelings," Julia suggested, brightening, "perhaps you love him more than you think you do."

Tess fixed a pair of thoughtful eyes on the hands folded in her lap. "I've been thinking about that possibility myself," she murmured. "I know next to nothing about love, you know. Only what I've read in novels. I'm truly fond of Jeremy. I always have been, since the time we played together as children. But I've always thought these feelings weren't more than sisterly."

Julia sighed, the hopeful look fading from her eyes. "I don't think 'sisterly' is quite enough," she said frankly.

"Yes, but perhaps what I feel *is* more. Since I have no brothers, I don't know what sisterly feelings are, either. I most sincerely care for Jeremy and want to see him happy. It's just that my feelings are not . . . not . . ."

"Not what, my dear?"

Tess's dark lashes fluttered, and she lifted a pair of troubled eyes to her cousin's face. "Oh, Julia, how can I describe my muddled feelings? All I can say is that what I feel is certainly not what Mama refers to as the Grand Passion."

Julia's eyebrows rose in sudden amusement. "A grand passion?"

"Yes." Tess had to smile, too. "When Mama speaks them, those words always sound as if they're capitalized. Do you think what you feel for Edward is a Grand Passion?"

Julia laughed in relief. "Good heavens, my love, I should say not! Is *that* what you think wifely love is? Grand Passion? My dear little innocent, Grand Passions are reserved for the heroines of Italian operas, for members of royalty who are forever being forbidden to marry whom their hearts desire, and for those whose love is unrequited. We ordinary mortals who meet, love, and marry in the ordinary way do not struggle enough or suffer enough to call our affairs Grand Passions."

"But, Julia, didn't you feel a Grand Passion for Edward even at first?" Tess asked, unable to disguise a feeling of disappointment at Julia's unromantic practicality.

Julia gave the question serious consideration. "I don't think so," she answered after a moment. "Oh, I fell in love with him right away . . . and I knew without question that it was love I felt. But to call it a Grand Passion would be, I think, an overstatement. If *that's* all you think is lacking in your feeling for your Jeremy, then don't give the matter a second thought. If you ask me, a Grand Passion is probably more trouble than it's worth."

"Do you really think so?"

"I'm certain of it. All that rodomontade . . . all those declarations, accusations, misunderstandings . . . all that rending an emotion to tatters . . . all those bitter quarrels and weeping reunions . . . ! I tell you frankly, it would all be too much for me."

Tess grinned. "Yes, I see what you mean. It sounds just like the sort of thing Mama enjoys. I would hate it!" She smiled at her cousin as a cloud seemed to lift its shadow from her face. "I must admit that you've lightened a load in my heart. I was truly fearful that something essential was missing from my life."

"I'm glad that I have." The cousins embraced warmly. "And *I* must admit," Julia added, "despite the dreadful things I said before about the state of matrimony in general and my life with Edward in particular, if you and Jeremy do as well as Edward and I, you may look forward to a great deal of happiness! Now, let's make haste and go upstairs. It's almost time for the nuptials! I want to take a look at your gown before we dress."

They ran up to Tess's bedroom, but Julia's exclamations over the beauties of the lace and seed pearls which so lavishly trimmed the gown had hardly been expressed when they were interrupted by a knock at the door. "Sorry to bother you, Miss Tess," Mercliff said from the doorway, "but there's a gentleman downstairs waiting to see you."

Tess noticed an unusual pucker in Mercliff's brow. "A gentleman?" she asked, suddenly apprehensive.

"Yes, miss. Said his name's Pomfrett. Doctor Pomfrett."

"But I don't know any Doctor Pomfrett. Why didn't you call Mama?"

"He asked most particularly for you, Miss Tess. He didn't want to see anyone else. Said it was urgent. He's waiting in the morning room."

Tess threw Julia a quick glance. "Will you come with me, please?"

"He said only you, Miss Tess," the butler said.

"Never mind," Tess snapped. "He'll talk to both of us or not to anyone!"

Tess's feeling of apprehension increased as she hurried down the stairs. Julia, following closely behind, could almost see the tension in the tightness of her cousin's clenched hands and the erectness of her carriage. But the gentleman awaiting them in the morning room did not have a threatening aspect. He was, in fact, a kindly looking man with a tall hat in one hand and a bouquet of flowers in the other. The flowers surprised Julia; where on earth had the fellow managed to find so many varied blooms in the middle of winter?

Tess was also staring at the flowers. Some of them were crushed, and there was a peculiar red smudge on the tissue paper . . .

"Are you Miss Brownlow?" the gentleman was asking, obviously trying to keep his face impassive by the exertion of great effort.

Tess nodded, unable to speak. Something had frozen the blood in her veins, making her feel as stiff as a statue.

"I regret . . ." the doctor mumbled. He pressed his lips together and turned to Julia as if hoping for some assistance. "I only wish . . ." He paused, turned back to Tess, and after a deep breath, plunged ahead. "It happens, ma'am, that I was traveling on the London–Manchester stage last night—"

"With . . . Jeremy?" Tess managed, her tongue dry.

"Jeremy Beringer, yes. He mentioned your name, you see—" The doctor's eyes fell from her face. "I didn't know who else to . . ." He paused again, unable to go on. This was even more difficult than he'd imagined it would be.

The silence hung in the room like an ominous cloud. "That's blood, isn't it?" Tess asked numbly.

"Blood?"

"On the paper there?"

The doctor, startled, looked at the wrapping of the bouquet. "Oh! Yes, I . . . I hadn't noticed. I'm terribly sorry . . . !"

"Oh, my God!" Julia cried in sudden understanding. "Have you come to tell us that something has happened to Mr. Beringer?"

But Tess had already seen the answer in Dr. Pomfrett's eyes. There was not a hint in those eyes of any hope at all. The doctor, his expression of controlled detachment giving way to one of agonized sympathy, wordlessly held out the flowers. Tess took a shaking step backward. All she could see was the dreadful red smudge that seemed to her to be growing larger and darker as she stared. Her knees buckled and a low moan sounded in her throat as the darkness swelled up, over and around her until it enveloped her completely.

❧ Six ❧

Throughout the bleak winter months that followed, Julia sent repeated invitations to Tess to come to stay with her in London, but it was not until spring that Tess finally came. Within a few days of her arrival, however, Julia began to regret that she'd invited her friend.

Julia and her husband were a down-to-earth, practical couple who had not a touch of romantic nonsense about them. Sir Edward Quimby, a gentleman of means whose good mind was made even better by an excellent education, did not indulge in the excesses and fripperies of most of the men of wealth in London. He didn't play cards, engage in fisticuffs, or pursue lightskirts. Instead, he was an active member of the London Historical Society and spent a good part of his time in research for a book he was writing on British naval battles. His only interest in fashion was the cut of his hair. Prematurely gray, he took pride in the impressive dignity his hair color imparted to his otherwise unnoteworthy appearance. The coats he wore on his stocky frame were unremarkable, his waistcoats were dull, and his boots no more than serviceable, but his hair was always cut, brushed, and combed in the latest mode. If one saw him strolling on the street, with his out-of-fashion beaver perched squarely on his brow and his spectacles dangling from a black ribbon round his neck, one would take him for a schoolmaster rather than a well-to-do baronet.

Julia, however, found his appearance perfectly satisfactory. She was quite content with her husband and their quiet life. She spent her days rewriting her husband's notes, visiting the wonderful London museums and shops, or, occasionally, taking tea with Lady Wetherfield or one of her other London acquaintances. Although the couple would have been readily granted full membership in the *haute ton* under the aegis of Lady Wetherfield (who was a distant connection of Julia's father, and who had not only been instrumental in matching Julia with Sir Edward but who'd befriended her from the first day of her arrival in this huge, frightening city), they did not choose to take advantage of the benefits of mingling in society. They were quite content to remain quietly on the fringes. But when Julia learned Tess's purpose in coming to London, she had an uncomfortable premonition that the quiet life she and her husband so much enjoyed was in danger of coming to an end.

She said as much to Edward at breakfast on a sunny May morning a mere four days after Tess arrived. The two of them were, as usual, breakfasting early, although Julia had not yet dressed for the day. Clothed in a filmy morning robe, with her hair undressed, she sat staring gloomily at her coffee cup, leaning on the breakfast table with chin in hand. "I'm almost sorry I invited her," she muttered.

"Mmmph," Edward responded, not looking up from *The Times*. The hour after breakfast was the time he devoted to a thorough perusal of the newspaper from front page to last, and he did not readily permit anyone to distract him. Since his wife was by this time quite accustomed to this ritual, Edward assumed that she was merely talking to herself, and he didn't bother to pay attention to her.

"I think she's going to cause some sort of stir, and we shall find ourselves in the suds," Julia muttered. "Perhaps I should avoid trouble before it happens and send her back home right now."

Edward heard just enough to be startled. He knew how fond his wife was of her cousin, so her last few words were completely unexpected. His attention was caught. "Send her back home?" he asked, his spectacles dropping from his nose. "Is *that* what you said?"

"Mmm." Julia was so intent on her problem that she didn't

even acknowledge the concession Edward had made in listening to her. "You've no idea how obsessed she's become."

"Obsessed?"

"Yes, obsessed. She speaks of nothing but vengeance for the accident to Jeremy. She *thinks* of nothing else."

Edward put aside *The Times,* returned his spectacles to their place on his nose, and blinked through them at his wife across the table. "Vengeance? What on earth are you talking about? Vengeance against whom?"

"Against the driver of the coach."

Edward was completely confused. "Coach? What coach?"

His wife glared at him in disgust. "What coach do you think? The one that caused Jeremy's death! Tess has spent all these months brooding about something she overheard at his funeral. Do you remember my mentioning the gentleman who brought her the news?"

"Yes, I think so. It was a Dr. Pomeroy or some such name."

"Dr. Pomfrett. Well, it seems that he remarked to someone in Tess's hearing that the coach was driven that night by a drunken nobleman who liked to play at being a coachman."

"Ah, yes. An FHC man. Coach driving is a popular sport in those circles, you know."

"I didn't know. What an absurdity!"

"Yes, I suppose it is. But not worse than other absurdities of the Corinthian set, like boxing or cockfighting or dueling. However, I can understand why Tess feels bitterly toward the idiot who caused the accident. To endanger one's own life for sport is one thing; to cause death and injury to innocent bystanders is quite another."

Julia peered at her husband in some surprise. "Are you saying you think Tess is *right* in pursuing this . . . this madness?"

"In seeking some sort of revenge? No, of course not. I'm only saying that I can sympathize with her feelings."

"Thank you for that, at least, Edward," came a voice from the doorway, and Tess entered the breakfast room in an angry flounce of ruffles and ribbons (having been told by Julia that a morning robe was the most appropriate manner of dress for breakfast), sat down at the table and reached for the coffeepot. "At least *someone* in this house has some sympathy for me in my 'madness.' "

"You needn't climb on your high ropes with me, my girl," Julia said, feeling not the least embarrassment at having been overheard. "If your scheme is not mad, it is something very close to it! And I would not be a friend if I didn't stop you from pursuing it."

"I don't see how you can call a scheme mad before it is even concocted," Tess retorted, pouring her coffee with a completely steady hand.

"The fact that you even *contemplate* concocting such a scheme is mad," Julia replied.

"Julia's right, of course," Edward put in calmly. "Even assuming you could identify the culprit—which in itself sounds an impossible task—there isn't much you could do to him. It was an accident, after all. There was no law broken."

"Exactly so," his wife agreed. "What would you do if you found him? Challenge him to a duel?"

"Something much worse," Tess muttered grimly. "In a duel he'd have a fighting chance. I intend to concoct a scheme in which he'll have no chance at all!"

"Do you see?" Julia demanded of her husband. "Was I not right? The girl's obsessed! Quite mad! Tess, my dear, what shall I *do* about you?"

"What you should do is to remain my friend and try to understand," Tess said. "You really don't, you know. If you did, you'd know that though I'm not quite mad yet, I shall certainly become so if I don't *do* something about the monster who caused all this."

"Feeling compelled to do something *is* an obsession," Julia pointed out reasonably. "Don't you see that?"

Tess shook her head. "I don't care what you call it. Perhaps I *am* obsessed. But there's a lump of pain inside me that I've been carrying about since the day Jeremy died, and I know it won't ease until I've done something about the perpetrator." She stood up and walked to the window. The bright sunlight made a dazzle of the small, walled garden at the rear of the Quimbys' town house, but Tess didn't even see it. Her eyes were fixed on something else . . . on a dark vision that she'd seen only in imagination but that had not left her mind for months. "A reckless, drunken gamester took a drive that night for sport—only for sport, mind you!—and by morning had ruined several lives. Several, not just one!"

Julia's firm, practical, commonsensical attitude began to wilt. "I *do* understand, dearest, truly I do. You mustn't believe I lack sympathy. But—"

"Jeremy was only twenty-four, you know. Only a boy, really. Only just beginning to live."

"Tess, *don't*—!"

Tess didn't seem to hear. "His mother is quite lost," she went on, her voice strangely empty even of sadness or self-pity. "Poor, dear Lady Lydia . . . she's only a shadow of herself. She has none of her old vitality. She hasn't left her house since that day. Mama walks over there every afternoon to make certain she takes some nourishment. I don't visit very often anymore, you know. The sight of me only makes her weep."

Julia's eyes misted. "Oh, my dear! I know the pain must be insupportable for you both."

"Yes, it is. Quite insupportable. For me it's bad enough, but I was not yet Jeremy's wife. For his mother, however . . ." She couldn't go on, although neither her stance nor her voice wavered.

Julia had to restrain herself from getting up and enfolding her cousin in a comforting embrace. But she knew that such an act would only encourage a flood of emotions, and she didn't see any good in that. "I know, love, I know," she could only murmur helplessly.

"My own pain is mostly regret for what I never did for him. Especially when I remember how happy Jeremy was about . . . about the wedding." Tess's head slowly lowered and her hands clenched tightly. "But before he . . . before I had a chance to . . . to *give* him anything—"

"Please, Tess, don't think about it. I know the timing of the accident was terribly unfortunate—"

"*Unfortunate!*" Tess wheeled about and glared at her cousin. "I find that word utterly inadequate."

"I only meant to say, love," Julia explained, "that you mustn't permit *yourself* to feel guilty. The accident—and the timing of it—were not your fault."

For a moment Tess stared at her cousin, arrested. Then she seemed to shake away the thought she was having. "Yes, you're right. That's why I must concentrate my thoughts on the one who *is* at fault."

Edward shifted uncomfortably in his chair. "You shouldn't

dwell on it so much, Tess. In time, you know, the pain will subside."

Tess stiffened her shoulders and held her head erect. "I don't *want* the pain to subside. The pain will keep me to my purpose. I want to feel it just this way . . . until I can make things right."

"But you can't make things right, my dear. You can't undo—"

"But I *can* make the murderer pay for his crime!" She turned her face back to the sunlit garden, adding more quietly, "Somehow."

Edward and Julia exchanged helpless looks. Julia sighed inwardly. What *was* she to do about the girl? Silhouetted against the light, looking as tall and erect as a soldier on parade, Tess appeared unshakable. The sunlight streaming in the window made her pale face seem almost colorless, but it touched the curls of her dark hair with little aureoles of flame. All at once she seemed to have become older, stronger, and more imposing. Tess Brownlow had been plucky and resolute enough as a girl, but now she'd become a woman of unyielding purpose. She'd found a goal.

Julia had the sinking feeling that this glorious woman in the window would not easily be deflected from that goal. As Tess looked now, outlined in brilliance, she seemed to Julia to be gallant, intrepid, even heroic. Perhaps she was mad, but many heroic figures must have seemed mad to their contemporaries. One had only to think of Joan of Arc; even against their will, her soldiers had the urge to follow where she led. Julia felt something of that urge now. Tess's will was compelling.

Tess returned to the table. "Well?" she asked, looking from one to the other. "Do you intend to send me packing? It won't matter, you know, whether you do or not. If I can't stay here, I shall move into a hotel."

"Of course we shan't send you packing," Edward said, rising from the table, "but whether we can support you in any wild enterprise you may concoct is quite another question."

"As to that, Edward," his wife murmured, her resolve to bring Tess to her senses considerably dissipated, "let's wait to discuss that problem *after* she concocts the wild enterprise, shall we?"

Edward frowned at his wife in surprised disapproval.

"You've certainly had an amazing about-face in the last few minutes. Why have you changed your perfectly sensible views?"

"I wouldn't go so far as to say that I've changed them, exactly—"

Tess reached across the table for her cousin's hand. "Oh, Julia, you *are* a friend! I shan't ask you to do anything dreadful, really I shan't. Only come with me today to see Dr. Pomfrett."

"Is that what you plan to do?" Julia asked. "See Dr. Pomfrett?"

"To learn the identity of the driver, yes."

"And is that all?" Edward inquired.

"That's merely the first step."

"No doubt," Edward said dryly. "And what's the next one?"

"After we learn who the man is, then we shall see what we shall see."

Edward looked down at his wife. "Is *that* a satisfactory answer for you?"

Julia shrugged helplessly. "I suppose it must be."

Tess squeezed her hand in gratitude. "Then you'll go with me?"

Julia returned the affectionate pressure of the handclasp. "I suppose I am the greatest fool alive, or that your madness is contagious, but of course I'll go with you!"

The two women smiled at each other, happy to have recovered the closeness that had disappeared during the past few days. But Edward let out a disgusted breath. "Julia! Have you suddenly grown more hair than sense? Did you not say, less than fifteen minutes ago, that this business will land us all in the suds? Are you now intending to *support* your cousin in what you earlier called her 'madness'?"

Julia bit her lip. "No, of course not. But you see, my love, I—"

"Never mind. Don't say anything more." He strode angrily to the door and shouted to the butler with unusual asperity to bring him his hat and stick. Then he turned back, shook his head, and favored both women with a look of pained severity. "Females! I'll never understand the ways in which your minds work!" He was about to say more, but the butler appeared in the doorway. Edward took his things and waved the fellow away. "Madam Wife," he said, clapping his hat on his head, "I'm off to the Society meeting. I shall be gone all day. That gives you plenty of time to plot your mischief. But if and when the two of you decide on some sort of heinous scheme for revenge, I don't want to know *anything* about it!"

He marched out into the corridor, stopped, turned, and marched back to the doorway again. Taking a stance on the threshold and gesturing with his cane, he added in a voice of dire foreboding, "But if this business ends with the two of you dangling from a gibbet, I shall not be a bit surprised!"

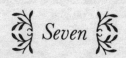

Seven

Dr. Pomfrett proved to be a reluctant informant. "I don't see what good it will do for you to know the gentleman's identity," he said to the two young women seated on stools before him in his modest surgery on Brooke Street. "There's nothing you can do to bring him to justice. I would certainly have done something about it already, if there were something to be done."

He had brought them into his surgery to save time; in the surgery he could at least clean and rearrange his instruments while they spoke. He was not happy to see them. For one thing, they were stealing precious time from his day. Two patients were already waiting in the anteroom to see him, and there would undoubtedly be one or two more before the ladies took their leave. And for another thing, they were forcing him to remember an experience he would prefer to forget.

The surgery was small and sparsely furnished. The two stools the doctor had pulled up for the ladies were the only seats. Besides an examining table and a number of wall shelves on which were stored hundreds of bottles of chemicals and medications, the room's only piece of furniture was a large glass-doored cabinet containing a frightening array of scalpels, knives, probes, splints, and other bewildering paraphernalia. The only decoration in the room was a vulgarly colored chart of a human body without the skin, displaying a great number of muscles, veins, and organs. At the level of Tess's eyes was the body's midsection, in which the bulbous, ropy intestines were blatantly revealed. Repulsive as the picture was, Tess could not seem to keep her eyes from returning to it.

The doctor stood at his examining table, two trays of instruments before him. "Since you are no more able than I," he was saying, "to do anything about the matter, I see no point in merely satisfying your curiosity." As he spoke he kept his hands busy cleaning some small-handled knives and scissors that he took from the first tray and, when cleaned, placed in the second.

With an effort Tess tore her eyes from the ugly wall chart and fixed them on the doctor's face. His graying, streaked hair was unruly and seemed to want to stand up on end; his eyebrows, almost white, were fuzzy and thick; and his lips were tightly compressed into a forbidding frown. But something about his eyes suggested that this was a man who had seen much of human suffering and had done what he could to ease it. Tess sighed, disliking to disagree with such an obviously good man, but there was no help for it. "Perhaps there *isn't* anything I can do," she argued, "but I must know! Not in order to satisfy my curiosity, sir, no. Not for that reason, but for my peace of mind."

The doctor frowned down at the blade of the knife he was polishing. "I don't see how the information can bring you peace of mind, ma'am. I think it will only create a greater agitation in your mind than there is now."

"I don't think it *possible* to feel greater agitation, Doctor Pomfrett."

"She's right, Doctor," Julia said in support. "The thought that the man responsible for bringing so much pain to two families is walking about among us unpunished and unscarred is enough to agitate anyone!"

The doctor's hand stopped. "Yes, Lady Quimby, it is," he said, shaking his grizzled head. "If I let myself dwell on the memory of that night, I, too, become agitated. That's why I believe the best solution is not to dwell on it at all."

Tess leaned forward. "But you see, I can't *help* but dwell on it. Julia—Lady Quimby, here—says I'm obsessed."

"I'm truly sorry for it, ma'am. Truly." He put down the cloth and the scalpel he'd been cleaning and stared ahead of him at nothing. "I, too, could become obsessed if I permitted myself . . ." He walked round the table. "I admit that there were many nights during which I lay awake reliving the . . ." Half absently, he took Tess's hands in his. ". . . wondering if I should have done more to prevent . . ."

"There, you see? You, too, are obsessed by it! And blaming yourself!" She looked up into his face earnestly. "Why should we berate ourselves, Doctor? We are not at fault! *He* is!"

The doctor shook himself from his reverie and peered at her curiously. "Do you berate *yourself,* ma'am? Surely *you* have no reason for guilt. You weren't even there."

Tess dropped her eyes and withdrew her hands so that he wouldn't feel the tremor of her fingers. "Reason has very little to do with it," she murmured.

"Surely, my dear young lady, you can't blame yourself because Mr. Beringer chose to go to London to bring you flowers!"

She shook her head. "That's not it. My guilt comes from a deeper source. You see, I could have married Jeremy months before . . . when he first asked. If I had, then perhaps he would never have *been* on that coach!"

"Good God, ma'am," Dr. Pomfrett exclaimed, appalled, "I've never heard such . . . such balderdash! To blame yourself—"

"Is it greater balderdash than your lying awake blaming yourself for not preventing what happened?" she countered.

"Dr. Pomfrett," Julia interjected, "you are *both* inflicting punishments on yourselves that neither of you deserves. And that's what Tess has been trying to say. If you can aim this need for punishment in the right direction—toward the true culprit!—then perhaps you *both* can find peace of mind."

Dr. Pomfrett leaned back on the examining table, considering her words. "But, Lady Quimby, you keep ignoring the fact that there is no way to administer such a punishment."

"If I knew who the man was, and what his circumstances are, I might find a way," Tess said.

The doctor shrugged sceptically. "What sort of way?"

"I don't know . . . yet."

"But there is nothing that anyone legally can do—"

"The law is not the only route for the administration of justice. If one has a bit of imagination . . . and determination . . ."

"And Tess Brownlow is nothing if not determined," Julia muttered dryly.

The doctor stared at Tess speculatively. Then he clasped his hands behind his back and paced about the table. When he'd made a full circle, he paused. "No," he said. "The thing is best forgotten. In the eyes of the law it was an accident, not a crime. That is how we must accept it."

"But you *know* it was a crime," Tess protested. "You said he was drunk!"

The doctor sighed. "Yes, he was. Completely cast away."

"In my view that would be unforgivable even on an ordinary day. But on a night such as that one, his drunkenness was criminal, was it not? On moral if not legal grounds?"

"I suppose it was," the doctor muttered with head lowered. "But if it was, then we must leave it to heaven to administer the punishment."

"I don't wish to wait so long," Tess retorted.

Dr. Pomfrett raised his eyes. "I'm sorry, ma'am. I'm convinced that this matter is best not pursued. I see no good in it. Now, if you will forgive me, I have patients to attend."

Tess stiffened and would have continued to argue, but Julia's hand on her arm brought her to her senses. It was clear that Dr. Pomfrett was dismissing them. He'd made up his mind, and there seemed little hope that Tess would be able to persuade him to change it; she'd already used all the arguments she could think of.

The doctor remained mulishly staring down at his instrument trays while the ladies rose to leave. "I shall try some other avenues of inquiry, Dr. Pomfrett," Tess said at the door. "You may be inclined to push this matter out of *your* consciousness, but I cannot."

Julia quickly bustled through the anteroom and out the door, Tess trailing reluctantly behind. Tess's mind was already grappling with the problem of where to turn next. She could, she supposed, interview the drivers of the mail until she found the one who'd relinquished his post to the drunken nobleman, but she had no certainty that the search would end in success. The doctor's refusal had certainly made her task more difficult and would considerably delay her plans.

The Quimbys' phaeton was waiting for them outside Dr. Pomfrett's door. Julia cast her cousin a look of sympathy and, with a sigh which was supposed to express disappointment but seemed to Tess to reveal relief, climbed up the carriage steps and took her seat. Tess, following, had climbed up the first step when Dr. Pomfrett shouted from the doorway, "One moment, Miss Brownlow, please!"

He came slowly toward her. "There's something else I ought to say," he muttered, taking Tess's arm and helping her down, "especially since you seem determined to pursue this matter . . ." He hesitated, his brow furrowed worriedly.

"Yes? Go on," Tess urged.

"Hasn't it occurred to you that the gentleman in question may have already been punished?"

"Already? How?"

The doctor's face took on an expression that she could only describe as tortured. "I have a strong recollection of his face after the accident," he said in a low voice. "The man had sobered up by that time and seemed to be quite agonized. There are some people, you know, who in such a situation cannot forgive themselves. They live in a hell worse than any we could create for them. If this is such a man—"

"Is that why you will not reveal his identity?" Tess asked, studying the doctor's troubled eyes. "Because you think he may have punished himself?"

"Don't you think it a possibility?"

"I hadn't thought before of *his* feelings," she admitted. "Yes, I suppose it is possible."

He seemed pleased by her answer. "Then you agree that the matter is best forgotten?"

"No! I don't agree at all!" Tess said vehemently. "I only agreed it was *possible* the man is consumed with guilt. But suppose the fellow has no regret at all? Suppose he has gone on with his life as though nothing untoward had happened? Should you wish, then, to forget the matter?"

Dr. Pomfrett ran his fingers nervously under his collar. "No, I shouldn't," he said frankly. "Though I think it highly unlikely that any man could go on with his life as though nothing had happened."

"Are you sure, Doctor, that you're not judging other men by your own character? You are a good man, suffering from the accident almost as much as if you'd been responsible for it. But is the perpetrator such a man as you? If he were, would he have driven that coach in the first place? And while inebriated?"

The doctor shook his head. "That's what has tormented me since that day. I don't know."

"If I discover his identity," Tess said, eagerly pursuing what she recognized as an advantage, "I shall ascertain just what sort of man he is before I act. If he is indeed living in a hell of his own making, I'll know it at once. And my undertaking will end right there."

"You're sure of it?"

"I'm not so obsessed, Doctor, that I would rub salt in an injured man's wounds. If the man shows signs of true repentance, my mission is at an end. You have my word on it."

The doctor stared at her for a long moment. Then he clasped his hands behind his back, turned away from her, and walked slowly back to his door.

Tess, fearing she'd lost the struggle again, took a step after him. "Doctor—?"

"Lotherwood," the doctor said over his shoulder. "That's the name your Mr. Beringer called him. Lotherwood. And may God forgive us all."

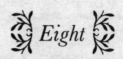

Eight

Quimby House
15 May 1812

Dear Dr. Pomfrett:

I have two reasons for writing. The first is to offer my most
sincere thanks to you for giving me The Name. You departed
from me so abruptly yesterday that I did not have the opportunity to express properly my gratitude to you for revealing
the identity of the driver of the stage that fateful night. I know
that you forced yourself to overcome some basic qualms
before you could name The Name. That you overcame those
misgivings for my sake was more than kind of you, and for
that I shall always bless you in my thoughts.

Your misgivings, however, give me my second reason for
writing. Your last words to me revealed all too clearly your inner reluctance to involve yourself in an enterprise whose
morality you find questionable. I am writing to assure you,
therefore, that you may put those qualms aside. It has turned
out that your misgivings can be put to rest. When I tell you
what I have discovered, I think it will be possible for you to
close your eyes at night with a clear conscience.

Herewith, my tale:

When I revealed The Name to my cousin Julia (the Lady
Quimby, whom you met in my company), she was very much

shocked, for she not only had heard of Lord Lotherwood but is somewhat acquainted with him. Her friend, Lady Wetherfield, is Lotherwood's aunt. The gentleman is apparently so sought-after and respected in society that Julia refused at first to believe you had remembered the name correctly. However, when I described what I knew of his physical appearance (details I had garnered from remarks I'd overheard at Jeremy's funeral), the description matched perfectly with Julia's knowledge of Lotherwood's person. And when we discovered that his lordship is indeed a Corinthian of widely touted sporting talents, a racing driver of some repute, and a member of the Four-in-Hand Club, there seemed to be no question that we'd found our man.

I immediately prevailed upon Julia to extract what information she could from her friend Lady Wetherfield. And judging from the information Julia gleaned when she took tea with her ladyship, Matthew Lotherwood, Marquis of Bradbourne, seems not at all to be a man living in a private hell! A man who is seen at all the important social functions, who is active in sports, who has a wide circle of friends, and (most significant of all) whose betrothal is this week to be officially announced in The Times, must be a man content with his life. Such a man could hardly be believed to be suffering the agonies of self-torture.

Under the circumstances, Dr. Pomfrett, I hope you will not continue to berate yourself for assisting me in the most important first step in my attempt to devise an appropriate retribution. However painful that retribution turns out to be, it seems to me that this Lord Lotherwood fully deserves it.

Yours in gratitude,
Teresa Brownlow

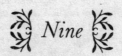

Nine

To Tess, the name Lotherwood suggested nothing more than a faceless enemy; she'd never heard it before and had no inkling of the personality of the man to whom it was attached. But to Julia, who'd heard only good things of him from her London benefactor, Lady Wetherfield, the name stood for everything that was enviable and admirable in London society. Tess's plan for revenge seemed more fraught with danger than ever.

After mulling over what she'd learned from her tête-à-tête with Letty Wetherfield, Julia could not disagree with Tess's conclusion about Lotherwood: there was nothing in the gossip concerning him that could possibly be interpreted as a sign that his lordship was suffering the slightest remorse for the accident he'd caused less than six months ago. But Julia was nevertheless unhappy that it was Lotherwood whose life Tess wished to damage. Matthew John Lotherwood, the Marquis of Bradbourne, besides being the apple of his aunt's eye, a darling of the *ton* and a gentleman of impeccable reputation, was too formidable a match for a country girl like Tess. The whole situation was certain to become an impossible muddle.

For two days after the meeting with Dr. Pomfrett, however, everything was quiet. Tess remained closeted in her room most of the time, unable to concoct even the beginnings of a scheme for her revenge, though her mind was desperately concentrating on the problem. Julia was almost lulled into believing that the whole crisis would fizzle away to nothing. But on the third day an innocuous incident occurred that set off a train of ideas in Tess's head—ideas that would lead to a plan destined to destroy Julia's euphoria, upset the peace of the Quimby household, and change the life of the unsuspecting Lord Lotherwood forever.

That day, shortly after noon, Julia invaded Tess's room in the hope of rousing her from her cogitations and enticing her to go out on a shopping expedition. She found Tess ensconced on the window seat weeping over a copy of *Childe Harold's Pilgrimage,* a work of poetry which had burst on the world only a month before and made its author, Lord Byron, an overnight sensation. "Listen to this, Julia," Tess said, wiping her eyes. "One would have thought the man wrote it for me:

"What is the worst of woes that wait on age?
    What stamps the wrinkle deeper on the brow?
    To view each loved one blotted from life's page,
    And be alone on earth, as I am now."

"Written for *you?*" Julia tossed her head scornfully. "As if you were an aged crone, alone in the world! I love the poem as much as anyone, but I will not let you wallow in self-pity over it. Besides, I didn't come up to discuss poetry. I've received an invitation card for the Wetherfield Ball! And Lady Wetherfield has included a particular invitation for my houseguest. Was that not kind of her?"

"I suppose so," Tess murmured unenthusiastically, closing her book.

"We must find you a wonderful new ballgown, my love," Julia said, pulling Tess to her feet. "Letty's balls are always quite special. I'm sure it's just what you need to shake off your doldrums."

"No, no, dearest, I've no wish to go," Tess said, resisting the tug at her arm. "Please send Lady Wetherfield my regrets. I've no interest in such nonsense."

"But you *must* take an interest, Tess," Julia persisted. "Letty is one of the very best hostesses in town. She always provides a special sort of entertainment for the evening that sets her galas apart from the others."

"Oh? What sort of entertainment?" Tess asked, more to please her cousin than to learn the answer.

"One never knows beforehand. I've been told that a few

years ago she set up a maze of mirrors through which every guest had to find his way. Last year she employed a troupe of acrobats and jugglers. The acrobats swung about on trapezes right over the dance floor, while the jugglers tossed their balls to one another over and around the guests while they danced. It was a veritable circus!"

"It all sounds very silly to me."

"Actually, it was a charming diversion. Even Edward enjoyed it."

"Mmm. What will the woman be doing to surprise her guests this year?"

Julia grinned. "Actually, it's supposed to be a secret, but Letty confided to me when we took tea the other day that she's hired a gypsy to tell fortunes! I think it should be great fun!"

Tess made a dismissive gesture with her hand and returned to her place on the window seat, asking, "Are these the absurdities with which your London circle concerns itself, Julia?"

"It's not *my* circle, goosecap. It's Letty's. I'm only on the fringes. I assure you, Edward and I are rarely tempted to waste away our evenings at the usual squeezes. Letty's ball was one of very few we attended last season. But I should have thought *you'd* be eager to be part of Letty's circle. After all, it includes Lotherwood."

Tess's bored expression changed abruptly, and she jumped to her feet. "Good God, I'd forgotten!" she exclaimed, a light springing to life in her eyes. "He's her nephew, isn't he?"

"Yes," Julia admitted, wishing she'd bitten her tongue off before making that last, thoughtless remark. Why had she been so idiotic as to bring up the subject of Lotherwood when she'd been hoping that Tess would forget the whole thing?

"Will he attend her ball, do you think?" Tess inquired, now all attention.

"I suppose so," Julia answered with a helpless sigh. "For one thing, he wouldn't be likely to offend his aunt by not making an appearance. And for another, his betrothal has just been announced. Letty's ball is the perfect place for the couple to receive the congratulations of the *ton*."

"In that case, Julia," Tess said with a wicked smile, "it is very possible that I may agree to attend the ball after all." She placed her hands on her cousin's shoulders, turned her about, and gently urged her to the door. "Will you excuse me for a while, my love? I have some thinking to do."

"Thinking?" Julia echoed with a sinking heart.

"Yes. I must decide how to put this very fortuitous invitation to the best use."

Julia went downstairs to the sitting room with lowered head and faltering steps. In spite of her misgivings, Julia was quite in sympathy with her cousin's feelings. The more she heard of Tess's story, the more she understood. Tess's need for revenge was caused by something even stronger than grief. It was guilt. Julia was beginning to see that Tess was suffering from deep-seated feelings of self-blame, not only because she regretted not having married Jeremy earlier—*that* guilt even Tess herself recognized—but because she still wondered if she had loved him enough. In a hidden part of Tess's mind lay a painful awareness that her response to Jeremy's love for her had been inadequate. It seemed to Julia that Tess had convinced herself that revenge for Jeremy's death would somehow be an *atonement* . . . a sacrificial offering that she could place on the altar of Jeremy's memory that would convince not only his ghost but Tess herself that she truly loved him!

Julia sat down in her favorite chair in the small sitting room and pulled over her embroidery frame. While her fingers worked on the tiny stitches, her mind struggled with the problem of what her part in Tess's mission should be. She had to face the certainty that Tess would eventually—more probably very soon!—devise a plan that would accomplish her purpose: to make Lord Lotherwood suffer as she had suffered. And if Julia refused to assist her in her goal, Tess would undoubtedly depart from the Quimby house and proceed on her own. Julia admitted to herself that it might be better for her own and Edward's peace of mind to let Tess go on alone, but she knew she couldn't. Tess was as dear to her as a sister, and her sense of loyalty as well as her affection demanded that she remain her cousin's ally. Jabbing her needle into the fabric with a firmness that reflected her sudden decisiveness, she resolved to offer Tess all the sensible counsel and support of which she was capable. And, more important, she would make herself available to help pick up the pieces after this inevitably destructive adventure had run its course.

The afternoon shadows had begun to lengthen by the time Julia heard Tess's step on the stairs. Tess entered the sitting room with an air of decided elation. "You've thought of something, I suppose," Julia murmured, looking up from her needlework. Despite her decision to offer Tess her support, she couldn't help feeling alarmed, and the feeling revealed itself in the wrinkling of her brow.

"Yes, I have," Tess answered, very pleased with herself. "But don't look so frightened. I shall not cause you the least difficulty. At least, not very much. Will you do only two small things for me?"

Julia put aside her needlework. "What things?"

"First, when you accept the invitation from Lady Wetherfield, I wish you to tell her that my name is . . . let me see . . . what shall I call myself? It must be something a bit mysterious and inviting. Romantic, even. How about Rosamond? Or Sybil? What do you think, Julia?"

"I think you are being excessively silly. Why should you wish to take another name?"

Tess perched on the nearest chair and leaned toward her cousin eagerly. "It is the most important part of my plan. You *must* promise me never to reveal my true identity . . . and you must make Edward promise, too."

"Really, Tess, you're asking a great deal of me! You know that Edward will raise all sorts of objections—"

"Oh, pooh! You can twist him round your little finger! He does dote on you, you know. I have complete confidence in your ability to manage him. Now, let's get back to names again. What do you think of Clarissa?"

"I think it sounds like an old dowager," Julia muttered sourly, wondering if she'd made a wrong decision after all.

"Patricia, then. Or Gwendolyn. I've always thought that Gwendolyn had a rather medieval aura."

"Gwendolyn is an ugly name. And Patricia is so ordinary."

"Then what do you say to Olivia? No? Ophelia? How about Imogen?"

A reluctant giggle escaped Julia. "*Imogen?* How can you call that romantic?"

"Then *you* think of something," Tess said, getting up from her chair and beginning to pace.

Julia watched her for a moment, feeling again the dynamic strength her cousin seemed to exude. "I've always liked Sidoney," she suggested at last, shrugging and permitting herself to surrender to the game. "It always seemed to me to sound like a foreign princess."

"Then Sidoney I shall be," Tess said briskly. "Sidoney Ashdown . . . Atwood . . . Arnold . . ."

"Ashburton!" Julia smiled with satisfaction. "Sidoney Ashburton! It's a lovely name. I can't imagine one more mellifluously romantic."

Tess dropped a graceful curtsy. "Sidoney Ashburton, at your service, ma'am." She threw Julia a mischievous grin. "So will you write to Lady Wetherfield that Sir Edward and Lady Quimby will be delighted to attend her ball in the company of their houseguest, Miss Sidoney Ashburton?"

Julia sighed in reluctant agreement. "Very well. What's the second thing you wish from me?"

"Only a bit of information. Do you think you can discover from Lady Wetherfield the name and direction of the gypsy she's hired?"

"Yes, I suppose I can. But what on earth will you do with that information?"

"I will go to see her, of course. The gypsy is the centerpiece of my scheme to become acquainted with Lotherwood."

"You don't need a gypsy for that, silly. When Lotherwood appears on the scene, I can quite easily point him out to you myself. By the end of the evening you will have accomplished at least one goal: you'll have learned to recognize your enemy."

"Ah, but with the help of my gypsy, I shall have accomplished more than that," Tess chortled, striking an attitude of triumph. "My enemy will have learned to recognize *me!*"

❧ Ten ❧

When Lotherwood came down from the balcony after his visit with the gypsy, he found Dolph and Viola eagerly awaiting him at the bottom of the stairway. "Oh, *Matt*," Viola breathed, a pretty flush still coloring her cheeks, "she kept you *such* a long time! What did she say? Was she not remarkable?"

Lotherwood had laughed all the way down the stairs, thinking of the gypsy's ludicrous prediction that a perfect stranger would be his "true bride." But now, looking down at his betrothed's eager face, his smile faded. Viola seemed to have such innocent trust in the gypsy woman's ability. How would she feel if she learned that the gypsy had predicted his marriage to someone else?

"Well?" Dolph was prodding, almost as eagerly as Viola. "What city did she predict would be your honeymoon site? Geneva? Venice? If she hit the mark, you'll have to admit she has a gift."

"Gullible flats, the pair of you," Lotherwood said, smiling but evasive. "I refuse to permit you to dwell any longer on that sham of a fortune-teller. Besides, you and she have kept me from the buffet long enough. If you don't mind, I'm for the lobster cakes before they're all gone."

"Matt! Don't be such a tease!" Viola put a hand on his arm and looked up at him with a beguiling kittenishness. "*Tell* us!"

He shook his head. "There's nothing to tell, my dear," he insisted, drawing her arm through his and starting for the buffet. "She was so far off the mark that I suspect she mistook me for someone else."

Dolph hooted in amusement, but Viola's face fell. "Oh, Matt! Really? Just what did she say that was so far off the mark?"

"Everything. Vi, my love, there's really no point in going over it. You're a silly chit for putting so much credence in the woman's performance in the first place."

"He's right, you know," Dolph said gently. "No need to take it to heart. Those gypsies are made of nothing but humbug and chicanery."

"But she was so wonderful with *me,*" Viola said, crestfallen. "Are you certain, dearest, that there was nothing pertinent to you in what she said?"

Lotherwood stared down at her a moment in speculation. Perhaps he *should* tell her what the gypsy woman had said. The girl was too trusting by half. Hearing the full story might help her to become a little less gullible. "If you truly wish to know, Miss Innocence, the gypsy told me I was to be married before you."

Viola gaped at him. "*Before* me? How can that be?"

"That's just what I asked her. She replied by telling me that my betrothed would not be my true bride." He dropped her arm, took a stance in imitation of an old crone huddled over a crystal ball, and said, in an accent quite like the gypsy's, "Yer bride'll be somevun else entire."

Dolph burst into appreciative laughter, and Lotherwood was about to join in with him when a glimpse of his betrothed's face stopped him. The girl was positively aghast. She was staring up at him with eyes filling with tears. What was worse, her cheeks, which had until a moment ago been so charmingly rosy, were now white as chalk. "Vi!" he said, shocked. "You can't be taking this *seriously!*"

The poor girl merely shook her head, made a small gesture with her hands, and let her tears spill over. Dolph's laughter faded. "Vi! Don't you think it's *funny?*"

"I s-suppose I'm being g-goosish," she said, wiping a cheek with the back of her hand, "b-but what if it's *t-true?*"

"There's nothing true about it!" Lotherwood said flatly. "Goosish is a very apt word for such a question."

Viola, not finding in his tone enough of the reassurance she needed, felt a fresh flood of tears rise to the surface. "I th-think I'd like to s-sit d-down," she mumbled, reaching tremblingly for the handkerchief tucked into her bosom.

Dolph pressed his own handkerchief into her hand while Lotherwood led her to a seat behind a potted palm. "I think I'll give my aunt Letty a good dressing-down for hiring that troublemaking fortune-teller," he muttered, kneeling down beside his betrothed and taking the handkerchief from her fingers. He carefully dabbed at her cheeks while he added, "And I ought to give you one, too, for allowing yourself to be carried away by such nonsense."

The affection in his tone of voice was comforting, and after listening to his and Dolph's teasing for several minutes, Viola was able to regain her equilibrium. When her cheeks had finally dried and her usual, cheerful expression had returned to her face, she rose unsteadily. "I think we can go to the buffet now," she said. "I'm feeling much better."

"I should think so," Dolph said, helping her up. "As if anyone could steal Matt's heart from such a pretty package as you!"

"Right, Dolph," Lotherwood agreed, getting to his feet and brushing the dirt from the knees of his satin breeches. "I couldn't have said it better. Besides, you goose," he added, taking Viola's arm again, "our betrothal has been announced in *The Times*. The only way to untie the knot now is for *you* to cry off."

"I know," she said, smiling up at him tremulously. "It's just that a gypsy's prophecy has such a feeling of . . . of *foreboding* about it. I know I've been goosish. Now that I've had time to think, I don't really believe any more that the prophecy will come true."

"Well, if it *does,*" Dolph chortled, taking her other arm, "you can always have me, Vi. Remember, I'm next in line."

With two gentlemen to tease and cajole her back into good spirits, Viola was able to recover the happy excitement she'd felt earlier in the evening. And when, a short while after midnight, the Prince Regent put in an appearance and came directly over to them to express his delight at their betrothal, nothing else that had happened that evening seemed to matter. Prinny had seen the announcement in *The Times,* and he not only kissed Viola's hand and twitted Lotherwood on his loss of freedom, but he promised to send them one of his favorite ormolu clocks as a betrothal gift.

By the time Lotherwood suggested it was time to take their leave, it was two in the morning. Viola was in such high spirits that it was clear she'd forgotten the entire incident concerning the gypsy's prophecy. Dolph (who'd walked the short distance from his rooms to the Wetherfield house) requested a lift home, so the three went to the doorway together. A number of other guests were departing; Lady Wetherfield's marbled, round entryway was filled with people. Every one of her huge staff of footmen was required to find hats and cloaks and to assist the guests to go promptly on their way. After only a short wait, the butler himself went to find Lotherwood's and Lord Kelsey's hats and canes, while one of the footmen brought Viola's hooded cape. Lotherwood, having taken the cape from the footman's hand, was helping her put it on when his eye fell on a tall young woman standing in the doorway. He recognized her at once. It was the girl the gypsy had designated as his "true bride."

A footman had just placed a velvet cloak over the young woman's shoulders, and she was in the act of hooking a clasp at its neck when their eyes met. Her black curls made a dark, feathery halo about her pale face, and her extraordinary eyes gleamed like a cat's. For what seemed like an eternity those eyes studied him. Despite his intention to turn his eyes from her, he found he couldn't look away. For the second time that evening, he felt a sensation like the stopping of an inner clock. If someone had told him at that moment that the girl was a witch and was turning him into stone, he would have believed it. But then, with a last look (which Lotherwood later described to himself as one of absolute loathing), the lady turned away and was gone.

As soon as he regained a sense of mobility, he looked down at Viola with an unaccountable feeling of guilt, ready to offer an apology for his long period of abstraction, but she was calmly tying the strings of her hood. Dolph, too, seemed to have noticed nothing. And the butler had not yet returned with their hats. Was it possible that only a few seconds had elapsed since he first saw the girl? *And good God,* he wondered, *who the devil was she?*

A few moments later, after Viola had climbed into his carriage, Lotherwood kept Dolph from following by putting a hand on his arm. "Who was that lady in the doorway, do you know?" he asked in a low voice.

"What lady?"

"The one standing in the doorway just now. Wearing that long cloak. You must have noticed her. She was tall and dark, with the oddest light-blue eyes."

Dolph shrugged. "I didn't notice anyone. But why do you ask?"

"Never mind," Lotherwood sighed. "Let's go home."

Lotherwood did not sleep well that night. He couldn't seem to get the girl with the ice-blue eyes out of his mind. He paced about his bedroom for a long while, trying to rid himself of the pernicious feeling the gypsy woman's prophecy had left with him, but the harder he tried, the more persistent was the feeling. And his annoyance with himself for falling under so ridiculous a spell was compounded by a feeling of disloyalty to Viola. Why, he wondered, did he feel as if he were being, somehow, unfaithful?

The thought troubled him all night long. The evening's experience even invaded his dreams. The face of the girl with the strangely light eyes made a part of every dream-image his brain conjured up, and the next morning his wide-awake mind still found itself haunted by that vision. His mouth felt dry, his tongue furry, and something was hammering away inside his skull right over his left eye. More annoyed with himself than ever, he cursed the gypsy woman under his breath. Why had he permitted himself to fall under her spell?

After another hour of pacing, he dressed himself in a long, frogged dressing gown and made his way down to the morning room. Bradbourne House, the Lotherwood London residence, was much too large for the needs of a bachelor, and his lordship kept most of the rooms closed. In that way he could keep his London staff to a minimum—just a cook, a couple of housemaids, the stable staff, two footmen, and his man Rooks, who served as butler, valet, and general overseer. But this morning, just when he was needed, Rooks was nowhere about.

Lotherwood's only hope of clearing his head was a cup of good, strong coffee, and to his good fortune, he found one of the footmen just bringing a pot to the morning room when he arrived. "Tell Rooks not to send up anything else," he said to the footman. "Coffee is all I want this morning."

But the sideboard had already been set with covered plat-
ters, undoubtedly containing shirred eggs, fish, ham, and
several other foodstuffs that he had no wish to consume. With
a groan, he sat down at the table with a cup of coffee, but
before he'd taken his first sip, Rooks came in. "Lady Wetherfield, my lord," he announced with an air of sympathy.

"What? Here? So early?"

Before Rooks could answer, his aunt sauntered in. Her eyes
were bright, her gray curls bounced under a pretty, beribboned bonnet of yellow straw, her step was light and graceful
for a large-boned woman of sixty-two years, and she swung
her folded parasol back and forth like an energetic young
schoolboy swinging his first cane. No one would have guessed
that she'd entertained one hundred and fifty of London's
most select company the night before.

Lotherwood eyed her with unwonted irritation. "You are
much too cheery this morning, ma'am," he muttered, "considering what a shambles your party was."

"Shambles? What on earth are you talking about?" She
calmly helped herself to a bun from the pile on the sideboard
and perched on a chair.

Rooks and the footman hovered over her to offer her tea or
coffee, but Lotherwood dismissed them both with a wave.
"Your inspired idea to hire a gypsy fortune-teller is what I'm
talking about," he said, pouring his aunt's coffee himself.
"Her blasted prophecies have put everyone in a foul mood."

"Have they indeed? Not that *I'm* aware of. Princess
Esterhazy said the party was my greatest success. Lady
Cowper insisted on taking down the gypsy's direction; she intends to go to see her for an additional reading! As for Prinny,
he left the party positively beaming. Madame Zyto told him
his debts would be cleared by the end of the year." Lady
Wetherfield had already breakfasted, but she buttered her bun
and, to ease her conscience, only nibbled at the edges. "He intends to purchase a rosewood pianoforte for the music room
at Brighton entirely on the strength of her prediction."

"Then His Royal Highness is reaching his dotage sooner
than expected." He eyed his aunt over his coffee cup as if she
were responsible for the Regent's profligacy. "And if I know
Prinny, he'd have bought the pianoforte anyway."

"You may be right about that, Matthew," she agreed, cock-ing her head at him curiously, "but I find it hard to believe that the gypsy could have said anything to put *you* in a pucker. You've never been the sort to let a fortune-teller flummer you."

"I wouldn't say she flummered me, exactly. But what she said to me upset Viola more than I like to admit."

"Upset Viola? How can that be? I saw her not thirty minutes ago, and she was beaming like a mooncalf. All she talked about was the ormolu clock Prinny promised to send."

"You saw her? This morning?"

"Yes, I stopped at the Lovells before I came here, to deliver a dinner invitation. I'd invite you as well, if you weren't such a Friday-faced old grouch."

"You needn't bother," he retorted ungraciously. "I want no more of your blasted invitations."

His aunt was not the least put out. She merely leaned back in her chair and raised an eyebrow. "What on earth did my gypsy say to you that's put you so far out of frame?"

"She said, my dear aunt, that I shall not wed my betrothed but someone else entirely. And she even went so far as to point out to me the very person she insists I shall wed."

Letty Wetherfield gave a trilling laugh. "You don't say! How very entertaining! Who is it she picked out for you? Don't tell me it was the Sturtevant chit."

Lotherwood made a face. "Will you forget the Sturtevant chit? You've been trying to push her at me since I was in short coats."

"Well, I still think she'd be better for you than your Viola Lovell. At least the Sturtevant girl has some spirit, which is more than you can say for Miss Lovell."

"Now, see here, Aunt Letty—" Lotherwood cut in, pushing back his chair.

But Lady Wetherfield went right on as if he hadn't said a word. "All that insipid sweetness! She'll be like a steady diet of jellies and clotted cream—they both can corrupt your blood before you're fifty."

Lotherwood rose in offended dignity. "Listen to me, ma'am," he declared in an awesome baritone, "you may have stood in place of a mother to me all these years, and you may have a claim to my greatest affection and respect, but I cannot sit by and let you malign the woman who is my affianced bride."

"Oh, sit down, Matt," she retorted, not a whit impressed. "If you want to spend your life saddled to a piece of pretty sugar-fluff, I'll say no more. I've accepted your decision, have I not? I've had her to tea, invited her entire family to my routs, taken her shopping, and done everything else a devoted aunt could do. So stop glowering at me. Sit down like the dear boy you are and finish your coffee. Yes, that's better. Now, where were we before you climbed on your high ropes?"

"Talking about your gypsy," he muttered, refilling his cup.

"Ah, yes. The gypsy. If it wasn't the Sturtevant girl, who *did* she choose for you?"

"I don't know her name. I'd never seen the creature before last night. Where do you manage to find all those eccentrics you invite to your galas?"

"I *don't* find eccentrics! But I do like to have interesting people about me. I see nothing wrong in that. What's more, if there were anyone very odd at my party, I surely would have noticed. Are you saying there was someone there last night who was truly eccentric, and that the gypsy tried to match you up with her? What was eccentric about her?"

"She was seven feet tall, had striped skin, and wore two orange circlets in her nose." His expression remained perfectly serious; only his eyes had a glint. "Is that eccentric enough for you?"

"Come now, Matt, don't tease. I want to hear about this. Did my gypsy really pick out a bride for you?"

"I've already said she did. And I've also said I don't know who the girl was."

"What did she look like? Was she actually eccentric?"

Matt shrugged. "She had very strange eyes. They were the palest blue, and when she looked at me, I had the feeling she could see right through me."

Letty's face lit up. "Oh, of course! That must be Julia Quimby's houseguest. Her name is . . . let me think . . . Ashburton. Sidoney Ashburton."

"Sidoney?" Matt's eyebrows rose in mock horror. "Are you teasing *me,* now?"

"What's wrong with Sidoney?"

"Nothing at all," he replied with a half smile. "*Sidoney.* Of course! One couldn't expect her to be called something ordinary, like Anne or Jane or Bess."

"You're quite right," his aunt said with a brisk nod. "An

exceptional name for an exceptional girl.''

Matt, who'd been so diverted by his aunt's presence that he'd forgotten his headache, now felt it returning. "Yes, I suppose she is exceptional. *I* certainly found her so.''

"Did you?" Letty looked at him interestedly. "In what way?''

"In every way, but particularly in her attitude toward me.''

"Oh?" his aunt queried. "Did she say something offensive to you?''

"No—we had no opportunity to speak at all. But considering that the girl had never met me and knew nothing about me, she nevertheless looked at me as though I were a worm.''

"That's ridiculous. Why would she do that?''

"I haven't the slightest idea.''

"Well, if I decide to invite you to my dinner party, you will meet her there and can ask her why.''

"Good God, woman," he exclaimed, "have you come this morning to invite me to a dinner party which includes that . . . that *witch?*"

Letty looked at him with an intent amusement. "Why do you call her that? Because she has speaking eyes, or because she doesn't seem to like you?''

Matt, in the act of lifting his cup to his lip, paused. "For both reasons," he said thoughtfully. Then, laughing at himself, he added, "Or neither.''

"Well, which is it?" his aunt insisted.

"How can I answer such an improbable question?" he said, shaking his head as if to clear the cobwebs from his brain. "Let's drop this subject, shall we? I hope you realize, Aunt, that this has been the most nonsensical conversation we've ever had.''

"Perhaps. But before we drop it, don't you want to know the day and time of my invitation?''

"No. Thank you, but no.''

"What? What do you *mean?*" She put what was left of her bun (now nibbled down to a mere nub) down on her plate and rose majestically to her feet. "Are you saying you are *refusing* me?''

"Yes, ma'am, that's just what I'm saying.''

"But, Matt, you *must* come! Your betrothed and her parents have already accepted, and you know perfectly well that I only asked them for your sake.''

"Sorry, my dear," Matt said firmly, getting to his feet to escort her to the door, "but I have no intention of going anywhere *near* your Miss Sidoney Whatever-her-name-is."

Letty gaped at her nephew in disbelief. "*Matt!* Has your brain gone *maggoty?* Surely you're not taking my gypsy *seriously!*"

"If you mean to ask if I believe she really has a gift of prophecy, the answer, of course, is no. But there is such a thing as a self-fulfilling prophecy. You've heard the phrase, have you not?"

"No, I don't think I have. What does it mean?"

"It means," Matt explained as they strolled toward the door, "that one can make a prophecy come true by one's own behavior that never would have come true if one had gone about one's business in the ordinary way. For example, let's say your gypsy tells you you'll find something you thought you'd lost forever. So you think: now what have I lost that I've given up hope of finding? Ah, an opal ring. Then, *expecting* to find it because the gypsy said so, you keep your eyes open and look about you more carefully than you would otherwise have done, and thus you discover it in the back of your jewel case. And you declare to the world that the gypsy is a true seer, but in reality, you *yourself* have fulfilled the prophecy."

They had reached the outer doorway, but Letty was not ready to make an exit. "Are you telling me, Matthew Lotherwood," she demanded, poking at his shoulder with the tip of her parasol, "that you're *afraid?* Afraid that you yourself might make my gypsy's prophecy to *you* come true?"

"Call me cowardly if you wish, my dear aunt, but I don't intend to go anywhere *near* that girl," he answered, removing the parasol from her grasp and opening it for her. "If that blasted prophecy comes true," he added as he watched his aunt march down the front steps in offended dignity, "it won't be through any doing of mine!"

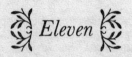

Eleven

Brooke Street
20 May 1812

My dear Miss Brownlow:

I am in receipt of your letter of the fifteenth. I am afraid that your conclusions were not based on evidence strong enough to enable me to put aside my qualms. A man who goes about his business in the ordinary way and is seen in society with a composed demeanor may still be greatly troubled in his soul. I beg that you will consider the matter further before taking any action.

Yours, etc.,
Josiah Pomfrett

❧ Twelve ❧

Lotherwood was forced to change his mind and attend Letty Wetherfield's dinner party after all. Viola had been dreadfully upset when he told her he would not be escorting her to the affair, and when he tried to explain his motives, he realized how foolish he sounded, especially since he was avoiding all mention of the girl with the ice-blue eyes. As he explained to his aunt when he informed her of his change of intention, he'd been unable to justify himself and thus had finally agreed to go. "How could I explain myself to Viola," he asked his aunt, "without seeming to make more of the whole gypsy incident than it deserves? Besides, I *am* making more of it than it deserves."

"Yes, I suppose you are," Letty said, trying not to show the extent of the satisfaction she was feeling. "I'm delighted you're coming, of course. I think that when you meet Miss Ashburton and talk to her in the ordinary, everyday way, you'll get over this feeling of having to avoid her."

Letty Wetherfield was, in truth, hoping for an even more satisfactory outcome than that. She was quite gleeful about the whole gypsy incident. She didn't put much stock in gypsy fortune-telling herself, but this was one time she hoped there was something in it. She'd never felt that the sugary Miss Lovell would make a suitable spouse for her beloved nephew (Viola being, like sugar, the sort who would completely disintegrate in the least shower of trouble), and anything that might come between that insubstantial female and Lotherwood had her approval, even gypsy witchery.

She glanced at her nephew from the corner of an eye and asked nonchalantly if Viola knew that Miss Ashburton was the "predicted" bride.

"Good God, Aunt Letty, of course not!" Lotherwood answered, appalled. "I hope you're not thinking of telling her!"

"Well, I won't if you don't wish it, but why do you think it necessary to keep her in ignorance?"

"*Why?*" Lotherwood echoed in some disgust. "I should think the reason would be obvious. Would it not be upsetting for a gentle, sensitive female like Viola to have to make polite conversation with someone who's been singled out as fated to make off with her intended spouse?"

"Surely she doesn't take all that nonsense seriously!"

Matt sighed. "I'm very much afraid she does. She was visibly shaken when I told her the gypsy said I would marry another. If she were to discover that the 'other' was a specific person—and someone with whom she was expected to sit down and dine!—well, I don't know how she might react. I think it better to leave her in ignorance about your Sidoney, don't you agree?"

Lady Wetherfield agreed. And when she was called upon to introduce the betrothed couple to Miss Sidoney Ashburton in her drawing room a few days later, she took a great deal of inner delight in the scene. Her drawing room was already crowded when Lotherwood and Viola arrived. Lady Cowper had come first, escorted by Lord and Lady Fenwick. Then Dolph Kelsey had appeared, looking as usual like an overdressed dandy in a silk waistcoat of bilious green. Mr. and Mrs. Lovell had arrived next, followed soon after by Sir Edward and Lady Quimby and their guest, Miss Ashburton. Letty Wetherfield gave the girl's face a thorough scrutiny and decided that Sidoney Ashburton was a woman of character. Earlier she'd only hoped that the gypsy prophecy would make trouble between Viola and her nephew; now she wished it would come true.

When the betrothed couple entered her drawing room, Letty hurried over to greet them and grasped Viola's arm. "Viola, my love," she purred, leading her across the room to where Tess was sitting calmly sipping sherry from a long-stemmed glass, "I want you to meet Julia Quimby's guest, Miss Sidoney Ashburton. Miss Ashburton, this is Miss Lovell, who is to wed my nephew. You've met my nephew, of course, haven't you?" she added wickedly.

"No, I don't believe I have," Tess answered, smiling up at Viola and making room for the girl beside her on the love seat.

"Then you must meet him at once." Letty turned and strode across the room. Abruptly breaking in on the conversation Matt had just begun with Edward Quimby and Dolph Kelsey, she said loudly, "Matthew, come and say hello to Julia's guest." Without giving him a moment to excuse himself, she snatched his arm and hauled him into Tess's presence. "Miss Ashburton, this is my nephew Lotherwood."

His aunt's abrupt action was disconcerting enough to Lotherwood, but his first close look at Miss Ashburton was more so. It was fortunate that his air of assurance and social facility was ingrained, for when Miss Sidoney Ashburton looked up at him and put out her hand, he experienced again that peculiar sense of shock that had struck him twice before when he'd looked at her—the feeling that all his inner mechanisms had stopped at once. If he were a callow youth, he would probably have gaped and stammered like an idiot. But years of training and experience stood him in good stead, and he was able to bring forth a perfectly normal how-de-do and bow over her hand with adequate aplomb. If he stared into those witchlike eyes a moment too long, no one noticed. Even Viola (who had no suspicion that this was a fatefully significant moment) watched with complete complacency as her betrothed performed the rituals of introduction with outward sangfroid.

When Miss Ashburton released his hand and turned away to resume her exchange of pleasantries with Viola, Lotherwood quickly escaped. Needing a drink and a moment of solitude to recover his composure, he sought out the footman with the tray of sherry glasses. *She is not so very beautiful,* he told himself with relief as he downed his glass of wine in a quick gulp. Her chin was a little too prominent for classic taste, and her skin was so pale as to seem almost colorless (and couldn't hold a candle to Viola's peaches-and-cream rosiness). There was no reason for him to react like a love-stricken schoolboy every time she looked at him. It was not the girl herself but the gypsy's prophecy that was to blame; it seemed to have affected him like some sort of malignant curse.

Lotherwood had quite recovered himself by the time the butler announced that dinner was served, so that, when his aunt clarioned, "Matt, you must give Miss Ashburton your arm, and Sir Edward will take Viola," he was able to return to Miss Ashburton's side with his usual equilibrium.

But he didn't hear the rest of his aunt's arrangements for the parade of her guests into the dining room, for Miss Ashburton had risen and was standing beside him, and her nearness was affecting him again. She was almost as tall as he, and the first thing he noticed was the fragrance of her hair. He did not dare to look directly at her, but he was aware of a shapely bosom, small waist and long thigh outlined by her shimmering blue dress. He might have convinced himself a moment before that she was not particularly beautiful, but now he had to admit that she exuded an aura of alluring womanhood.

He followed the procession and seated her at the table without quite being conscious of what he was doing. The soup had been placed before him by the time the sense of being dazed had passed. With an inward shake, he forced himself into an awareness of his surroundings. He was not a green boy, he told himself, and he would not permit the foolish ramblings of a toothless old gypsy to make porridge of his brains. He'd been seated beside attractive women hundreds of times in his life, and he'd never lost his head. Now that he was betrothed, there was all the more reason to behave sensibly.

He was seated between Lady Cowper on his left and Miss Ashburton on his right, and he immediately turned to Lady Cowper and engaged her in a lively debate about the Regent's struggle to appoint a new prime minister. The topic was on everyone's mind, because the shocking assassination of Spencer Perceval had taken place only a few days before. "I hear Grenville and his crowd have refused to be absorbed into what is essentially a Tory ministry," Lotherwood remarked.

"A good thing, too. Grenville will only make trouble if he's not in first place," Lady Cowper responded promptly.

This caught the ear of Dolph Kelsey, who was seated opposite, and Sir Edward, just two seats down from Dolph, who both joined in. Soon everyone at the table was involved, trying to guess who would be the Regent's choice. Canning, they agreed, was too young and headstrong. "He's the one who revived the name Tory and calls himself such, but he remains on the Opposition bench with the Whigs," Lotherwood said.

"It will be Liverpool," Edward offered. "Despite his early flirtation with the Whigs, Prinny is too much under the thumb of the Hertfords."

"Liverpool! Good God!" exclaimed Lord Kelsey in disgust. This started everyone talking at once, for Liverpool, though highly regarded by staunch Tories, was highly despised by everyone else. It was soon clear, however, that the staunch Tories outnumbered the others at this table: only Matt, Sir Edward, and Dolph Kelsey were opposed to the idea of Liverpool. But they were strong debaters and managed to hold their own against violent opposition from Lord Fenwick, Mr. Lovell, and Lady Cowper and minor broadsides from everyone else.

Engrossed as he was in the debate, Matt did not fail to notice that only Miss Ashburton did not participate in the discussion, nor did she exchange even a private word with Lord Fenwick on her right. When the second course was brought in, and the discussion slowed down while everyone set to work on their glazed lamb cutlets and sautéed pheasant, Matt turned to her and murmured, "You are very quiet, Miss Ashburton. Are you not accustomed to political arguments at the dinner table?"

"Oh, I quite enjoy them," she said, putting down her fork and looking over at him with disconcerting directness, "but you were expressing my thoughts so well, I didn't think it necessary to offer you my support."

"I'm happy to learn that you agree with my views, ma'am, but you should have joined the fray, not only to add to the numbers on our side but to give the others the opportunity to learn where you stand."

"I can't believe that anyone here is interested in where I stand, my lord."

"Ah, but they are, I assure you. It's always interesting to learn what a beautiful woman has on her mind."

Miss Ashburton lowered her eyes in modest acknowledgment of his compliment. "Are you speaking for the others, my lord, or for yourself?"

"For myself most of all."

She glanced at him again. "Indeed? Why is that?"

He grinned at her. "If you promise not to repeat the nonsense, I'll tell you. I've been informed by good authority—the gypsy woman who made such a stir at my aunt's ball last week—that you will soon become my bride. Is it not natural, therefore, for me to be interested in your mind?"

The lady merely picked up her fork and played with the cutlet on her plate. "I see," she murmured.

Lotherwood was startled by her lack of reaction. "You seem not at all surprised, ma'am. Is it not shocking to you to learn that *I* am your *fate?*"

Her lips curled. "I am not shocked, my lord. You see, I—"

But their brief tête-á-tête was interrupted at that moment by Lord Fenwick, who was demanding Lotherwood's attention. "I was saying, Lotherwood, that I've placed a hundred on you for Sunday's match with Sherbrooke. You'd better not let me down."

"He won't let you down, Fenwick," Dolph said with authority. "When has he ever let you down in a race? Besides, didn't Matt outdo Sherbrooke by two minutes and a half last time?"

"Don't be too sure of me, Dolph," Matt warned. "Sherbrooke has a new pair of roans that are said to be magnificent."

"I'll still put my money on you," his friend insisted.

Julia, across the table from her cousin and near the lower end, had been listening to this exchange carefully. She'd been instructed by Tess to wait for just such an opportunity to bring up the subject of Lotherwood's prowess with horses. The moment Lord Kelsey's words had been uttered, she leaned forward. "I hear that you're a most distinguished horseman, my lord," she said to Lotherwood, and then threw a glance at Tess.

"Julia!" Sir Edward muttered warningly, lifting his spectacles to his nose and pointedly looking through them at his wife. "My wife knows very little about sports, my lord," he said to Lotherwood with a touch of embarrassment. "I don't know why she insists on speaking on the subject."

"But I am right, am I not, about your reputation?" Julia persisted. "Have I not heard that you're one of the outstanding members of the FHC?"

"He certainly is, Lady Quimby," Kelsey put in. "There's

no one in sporting circles who doesn't recognize Matt's talent."

"Thank you, Lady Quimby. And you, too, Dolph, for your kind words. But you both make too much of me," Lotherwood said with the matter-of-fact directness that was his nature. "I admit that I've won a few races, but I think I'm getting past the age for such sport."

"Balderdash!" Dolph grunted. "You can go on for years!"

"Do you like driving stagecoaches like a coachman, as so many FHC men do?" Julia asked, leaning on her elbow and looking down the table at Lotherwood with an intent stare, quite ignoring the fact that her husband was glaring at her. "I'm told one can do that at any age."

There was a moment of silence, during which Tess noted that Lady Wetherfield and Lotherwood exchanged looks. "Matthew doesn't approve of stagecoach driving," Lady Wetherfield said sharply, a tight expression about her mouth.

"No, I don't," Lotherwood said. "I think the stage should be driven by the men who are hired to do the job. It's a foolish hobby for FHC men."

"I quite agree," Sir Edward said, still frowning at his wife.

"And now," Letty said, jumping up abruptly and forcing a smile, "I think it's time, ladies, for us to take our leave."

Lotherwood rose to help Lady Cowper and Miss Ashburton from their chairs. "I hope we can continue our conversation later," he whispered in Miss Ashburton's ear. "Your remarks were cut off at a most inopportune moment. You're leaving me in unbearable suspense."

His lordship made the remark in a joking tone, but he found the words to be truer than he thought. The conversation of the men over their brandies seemed excruciatingly dull, and the hour that passed seemed endless. Never before had he been so glad to rejoin the ladies.

He had to pay court to his affianced bride first, but as soon as Dolph joined them, he excused himself and went to Miss Ashburton's side. She and Julia Quimby had been whispering together, but at his approach Lady Quimby rose, gave him a nod in passing, and went to join the group organizing a game of silver loo. "I hope *you* don't wish to play," he said to Miss Ashburton. "I've been looking forward to continuing the conversation we began at dinner."

She looked up at him, and for a moment there was something in her eyes that reminded him of the look she'd given him from the doorway the night of the ball. A look of loathing. But the impression was only momentary, and her words were decidedly inviting. "I don't care for cards," she said, moving over to make room for him beside her on the sofa. "Do sit down, my lord."

"Thank you." He took a place beside her and turned so that he could observe her face. "Now, ma'am," he said with a friendly smile, "I wish you will tell me why you took the news that I am fated to be your husband with such complacency."

"The answer is simple, my lord," she said. "I knew it already. You see, the gypsy regaled me with the very same prediction."

"You don't mean it!" He gave a shout of laughter and shook his head in self-deprecation. "Now, why did that possibility never occur to me?"

"I had the advantage of you, my lord. When I saw you looking down at me from the balcony that evening, I realized the gypsy woman had told you the same tale."

"So you knew about it all along!" He leaned back against the sofa cushions and grinned at her, feeling the comfortable closeness that comes when two strangers discover they share a secret. "Well, then, ma'am," he teased, "what was your reaction?"

She raised her eyebrows. "My reaction?"

"Yes. Were you pleased to learn what fate has in store for you?"

She gave him a cool, appraising look. "What a coxcomb you are, my lord! Do you expect me to say that I was delighted?"

He was taken aback. It was amazing to him how easily this creature could disconcert him. He had only meant his question as an innocent joke, but he could see now that she was right; it must have sounded disgustingly self-satisfied. He ran his fingers through his hair, feeling awkward and embarrassed. "I've not been called a coxcomb before, ma'am, but you are indeed justified to find me so. I beg your pardon." His expression became rueful. "I suppose I *did* expect you to say you were delighted."

"I couldn't very well say that, my lord. I knew from the first that you were betrothed."

"Yes, of course. But I was only teasing, you know. I didn't mean to sound like a coxcomb. I was certain that, like me, you're not the sort to take a gypsy's babble seriously."

Her eyes were fixed on the hands folded in her lap. "You're quite right. I have no faith in fortune-tellers."

"Of course you haven't. Nor has anyone with a grain of sense. But I must admit to you, Miss Ashburton, that I've found the entire incident vastly entertaining. The gypsy's prophecy seems to have taken hold of my imagination. It's distracted me for days."

"Has it?" She flicked a teasing little glance at him. "Then may I ask a coxcombish question of *you,* my lord? What was *your* reaction when the gypsy pointed me out? When you looked down at me from the balcony, you didn't look the least delighted."

"I was too startled to be delighted. It's your eyes, you see. They are the most disconcerting eyes I've ever seen."

She lowered her lashes again. "Yes. My mother says they are too piercing by half."

"Piercing is too mild a word. They are bewitching."

The bewitching eyes flashed up at him. "Do you mean that as a compliment, my lord?"

He stared at her for a moment, his brows knit. "I'm not sure," he said, surprising himself by his frank and unwonted lack of gallantry. But he was remembering that, twice now, a glance of loathing from those eyes had been as painful to him as a blow.

"Not sure?" She asked the question with more amusement than offense.

"No. I'm not at all sure. Sometimes they seem to flash a look of . . ."

"Of what, my lord?"

He shook his head and turned away from her, trying to phrase an answer. But finally he shrugged and gave an ironic laugh. "It's just as well that the gypsy has no real powers of prediction," he said wryly, "for I suspect you were far from delighted to hear her words. I have the distinct impression you don't like me at all."

"Oh? Do my bewitching eyes tell you that?"

He turned back and faced her squarely. "Yes, I think they do."

"I shall not argue the point, my lord," she responded,

rising regally to her feet, "especially since your Miss Lovell has been observing us for the past few moments with an expression which bodes you no good. If you'll excuse me, I think I shall play cards after all."

He scrambled to his feet and bowed. She gave him a small nod and walked away. But it was several seconds before he was able to shake off the spell in which she seemed to have enveloped him and return to his betrothed.

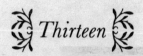

Thirteen

Quimby House
22 May 1812

Dear Dr. Pomfrett:

I am sorry that you still entertain the notion that Matthew Lotherwood, Marquis of Bradbourne, may be, in your words, "suffering in his soul." I have now met him personally, and I assure you that he is not suffering at all. In fact, I am beginning to wonder if the man has any soul in which to suffer. My cousin brought up the subject of stagecoach driving at the dinner table in order that she and I might observe closely how he reacted. He and his aunt exchanged glances that made it obviously clear that the question held a guilty significance for them, but aside from remarking that he did not approve of such sport, he showed not a flicker of remorse. I am not alone in that conclusion. I discussed the matter later with both my cousin and her husband, and they concur wholeheartedly. Even Sir Edward, who disapproves of this entire affair, had to agree with our interpretation of what we saw at the dinner table.

I hope this letter provides you with the assurance you need to allay your qualms, for I shall not be writing again until this affair is concluded. I intend that Tess Brownlow will disap-

pear for a while from the face of the earth. When you next hear from her, a just retribution for Lord L.'s crime will have been meted out. When that day comes, I trust you will find in the news the same satisfaction that I shall.

Your ever grateful

T.B.

Fourteen

When Tess asked Julia to accompany "Miss Sidoney Ashburton" to Islington the following Sunday in order to attend the Four-in-Hand Club race, Julia began to get an inkling of just what the mischief was that her cousin was planning. Tess had never before shown an interest in sporting activities, but now she positively glowed with excitement. She'd spread out on her bed a charmingly flounced afternoon dress of white cambric, a wide blue sash, and a wide-brimmed hat of natural straw trimmed round the crown with dried flowers and a long blue satin ribbon. The girl herself sat at the dressing table brushing her dark curls vigorously. It was plain that she was intent on impressing a man.

Julia took a stance in the doorway of her cousin's room and said in frowning disapproval, "Tess Brownlow, are you trying to make Lotherwood fall in love with you?"

"Of course not," Tess replied airily. "I'm trying to make him fall in love with Sidoney Ashburton."

"Very well, Sidoney, then. What do you intend to accomplish by that, pray?"

"I intend . . . that is, *Sidoney* intends . . . to get him to make an offer."

"An offer? Of . . . of *marriage?*"

"Exactly."

Julia began to feel a throbbing pain at her temples. "Oh,

dear. Tess, my love, do I need to remind you that the man is betrothed?''

"No, you needn't. That won't stop me. The whole idea of betrothals is that they may be broken under certain circumstances . . . as when the affianced man and woman discover they don't suit.''

"As when the *woman* discovers they don't suit," Julia corrected. "The man, once he's betrothed, cannot in honor break his word. That is the one advantage we women have in the marital stakes." Julia came into the room, sat wearily down on a corner of the bed, and leaned her throbbing head against the bedpost. "If your plan depends on the breaking of his engagement, Tess, it is hopeless. Viola Lovell will never release so good a catch as Lotherwood."

"As to that, Julia, my love," Tess said, smiling at herself in the glass of her dressing table, "we shall see what we shall see. I've been successful so far, have I not? My gypsy trick was more effective than I dreamed it would be!"

"Yes . . . but I don't know what you intend to gain by it, even if you are successful," Julia persisted. "Is it your intention to make him mad for you and then to refuse him? Is that your plan?"

"Do you think I'd let him off as lightly as that?" Tess's face took on the look of implacable purpose that Julia had seen before. "Oh, no, my love! I intend to set a wedding date. And on the eve of that day, I intend to arrange for someone to appear at his door with the news that I . . . or, rather, that Sidoney . . . was killed in a dreadful accident."

"Oh, Tess, *no!*" Julia gasped.

Her cousin turned and looked at her. "Oh, Julia, *yes!* Sidoney Ashburton will disappear from Lotherwood's life as suddenly and irrevocably as Jeremy Beringer disappeared from mine. Why not?"

Julia put her fingers to her now aching temples. "It is too . . . too monstrous . . . !"

"Is it monstrous?" She shook her head and stared at her reflection in the mirror, frowning at it. "It doesn't seem so to me. Mama must be right . . . I am an unfeeling, cold person, like my father."

Julia's sympathetic nature was immediately aroused. "Tess! Your mother never meant that. You are *not* cold! Your feel-

ings are more tender than most. But you have been much
hurt—''

Tess sighed. ''Yes, I have. By Lotherwood most of all.
That's why I believe that my plan is the only suitable retribution. How else can I arrange for him to suffer as he made
others suffer?''

Julia had no answer. She knew she couldn't persuade her
obsessed cousin to change her mind. All she could do was to
hope that Viola Lovell would never give Lotherwood up. With
that hope to ease her mind, she rose and went to ready herself
for the outing to Islington.

It was Hugh Sherbrooke who'd issued the challenge to Lotherwood: a twenty-mile race which would match just the two of
them. Sherbrooke was a young hothead of twenty-two whose
prowess as a horseman was becoming the talk of the sporting
world. He would ride anything, drive anything, and bet on
anything. Lotherwood, who was becoming tired of the endless
competitiveness of sports, had initially declined the challenge,
but the officers of the FHC had begged him to accept. ''We
can't let these callow striplings think the world is theirs,'' the
white-haired Lord Osmond had pleaded. ''Let's show 'em that
they still have a thing or two to learn.'' Lord Osmond was a
legendary driver still active at the age of seventy-four, and
Lotherwood admired him too much to disappoint him. Thus
the match was set.

The FHC established the rules. The two contestants would
start out at Islington, each in a phaeton-and-pair. They would
drive north for ten miles, immediately add another pair of
horses and return to the starting line with four in hand. There
would be judges and timers at the ten-mile mark and the finish
line, and other FHC members would be stationed all along the
route.

Members of the FHC buzzed with excitement about the
match for weeks beforehand. The word soon spread beyond
the membership of the FHC; by the day of the race all the
members of White's, Warkworth's, and even Brooke's had
become interested in the affair. Hundreds of bets had been
placed, and the betting men all made plans to be present at
Islington that day. Gentlemen of sporting proclivities would
not permit themselves to miss such an occasion either. Even

the young dandies, who cared more about their waistcoats than sporting events, decided it might be an entertaining outing to enjoy with their ladies. One dismayed hostess, who'd arranged a party for that day, had to cancel her plans, for most of the people she'd invited were bound for Islington.

The weather on the day of the race was fine—sunny and warm, with fresh westerly breezes. This encouraged the FHC to expect a notable turnout, but when, that afternoon, they discovered that the usually quiet road to Islington was thronged with carriages, they began to realize the crowd would be beyond their wildest expectations. By starting time the entire ten-mile stretch of road on which the race was to be run was fringed with carriages, and the area near the starting line looked like a fairground. Usually blasé Corinthians were perched on the tops of their coaches, excited and eager to get a good view; ladies in ruffles and bonnets were standing on the seats of their open phaetons, waving and calling to one another; sedate Londoners who, when in town, would not have gone on foot from one street to the next, now were abandoning their carriages (which could not be maneuvered closer than the outskirts of the throng) and making their way on foot to the starting line.

The air was full of the carnival noise of hundreds of voices shouting and laughing. There were even streamers and flags. A group of young bucks had made an enormous banner reading SHERBROOKE in large letters. Dolph Kelsey, not to be outdone, had procured a bedsheet on which he'd painted a huge LOTHERWOOD in red and gold. He'd attached the banner to the tops of two long poles and attached the poles to the roof of his carriage, one on each end. When Dolph raised that makeshift banner in the air, the crowd roared. Despite the loyalty of a number of young bucks who crowded together beneath Sherbrooke's banner, there was little doubt who the favorite was that afternoon.

Dolph's banner, hanging twenty feet in the air, was the first thing Tess saw on her arrival. Sir Edward had refused to go, and Julia and Tess, knowing nothing about sporting events, had not realized that they should have left home early. The Quimby coachman could not maneuver the carriage anywhere near the starting line. When he found a place to stop, the ladies couldn't see a thing. After abandoning the coach, they opened their parasols and set out on foot through the throng. Someone trampled on Tess's toe and didn't even look round to apologize. Someone else stepped on Julia's dress, ripping her hem. And when they came up to the starting point, there was such a crush in front of them that they could not even see the tops of the racing vehicles. "We may as well go home," Julia muttered irritably. "We shan't be able to make out a thing."

Tess was about to agree when they heard someone calling, "Julia! Miss Ashburton! Over here!"

It was Lady Wetherfield, perched on the back of a seat in the Fenwicks' open chaise, her feet cozily resting on the arm-cushions and her head protected by an open parasol. Lady Fenwick was seated right beside her and Lord Fenwick opposite. "Come here!" Lady Wetherfield shouted imperiously. "You'll see ever so much better from here."

Julia and Tess did not hesitate a moment. They climbed aboard the carriage with dispatch, thanked Lady Fenwick for making room for them, and perched themselves, like the others, on the the backs of the seats. After exchanging greetings, Julia joined the ladies in their gossip, while Tess and Lord Fenwick studied the situation at the starting line. Two light, open phaetons, highly polished and gleaming in the sunlight, were poised at the starting line, one yoked to a pair of nervous roans and the other to two perfectly matched grays. Tess could see Lotherwood checking the breeching and hipstraps of his grays. Sherbrooke had already climbed up on his vehicle and was waving gaily to his cheering friends. "He seems to be full of confidence," Tess murmured.

Lord Fenwick was thinking the same thing. "I suppose I would be, too, if I had a pair of roans like those," he said, brushing at his graying moustache with his fingertips. "Beautiful animals, both of 'em."

"Do you think he'll win?"

"No, but it'll be close. Those in the know're saying that Sherbrooke's favored in the first half because of those horses. But the betting is on Matt for the finish."

"Why is that, my lord? Do they change horses at the half?"

"No, they simply add another pair each. But even though Sherbrooke'll still have the roans, he doesn't have the skill. Take my word for it, Miss Ashburton, there's no one to equal

Matt with four horses in hand.''

"Yes, if he isn't drunk," Tess muttered bitterly under her breath.

"What's that you said?" Fenwick asked, turning to her.

"Nothing, my lord. I only said I hope you're right."

A cheer from the crowd drew their eyes back to the starting line. Lotherwood had climbed aboard his phaeton. He waved to the crowd and then lifted his hat to a carriage on the opposite side of the road. Tess realized that it was the Lovell carriage, for Viola was jumping up and down on the seat and waving her hat wildly. Then the two contestants picked up the reins and settled themselves on their boxes as the FHC officials circled the equipages for a final check. Lotherwood, taking a last look round, spotted his aunt and waved at her. In mid-wave, he saw Tess, and his hand seemed to freeze in place for a moment. Then, just as the starter took his place and raised his gun, Lotherwood, with a pleased smile, lifted his hat to her. The gesture, coming at a time when he should have had his eyes fixed on the starter, caught everyone's attention, and every head turned to see who it was who'd distracted his lordship. Tess felt the blood rush to her cheeks, but fortunately the gun went off at that moment. There was a great uproar, and the phaetons lurched forward in a thunderous surge of motion, making off up the road in a cloud of dust and gravel. The dustcloud did not completely obscure the vehicles, however, and it was soon apparent that Sherbrooke had taken a small lead. The crowd continued to watch and shout as the carriages sped up the road and over the brow of a distant hill.

It would be forty-five minutes or more before the phaetons were expected to return, so the crowd began to mill about. Picnic baskets appeared, and wine bottles were passed from hand to hand. Betting ledgers were produced as more bets were made, the odds narrowing from five-to-one for Lotherwood to two-to-one. The roans had evidently made a great impression on the crowd.

Viola Lovell, escorted by Dolph Kelsey, came up to the Fenwick carriage to exchange greetings with Lady Wetherfield and her hosts. She seemed much more subdued than she'd been before the race, and when she made her bow to Miss Ashburton, her manner was decidedly cool. It was clear to Julia that Lotherwood's betrothed had taken due note of his greeting to Miss Ashburton and had not been pleased.

After half an hour the FHC officials began to clear the crowd from the road. The starting line had now become the finish line, with a bright red ribbon stretched across the road to mark the place. The crowd closed in on the spot, and a hush fell over them. Dolph climbed up on the roof of his carriage with a stopwatch in his hand and shouted out the time every minute. Suddenly the sound of a distant shout wafted through the air, and cries of "They're coming!" rose from the crowd at the finish line. "Good God!" Dolph bellowed. "It's been only forty-two minutes!"

A small dustcloud was noticed at the crest of the hill at that moment, setting the crowd in an uproar again. Only one carriage appeared. "Which one is it?" Fenwick shouted, but the answer could not be determined for a moment. By the time it was clear that Lotherwood was ahead, the second carriage had made its appearance. The vehicles thundered down the hill, the noise of their wheels and the pounding hooves of eight horses rising over the roar of the onlookers' screams. Sherbrooke's phaeton was a full length behind Lotherwood's, but he was slowly closing the gap. As the racers came into closer view, Sherbrooke's first pair raced up to the right of Lotherwood's carriage, passed it, and came up alongside his rear pair.

Everyone in the crowd was screaming. Both drivers were on their feet and urging their horses to their utmost. Lotherwood began to draw ahead again, and with the finish line so close, it became apparent that Sherbrooke had no chance. Whether from desperation or simply poor horsemanship, no one knew, but Sherbrooke suddenly swerved to the right, making it necessary for Lotherwood to do the same if he was to avoid a collision between his phaeton and Sherbrooke's horses. Just as they thundered past the Fenwick carriage, Lotherwood veered. His phaeton swayed dangerously on only its two right wheels. The crowd gasped as if from one throat. But Lotherwood, manipulating the reins with cool concentration, managed somehow to right it. All four of his horses galloped over the finish line before Sherbrooke's.

Everyone in the crowd, cheering wildly, surged forward to get a glimpse of the winner as he climbed down from the phaeton. The Fenwicks and Lady Wetherfield jumped down from the carriage as soon as their hero crossed the finish line, in hopes of being among the first to embrace him. Julia, car-

ried away by the excitement, was about to follow when she
noticed that Tess had slumped down on the seat, her face
ashen. "Tess, my love, what *is* it?" Julia cried in alarm, kneeling down beside her stricken cousin.

"I don't know," Tess answered, breathing heavily. "It was
. . . dreadful. I thought the carriage would overturn. It made
me . . . *sick* . . ."

"Oh, my poor dear, you thought of Jeremy! It brought
everything back!"

Tess shivered. "Yes . . . Jeremy . . ."

"You're white as a sheet!" Julia took Tess's hands in hers
and rubbed them briskly. "We shouldn't have come."

"No, I suppose we shouldn't have. I didn't dream I would
find it so . . . so horrifying."

"Then, Tess, my dear, let's go home."

Tess shook her head, trying to pull herself together. "We
can't, Julia. Lady Wetherfield would think it strange if we
disappeared without a word of thanks or farewell."

"Oh, fiddle! Who cares for that? I can explain to her
another day that you were feeling ill—"

"No, I don't wish to draw such attention to myself. I don't
want to give anyone the least hint that a carriage accident can
affect me so. There must be no connection whatever between
Sidoney Ashburton and a coaching accident."

"But you surely don't want to stay! Letty will take one look
at you and know that something's wrong."

"Then, Julia, you stay. I'll go back to our carriage and wait
for you. Just say that all the excitement made me feel a bit
faint, so I went back to our carriage to avoid the noisy
crowd."

Julia didn't want to leave her cousin alone, but Tess, as
usual, managed to persuade her. Tess walked back to the
Quimby carriage on legs that shook, but her mind was more
troubled than her body. Why, she wondered, had she become
so upset by something that was so trivial? There had been no
accident. To everyone else the incident had been nothing but a
momentary fright. Was it that she'd been too dramatically
reminded of Jeremy lying dead under a pile of rubble? Or was
it something else . . . something that she was ashamed to admit
to herself?

She found the carriage deserted. The coachman had
evidently gone with the rest of the crowd to cheer the winner.

Grateful to be alone, she climbed inside and sank back against the squabs with a sigh of relief. She closed her eyes and tried to remember what had made her feel ill. She recalled the excitement of the last seconds of the race, the thrill of tension when Sherbrooke's horses seemed to be catching up to Lotherwood's, the chill of her blood when Lotherwood's phaeton swerved. She'd been certain that it would fall over. At that speed the accident would have been disastrous. In her mind's eye she'd seen the disaster quite plainly . . . the rearing horses, the horrible noise, the phaeton reduced to rubble, the bloody body buried beneath it. And she'd seen the victim's face, and the sight had made her ill.

Julia had easily explained it. The incident had brought Jeremy's accident to mind. But she had to admit one fact to herself that she'd not admitted to Julia . . . the fact that the face she'd seen in her mind was not Jeremy's. It was Lotherwood's.

❦ Fifteen ❧

Even without rousing herself from the depth of the carriage seat into which she'd sunk to look out the window, Tess knew that the crowd at the finish line was beginning to disperse. She could hear footsteps and voices approaching, and from all about her came the sounds of carriages starting to move along the road south to London. And soon Farrow, the Quimbys' coachman, tapped on the carriage door, indicating that he'd returned to his post.

"Lady Quimby is making her farewells," Tess told him, pulling herself up to a more dignified position and adjusting the angle of her hat. "She will be along shortly."

Farrow nodded and climbed up to his place on the box. But when the carriage door opened a few minutes later, it was not Julia who looked in. "May I come in, ma'am?" Lotherwood asked.

"But . . . my *lord,* what . . . ? Where's Julia? Is anything amiss?"

"No, nothing at all, Miss Ashburton. Lady Quimby is going home with my Aunt Letty in the Fenwicks' carriage. I insisted on seeing you home myself." And without waiting for her permission, he climbed up and sat down beside her. He was still in his riding clothes, though they looked considerably the worse for wear. His shirt was wrinkled, his hat was missing, and his neckcloth was undone and hanging loosely round his throat.

"Seeing me home yourself?" Tess echoed, feeling shaken and confused.

"Yes. I wished very much to speak to you. I hope you'll pardon my coming to you in all my dirt." He made an attempt to brush his trousers. "I must be a disheveled sight. I have no idea what's become of my hat."

Tess waved a hand in dismissal of the subject of his appearance. "I don't understand," she said, concentrating on questions of more importance than his lordship's disarray. "Julia—Lady Quimby—wouldn't desert me, especially knowing that I was not . . . er . . . not . . ."

"Not feeling quite the thing?" he supplied.

"Yes."

"So she told us. She hasn't deserted you, Miss Ashburton, I assure you. My aunt Letty and I had to use all our powers of persuasion to convince her to let me take her place." He tapped on the roof of the carriage with the handle of the riding crop he still carried, signaling the coachman to start off. Then, as the coach set promptly into motion, he sat back against the seat and looked at her.

Tess was disconcerted. It was bad enough that she still felt queasy inside, but to have to face Lotherwood in this unforeseen way was not to her liking. She needed to have her wits about her in her encounters with him; she could not afford to make a slip. If her scheme was to succeed, it was obviously necessary to see him frequently, but she wanted to meet him only according to her prearranged plans, not according to haphazard chance. "I still don't understand," she said, passing the back of her hand over her forehead. "Why should you wish to take Julia's place? You are the hero of the hour. Why are you not having a joyful celebration with your friends . . . and your betrothed?"

"I shall have my fill of joyful celebrations this evening. Lord Osmond is hosting some sort of gala, I believe. That will be quite enough." He smiled in the self-deprecating way she'd seen before, that she couldn't help liking. "This is not the first race I've ever won, you know," he said with a disarming lack of pride or affectation. "The celebrations do not seem as thrilling as they once did."

"But that doesn't explain, my lord, why you deserted your admirers to escort *me* home."

He hesitated for a moment before speaking. "You became

ill during the race, is that not so?'' he asked.

"Not exactly. To say that I became ill is putting too serious a face on it. I was merely a bit discomposed."

"No, you were more than discomposed. I saw you, you know."

She was startled. "*Saw* me?"

"It was just at the moment when my phaeton lurched. I saw your face. It was just for a fraction of a second, for, as you can imagine, my attention was fully occupied with the horses. But I did see you, as one might see a face in a lightning flash. Your expression impressed itself upon my brain."

"Oh?" She noticed that her fingers had begun, unaccountably, to tremble. "Why was that?"

"It was a look of pure horror, ma'am. I don't think I've ever seen such a look. And later, when I noticed you walking back to your carriage—"

"You *noticed* me?" She shook her head in disbelief. "But you were completely surrounded by your well-wishers when I—"

"Nevertheless, I noticed. You were so shaken that you were using your parasol as a cane. I realized that my little swerve had upset you badly, and that's why I've come. I wish to apologize for frightening you, and to make amends, if I can."

Tess did not know how to handle this unexpected kindness. Lotherwood had not turned out to be the sort of man she'd expected. *One's enemy should not be kind,* she thought ruefully. *It tended to muddy the purity of one's motive for revenge.* But of course, he had not been kind to Jeremy; *that* was what she had to remember. Even if in his sober moments he was generous and large-hearted, he had permitted himself to get drunk and had caused her sweetheart's death. And that was as far from kind as could be.

She turned her back on him and stared out the window at the long shadows cast by the passing trees in the late afternoon light. "You give yourself too much credit, my lord," she said coldly. "That little 'swerve,' as you call it, was not your fault. And my horror-stricken look—if it was indeed such a look— had nothing to do with you. So you see, you have nothing to apologize to me for. You've deserted your admirers to no purpose."

Lotherwood was completely taken aback by this icy response. "You have an infinite capacity to astound me, ma'am. If the look of horror that I saw on your face—and it was *indeed* such a look—had nothing to do with me, then what was the cause?"

"I don't like carriage racing, that is all. I should not have come today."

"But it's only a sport, like any other. What harm is there in it?"

"How can you ask so foolish a question?" she demanded, turning about abruptly and glaring at him. "Especially today, when you almost *overturned!*"

His brow cleared. "Are you implying, my dear, that the sport is too dangerous? Is that what troubles you? Please take my word that it is not. That swerve, today, was due to Sherbrooke's carelessness—or, perhaps, to his viciousness—but either way it wasn't dangerous. Part of the skill of driving four-in-hand is learning how to handle swerves. I used to spend hours in my youth practicing taking turns on two wheels. I learned how to handle just such emergencies. There was no real danger today."

His complacency seemed to her nothing but arrogance. This was just the sort of reasoning she expected from the driver of that ill-fated stagecoach. "You are overconfident, I think," she said, trying not to let her revulsion show in her voice. "What if you'd misjudged the situation today? What if, just this once, your much-admired skill had deserted you, and you'd turned over?"

"Then I would have been hurt, I suppose. But you said, ma'am, that your look of horror had nothing to do with me."

A feeling of fury flared up in her. "How arrogant you are, my lord," she hissed between clenched teeth, "to think that under those circumstances my concern would be for you! If I had a horror-striken look on my face, it was not at the prospect of injury to *you* but to your *victims!*"

He was utterly nonplussed by her venomous tone. "Victims, ma'am? What victims?"

"Might there not have been victims? Is it not possible that some innocent bystander might have been crushed if you'd overturned?"

"I think it extremely unlikely. Besides, I've never overturned a carriage in my life."

"*Never*, my lord?" She stared at him, narrow-eyed and scornful. "Yet one does hear of carriage accidents with fatal consequences, does one not?"

She had the satisfaction of seeing a startled look cross his face and his eyes fall from hers. "There are always coaching accidents, Miss Ashburton," he said quietly, after a moment, "but there are fewer accidents in sporting events than you would dream. We who indulge in this sport take the greatest care to avoid them."

Tess did not utter the contemptuous words that sprang to her lips. It would not serve her purpose, she realized, to call him a liar. In fact, she was uncomfortably aware that she might already have gone too far. He had withdrawn from her as far down the seat as he could go and was now staring out the window. She was sorry she'd revealed so much of her true feelings toward him and his "sport." If he was ever to offer for her, she had to make him believe she cared for him. The conversation of the last few minutes was bound to have been a setback.

She glanced over at him, but his face was turned to the window. She could see only that his jaw was clenched. Was it tight with anger? What could she now say to bridge the gap she'd so thoughtlessly erected between them? She tried various openings in her mind, but everything she thought of sounded too insincere to utter aloud.

They rode without speaking for a long while. They were almost home when she finally, somewhat desperately, broke the silence. "My lord, I . . . I should not have spoken as I did," she murmured lamely.

He turned from the window and faced her. The late afternoon sun was setting behind the roofs of the city, making the light in the carriage too dim for her to see him clearly, but she could make out the tight expression of his mouth. She braced herself for a barrage of angry words.

Instead, he gently picked up her hand and looked down at it. "On the contrary, ma'am," he said, surprising her by the lack of rancor in his voice, "you had every right to speak so. I forced my presence on you this afternoon. I realize now that it was arrogant. I seem always to play the coxcomb in your presence. But I did so only in the hope that I might ease your mind and allay the terror that I saw in your face. However, I seem to have upset you more than before. I'm very sorry, ma'am."

Her heart seemed to leap up in her chest. She hadn't expected so generous a response to what must have seemed to him a bitter, sharp-tongued set-down. She lowered her head contritely. "It is I who should be sorry. I have taken the joy from your triumph."

"Yes, you have. But only because I sense that you've taken a strong dislike to me, and I don't know why. Have I done something to offend you, Miss Ashburton, that I've stupidly overlooked?"

Under the sheltering safety of her wide hat brim, she smiled to herself. How lucky she was! The man was offering her the opportunity to regain the ground she'd thought she lost. "I don't dislike you, Lord Lotherwood," she said, looking up at him coquettishly from beneath the brim. "Whatever made you think something as foolish as that?"

But his lordship did not smile back at her. "I'd be foolish to think anything else," he said, regarding her suspiciously. "You're playing some sort of game with me, Miss Ashburton. I only wish I knew what game it was."

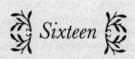

Sixteen

Viola Lovell's parents (having proudly watched their daughter embrace the victorious Lotherwood after the race) naturally assumed that the girl would return to London with her betrothed, and so they left Islington without her. But Viola, after surrendering her place beside Lotherwood to the dozens of other well-wishers who were surrounding him, discovered to her chagrin that he'd suddenly disappeared. One moment he was surrounded by a cheering mob and the next he was nowhere to be seen.

Deserted and bereft, she wandered about in confusion for a while, too embarrased to ask mere acquaintances if they'd seen him. But when she spotted Lord Kelsey, engaged with a circle of friends who were still crowing over their man's victory, she did not hesitate to draw him aside. "Do you know where Matt has gone?" she asked, not able to disguise the quiver in her voice.

"He must be somewhere about," Dolph answered cheerfully. "Can't have gone away already. He's probably hiding himself. Hates to have everyone clapping him on the shoulder, you know."

"But I don't see him anywhere! Can he have gone back to town without me?"

"Not likely, if he was expecting to take you up."

"Well, he *should* have been expecting to, should he not?"

She bit her underlip worriedly. "Mama and Papa have already left."

"Don't look so frightened, Miss Jinglebrain," Dolph teased. "You don't think you'll be left stranded here, do you? Look there! There's Lady Wetherfield with the Fenwicks. Wager my day's winnings she'll know where your fellow's hiding himself. Fenwick! I say, *Fenwick,* hold on there!"

Lord Fenwick, who had just ordered his coachman to depart, signaled the man to stop. When Lady Wetherfield realized it was she to whom they wanted to speak, she leaned over the side. In answer to Viola's breathless question about Lotherwood's whereabouts, the troublemaking aunt explained (with a barely visible smile of satisfaction) that Matt had excused himself to escort an ailing Miss Ashburton back to town.

"Miss *Ashburton?*" Viola gasped, her face paling.

Letty Wetherfield pretended not to notice her dismay. "Did you want a ride back with him? We can make room for you right here, can we not, Fenwick?"

But Dolph Kelsey, much moved by Viola's stricken expression, immediately offered her a seat in his curricle. "Much more room with me," he declared, giving Lady Wetherfield a reproving look.

"Thank you, D-Dolph," the girl said, her chin quivering. "That's very g-good of you."

The Fenwick carriage drove off, and Dolph and Viola went back toward his carriage. As they walked, Dolph threw several surreptitious looks in the girl's direction. Viola's face was clenched tightly to hold back tears, and her lips were pressed together in a tense line. Her hat had slipped off and was hanging by its ribbons on her back. She was obviously in distress, but Dolph thought he'd never seen a creature so endearing; a ride back in her company (during which he was certain to cheer her up) would make a charming end to a very pleasant afternoon.

After whispering to his friend Lord Merivan (who'd driven up to Islington with him) to find travel accommodations elsewhere, he helped Viola into his rig and climbed up beside her. As soon as they were on the road, the poor girl surrendered to sobs. "I'm s-sorry, Dolph," she stammered, sniffing into her handkerchief. "I c-can't seem to h-help myself."

"Oh, I don't mind," he said comfortingly. "Go ahead and blubber to your heart's content. Though I must say I don't see why. What is there in Matt's being gallant to someone who's taken ill to make you turn on the waterworks?"

"B-But it's . . . it's with M-Miss *Ashburton!*"

Dolph turned his eyes from the road to throw the girl a puzzled glance. "What's special about Miss Ashburton?"

"I d-don't know. It's just a f-feeling I have. Did you s-see him l-lift his hat to her today?"

"Lift his hat to her?"

"Yes. Just when the race b-began. His attention should have b-been on his horses, but there he w-was, smiling and d-doffing his hat to her as if there were n-nothing else on h-his m-mind. It s-seemed to m-me that everyone remarked on it."

Dolph's brow wrinkled. "Mmmm. Now you mention it, I *do* recall it. Thought at the time that Matt was going to lose a second or two on his start because of it."

"Oh, Dolph!" She burst into a fresh flood of tears. "You n-noticed it *too!*"

"Yes, but I don't see any particular significance in it. Certainly nothing to cause such a downpour as that."

She tried to stem the flood from her eyes with her already soggy handkerchief. "I s-suppose I'm making much of n-nothing, but I'm so m-miserable! Ever since Matt t-told us about the gypsy's prophecy, I've—"

"Prophecy? What prophecy? Do you mean that silliness about his marrying someone else?"

She peeped up at him with a glimmer of hope. "Do you really think it's silly?"

"It's utter rubbish! How can you even *think*—?"

"I don't know, D-Dolph. It occurred to m-me today that she . . . she . . ."

"She who? The gypsy?"

"No, you g-gudgeon, Miss *Ashburton*." She dropped her head in her hands. "What if she's the one the gypsy meant?"

Dolph gave a snort of disgust. "Vi, this is the outside of enough! If you insist on taking seriously the babbling of a gyspy woman, I wash my hands of you!"

Viola lifted her head and expelled a tremulous breath. "I s-suppose you're right. But even if we f-forget the gypsy, there is still t-today. He tipped his hat to her . . . and t-took her home. And the other night at L-Lady Wetherfield's, he sat p-prosing with her for hours and hardly sp-spoke to me at all!'' She brushed the wetness from her cheeks and turned to her escort with earnest intensity. "Tell me the t-truth, Dolph. Do you th-think he's *t-taken* with her?''

"Taken with her? Do you mean in an *amorous* way?'' He gaped at the girl beside him in complete surprise. "You must be touched in your upper works!''

"Why?'' Viola turned a pair of still-watery eyes up to his. "Don't you think she's beautiful?''

"Beautiful? Miss *Ashburton*? She's as tall as I am! Besides, she peers at everyone like a distrustful schoolmarm. Puts me in mind of a governess I had when I was a tyke. Frightened me out of my wits, that woman did.''

Viola glanced up at him gratefully. "You're n-not just saying that to c-comfort me, are you, Dolph? You truly don't believe that Matt is attracted to her?''

"When he has *you?* He'd have to be six ways a fool! See here, Vi, you're the prettiest creature in all of England, and everyone knows it. So you can put aside these addle-brained notions once and for all.''

"Truly, Dolph?''

"My word as a gentleman.''

She took a deep, trembling breath of relief and leaned her head on his shoulder. "Thank you, Dolph,'' she murmured. "You are my d-dearest friend in all the world! You've made me f-feel ever so much better.''

He looked down at the golden head resting on his shoulder, feeling very pleased with himself. Viola had been on the verge of a serious quarrel with her betrothed, but he'd calmed the ruffled waters. He had a golden tongue, he told himself. He'd managed to soothe the pretty creature beside him and to help his friend at the same time. "If you're feeling so much better,'' he said with benevolent self-satisfaction, "you can dry off those tears. I won't have you dampening my favorite coat!''

Dolph's golden tongue might very well have prevented a quarrel between Viola and her betrothed if Letty Wetherfield had not arranged an outing which brought Miss Ashburton again to Viola's attention. Nevertheless, for a fortnight following the race, Viola was able to dismiss Miss Ashburton from her mind. She and Matt did not encounter Miss Ashburton at any of the social gatherings which they attended, nor did her name cross anyone's lips in Viola's hearing. Matt certainly never mentioned her, and he gave no sign that he remembered her at all. So completely did Miss Ashburton seem to disappear from their lives that Viola allowed herself to hope that the girl had gone back to wherever it was she'd come from. It did not occur to her that Dolph had reported every word of their conversation to his friend, and that Matt had taken steps to keep Miss Ashburton out of their way.

But Lady Wetherfield did not intend to let Miss Ashburton disappear from their lives. Although Matt had twice refused to attend gatherings at her home, she did not give up. She racked her brain to find a way to bring her nephew and Miss Ashburton together again, but it was not until Julia remarked to her that her friend had not yet seen the Elgin marbles that Letty Wetherfield was able to concoct a successful scheme.

Lord Elgin had brought the magnificent Greek antiquities to England nine years before, in 1803, but since the sculptures were housed in a temporary building attached to his home in Park Lane, they were not commonly seen. Lady Wetherfield, being somewhat acquainted with Lord Elgin, had viewed them a number of times and had always found them breathtaking. When she learned from Julia that Miss Ashburton had never seen them, the idea of the outing took shape in her mind.

"Has Viola ever seen the Elgin marbles?" she asked her nephew when she paid one of her unexpected calls on him and caught him at breakfast.

"No, I don't think she has. Why?"

"I'm arranging with Lord Elgin to visit the exhibit again, with a small group of friends. Perhaps you'd like to join us."

Lotherwood eyed her suspiciously over his coffee cup. "Join whom?" he asked.

"I've only asked the Fenwicks and Lady Cowper so far. I'll include the Lovells, if you like."

"Very well, we'll gladly join you. I know Viola would wish to see the marbles. But I hope, Aunt Letty," he added, reaching for a slice of toast and buttering it with concentration, "that you won't ask anyone else. I dislike viewing works of art in a crowd."

His aunt said nothing else. She fully intended that the Quimbys and Miss Ashburton should be part of the group, but she saw no reason to mention it. Three more people would not

make a crowd, she told herself. She felt no touch of guilt. If
anyone had accused her of acting dishonestly, she would have
laughed and said that an evasive silence was not quite a lie.

Viola was not as enthusiastic about seeing the marbles as
Matt had expected. She and her mother had arranged to visit
the exclusive modiste who was making her wedding gown on
the day of the outing, and she explained to Matt that Madame
Durand was very temperamental and did not do her best work
for clients who missed appointments. But she promised to join
the group at Lord Elgin's exhibit as soon as her fitting was
over.

Lotherwood, having no lady to escort, arrived at the exhibit
before any of the others. Pleased at having the opportunity to
view the sculptures in privacy, he went immediately to the
alcove which housed his favorite of all the pieces, the fragment
from the east pediment of the Parthenon representing the head
of one of the moon goddess's chariot horses. Something about
this sculpture particularly moved him. The chariot that the
horse was supposed to be drawing had ostensibly sunk below
the horizon with the setting moon, and all that could still be
seen was the horse's head, looking tired and spent. Its great
eyes were wide with weariness, and its lower jaw hung limply
open almost as if the animal were gasping for breath. But
despite the weariness, the horse had a power and strength that
were unmistakable; there was a grandeur in the massive profile
that Lotherwood loved. He liked to imagine that, if the goddess had needed him, the tired animal would have summoned
the strength to gallop like the wind.

"I might have suspected that you'd be with the horses,"
said a low-pitched voice behind him. "You look as if you'd
like to stroke his nose."

He turned to find Miss Ashburton smiling at him, and
before he had a chance to reign in his emotions, he felt a surge
of gladness at the sight of her. She wore a dress of deep amber,
with a dark, wine-colored shawl thrown over it. One gloved
hand was untying the ribbon of her straw bonnet, while the
other was held out to him. Standing poised in the doorway of
the alcove, with the rays of sun from the high windows
lighting her face, she seemed magnificent, like the subject of a
Renaissance portrait or the heroine of an opera. His eyes
drank her in, as if they'd been starved for color by having
gazed too long at the pallid stones.

But he recovered quickly. "Good afternoon, Miss Ashburton," he said, removing his hat and bowing over her hand. "Yes, I have a strong affection for horses, even those of marble." He turned back to the sculpture, wondering why he didn't feel at all like murdering his aunt for lying to him. "This one is especially beautiful, don't you agree?"

She came up beside him and studied the sculpture. "Marvelous. But a little sad, too, I think . . . as if he'd been driven too long and too far."

"Yes, I feel that, too."

They stared at the horse's head for a long moment, Lotherwood finding himself unduly pleased at her reaction. "But you mustn't believe that I find horses the only work of art worth noticing. There are many pieces here I could recommend to your attention. Have you seen the Herakles in the next room?"

"Good heavens, my lord, you astound me. Are you an expert in classical sculpture? I thought you knew only horses."

"Now, that is a set-down if ever I heard one!" He laughed, taking her arm and strolling out toward the main room. "But you were quite right in your first assumption. I know very little about classical sculpture or anything else, other than horses. Of the four levels of gentlemanly types, I stand on the very lowest."

"Four levels?" she asked, looking up at him curiously. "What levels are those?"

"Haven't you heard of the four types of gentlemen? Then allow me, ma'am, to enlighten you. This method of classification may stand you in good stead when you decide to choose a husband. On the highest rung you will find the Religious Gentleman, who, even if he doesn't take holy orders, spends his days in doing good works for the benefit of humanity. One step below is the Scholarly Gentleman, who studies the classics, reads the great thinkers, and writes philosophical treatises in his mature years. On the third rung is the Military Gentleman, to whom the development of his mind and soul may not be of primary importance, but who is willing to give his life for the protection of his country and is therefore also admirable. But on the bottom rung, alas, we find the Athletic Gentleman, who has nothing at all to recommend him but his sense of sportsmanship and his well-developed muscles."

She laughed, a full-throated, gurgling laugh that delighted

him. "You are too modest, my lord. I know you have more to recommend you than that."

"Do you, ma'am? But didn't you just remark that you thought I knew about nothing but horses?"

"Yes, but I am already amending that opinion."

He stopped in his tracks in mock astonishment. "You don't say! Then tell me, please, what is it you've discovered?"

But before she could respond, they came upon the others in the group and had to separate. While Lotherwood made his greetings to his aunt and her guests, Lady Cowper took Tess's arm and led her to view some of the sculptures in the far corner of the room.

By the time they returned, an unexpected sight greeted Tess's eye. Lotherwood had evidently been describing to Lord Fenwick his theory of how the various marbles had appeared on the ancient Parthenon, and the others in the group had, one by one, come up behind to listen. Lotherwood did not know that his aunt, Lady Fenwick, Julia, and Edward were quietly grouped behind him and eavesdropping on his words. Lotherwood was suggesting that the sculptures of the Parthenon's West Pediment (which were so much damaged that it was difficult to make sense of them) represented the contest between Poseidon and Athena for possession of ancient Attica. He pointed out that the weathered torso of a huge, powerful figure could be the sea god, that the reclining figure (which had undoubtedly filled the left corner of the pediment) might be a minor god watching the contest, and that a third torso might represent the divine messenger Hermes, who, according to legend, had accompanied Athena to the contest. Tess could not help being impressed by his lordship's knowledge of mythology, his eye for sculptural detail, and the modest yet persuasive manner in which he spoke. And when Edward came forward (startling Lotherwood by declaring enthusiastically, "By heavens, old man, I'm dashed if you haven't got the right of it!"), she broke into applause with all the others.

Lotherwood flushed in embarrassment. "We're not likely ever to learn whether I've got the right of it or not," he muttered, looking about him for a way to escape, "so I'm quite safe in spouting my theories. Come, Miss Ashburton, I want you to see some other horses that I like."

As he ushered her boldly out of the room and into another

small alcove, Lady Fenwick threw Letty a quizzical glance. Lady Fenwick had been privy to much of the behind-the-scenes activity on the day of the race, and it suddenly occurred to her to wonder if the betrothed Lotherwood was showering too much attention on the attractive Miss Ashburton. She wondered if she should drop a word of warning into Letty's ear.

Meanwhile Lotherwood had stopped before a fragment showing the head of a horse rising up from the base of the pediment. In the midst of his explanation that this was probably the horse of the rising sun god, contrasting with the horse they'd seen earlier which drew the chariot of the setting moon goddess, he suddenly stopped speaking. Tess looked at him curiously. "Is something the matter, my lord?"

Abstracted, he shook his head. "Must you be forever calling me 'my lord'?" he asked in irritation. "My name is Matthew, although that's too biblical for me. I prefer to be called Matt."

"I don't think it would be suitable for me to do so, my lord, any more than it would be for you to call me Sidoney."

He gave a sudden laugh. "Sidoney. I should have great difficulty calling you that, even if it *were* suitable. Never have I heard a more ridiculous name."

"Then it's just as well you can't use it," she answered tartly.

"Very well, don't eat me. I meant no offense." He looked down at the hat in his hand and fingered the brim absently. "I suppose it was unsuitable for me to take you away from the others like this, too," he muttered.

"Quite unsuitable. I only hope there will not be talk to reach Miss Lovell's ears. We must be going back."

"Dash it all," he said, taking her arm as if to keep her from running off, "why is it I never find the opportunity to have a proper conversation with you?"

"I beg to differ, my lord," she teased. "Nothing we've ever said to each other has been *im*proper, has it?"

"I'm serious, ma'am." He dropped her arm and took hold of her chin instead, tilting her head up ever so slightly. "I have a keen desire to sit beside you somewhere in private, with no one about to disturb us and at least two hours of time ahead of us, where I can ask you questions and learn what goes on behind those eerie eyes of yours."

"That, sir," she said, removing his hand from her chin, "would be more unsuitable than anything else you've suggested."

He sighed. "I suppose it would. Do you ride?"

"What?"

"Do you ride? Perhaps we could meet one morning and ride in the park for an hour or so."

She shook her head and started toward the door. "That is quite impossible, and you know it. Come, my lord. Our absence will be noted."

When they returned to the group, they found that Viola and her mother had arrived. Viola was engaged in an animated conversation with Lady Cowper, but when she looked round and saw Miss Ashburton she turned quite pale. Lotherwood went over at once to greet her. "You are looking lovely, my dear," he said in her ear. "I'm glad you're finally here."

"I don't think you've m-missed me," she answered in a small voice.

"Yes, I have. I've been waiting to show you my favorite piece in this collection. It's in an alcove over there. It's an absolutely wonderful horse's head. Come and let me show it to you."

Viola kept her head lowered, but the position did not hide the pout of her lovely underlip. "I don't wish to see any old horses," she said in a shaking voice. "I want to go home."

"Are you sure, Vi? There are so many marvelous things here to see." He took her arm in his and leaned down so that he could see her face. "After spending an hour among these masterpieces, you'll feel so inspired that—"

She pulled her arm away petulantly. "I want to go home! If you don't wish to escort me, then I can go with Mama."

They were standing a little apart from, but in full view of, all the others. Lotherwood could see that everyone was aware of their quarrel and its cause. He reddened in embarrassment. "I'll be glad to escort you, if that is what you wish," he said quietly. "We need only to say our good-byes."

He put on a public face and moved among his friends with perfectly appropriate smiles and bows. He said and did everything he ought, but inside he felt ill. He found himself wondering if he'd made a terrible mistake in offering for Viola. The little incident had made her seem to him like a spoiled child; he felt as if he'd seen her throw a tantrum. He hated having been party to that public scene. The fact that he himself was very much to blame did not lessen his revulsion. One's own conduct is never quite as repugnant in one's eyes as someone else's.

He was, however, quite aware of his guilt. This afternoon's encounters had forced him to admit to himself that his attraction to Miss Ashburton was an actuality, stronger and more real than any gypsy could conjure up in a crystal ball. He felt more excitedly alive in her presence than he'd felt in any race, and in her absence his memory of her consumed him. In contrast to her, his betrothed seemed childish and dull.

But perhaps he was being unfair. He was infatuated, and Viola sensed it. She was jealous, and jealousy was known to distort one's character. It often made people behave in humiliating ways. He must be careful not to blame Viola for his own faults. And in any case, he was betrothed—shackled for a lifetime—and he knew he had no choice but to make the best of it.

He came up to Miss Ashburton to say good-bye, determined to make it their last encounter. If he kept himself out of her way, he was certain he could overcome his infatuation and face his betrothed with a clear conscience. "Good-bye, Miss Ashburton," he said, taking her gloved hands and looking intently into those bewitching eyes. "Thank you for making this afternoon so memorable for me."

She smiled and nodded with a gracious, mannerly detachment, moving her lips as if she were saying a perfectly polite good-day. But what he heard was, "I always ride on Wednesdays."

He was sure he hadn't heard properly, but his inner clock stopped again. "What?" he asked stupidly, wondering if everyone in the room could hear the strange thump of excitement in his chest.

Her smile widened by the merest millimeter. "At eight," she murmured, dismissing him with a wave of her hand. "Good day, my lord." Her voice was loud and clear as she walked away. "Thank you for an instructive afternoon."

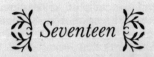

Seventeen

Tess departed from Lord Elgin's exhibit very pleased with herself, but as soon as she and the Quimbys returned home, Edward turned on her. They had barely set foot in the door when Edward rounded on the two women and loudly declared, "I've had just about enough of this business!"

Julia paused in the act of removing her gloves. "What business, my love?"

"What business? Can you ask? This business of Tess's. All this secret plotting, all this false-name nonsense, and now this latest mischief!"

"Mischief?" his wife asked with exaggerated innocence.

"Don't pretend you didn't see that scene between Lotherwood and Miss Lovell!" He lifted his cane and waved it beneath Tess's nose. "It's a *damnable* pass to upset so sweet a creature as Miss Lovell," he growled. "And as for Lotherwood, he's as fine a fellow as I've come across, whatever he's done in the past!"

"*Whatever* he's done?" Tess echoed indignantly, thrusting the menacing cane away. "Whatever he's done is not something to push aside so cavalierly!"

"Yes, really, Edward, I quite agree with Tess," Julia said, trying to placate him without taking his side. "You can't ignore what he's done as if it were a mere peccadillo, however fine you find him now."

"Quite right," Tess said, starting up the staircase, swinging

115

her bonnet saucily by its ribbons. "You know, Edward, I would like him, too, if I didn't know his secret shame. He has many surprising facets, I admit. If I didn't hate him so, I might really enjoy this flirtation."

"Flirtation? *Flirtation?*" Edward stalked to the stairway, perched his pince-nez on his nose, and glared up at her. "Is that what you're doing? Flirting with a man who's *betrothed?* And what do you intend to accomplish by this shocking behavior?"

"What I intend to accomplish, my dearest cousin-in-law, is to marry the man." She leaned over the banister and grinned into Edward's angry face. "Almost."

"*Almost?* What does that *mean?* What does she mean, Julia?"

Julia dropped her eyes and fiddled nervously with the gloves she'd just removed. "She means that she intends to entice him to offer for her and then to die on the eve of their wedding."

Edward's spectacles fell off his nose. "*Die?*"

Julia shrugged. "Well . . . *pretend* to die."

"*Miss Sidoney Ashburton* will die," Tess amended.

Edward gaped at her. "Die? I don't understand."

"It's quite simple, really. That's why I created her. To die."

Julia patted her bewildered husband on the arm. "I shall explain it all to you, my love, as soon as you make yourself comfortable. But Tess, I don't see why you are so complacent. If his lordship should *not* offer for you—and frankly, I don't see how he can, being betrothed as he is—you will have engaged in this elaborate masquerade for nothing."

"He will offer for me," Tess said with a serene smile. "In a fortnight or less." And with that arrogant prediction, she waved her bonnet at them in a gesture of adieu and sauntered up the stairs.

Julia, realizing that the time had come for Edward to know all, coaxed him into his favorite easy chair in the downstairs sitting room and ordered the butler to light a fire and bring in a cup of Edward's favorite Indian tea. This done, she perched on a footstool at his feet. "Promise me that you won't lose your temper," she urged, patting him fondly on the knee. "If Tess is correct in her prediction that Lotherwood will offer for her within a fortnight, the whole matter will be over in a month's time. She will, by then, have gone back to Todmorden, and we shall be at peace again."

He sighed deeply. "Very well, I shall *try* to stay calm. Just tell me what this 'dying' nonsense is all about."

"It's a rather clever plan, really. And the retribution is almost biblical in its fitness to the crime. An eye for an eye, you see."

"No, I don't see. Go on."

"Well, all depends on Lotherwood's offering for her, of course, but even *you* could see today that he's taken with her."

"Yes, even I could see that," Edward muttered dryly.

"Right. So when he does offer, she will set a prompt wedding date, telling him that since she has no family—"

"But she *has* a family. What about her mother?"

Julia frowned at him impatiently. "*Tess Brownlow* has a family. *Sidoney Ashburton* does not. And so she will ask Lotherwood to arrange a very private ceremony, which he no doubt will very happily do. Then, on the eve of the wedding . . ." Here Julia hesitated and looked up at her husband with trepidation. "Now, you will not fly into alt over this, Edward, will you?"

He groaned. "Go on. On the eve of the wedding—?"

"On the eve of the wedding we will go to Lotherwood's—"

"We? You and *I?* Listen to me, Lady Wife, I promised to stay calm, but I did *not* agree to play any part in this affair!"

Julia sighed. "Please hear me out, my love. How can we discuss this when you don't know all?"

"Very well. Proceed with this preposterous plot. On the eve of the wedding you and I are to go to Lotherwood's. For what purpose?"

"To inform him, with heartfelt sympathy, that there's been a carriage accident in which Miss Sidoney Ashburton has, most tragically, been killed."

Edward gaped at her in disbelief. "You've lost your wits. *Both* of you!"

"That's what I said, too. But when one thinks about it—"

"There's nothing to think about," Edward declared firmly, putting his teacup down on the nearest table with a finality that almost shattered the delicate china. "It's too ridiculous to consider."

"No, it's not. It can be accomplished quite easily. Just before we make the announcement to Lotherwood, Tess will steal home to Todmorden and never be seen in London again.

She says she doesn't care much for life in town anyway. Before she goes, she will arrange to bribe an actor to perform the role of a clergyman who will conduct a brief funeral service a few days after she leaves. It's rather neat, really. Sidoney Ashburton will be dead, Lotherwood will have been dealt a just retribution, and everyone will get on with their lives.''

Edward stared at his wife in horror. "It's . . . *ghoulish!* Positively ghoulish! I can make some allowances for Tess, considering the devastation of her loss, but *you*, Julia! I never would have believed that *you*—"

"I know, dearest. I reacted just as you are doing when Tess first explained it to me. But when I thought about it, I realized that it's a better plan than some others she might have concocted. No one is really *harmed*, you see."

"No one harmed? Are you *mad?* What about poor, adorable little Miss Lovell, for one?"

His wife threw him a look of disgust. " 'Poor, adorable little Miss Lovell' will have gained more than she lost. What happiness would she have had married to a man who doesn't love her enough to resist the first temptress to come his way?"

Edward was forced to concede the point. "There is something in that, I suppose," he muttered. "But there are several others who will be harmed. Tess, herself, will be forever banished from town. *We* will forever be deprived of her company. And all this is nothing compared to the harm to Lotherwood."

"Tess is willing to pay the price of banishment for the satisfaction of knowing that Jeremy's death is avenged. As to our loss, we will visit Tess in Todmorden, just as we've always done. But as to Lotherwood—"

"Yes, Lotherwood. How are you going to convince me that there's no harm *there?*"

Julia got up and went to poke the fire. "I can't pretend that Lotherwood won't be hurt. That is the intention, after all. Tess says it is simple justice: he will be made to suffer as she has suffered." She looked round at her husband with pleading eyes. "It *is* just, is it not, Edward?"

Edward tried to convince himself that there was some justification in all this, but he remained troubled. "I don't know, Julia. I am not a jurist. I only know that Tess has no right, either legally or morally, to play the avenger."

"I know, love," Julia said sadly, "but she will go ahead

whether we support her or not. If we refuse to help her, she may concoct some alternative that would be worse." She returned to the stool and sat down, resting her head on his knee. "It won't be too dreadful, will it? After all, Lotherwood *is* guilty of a terrible act. We mustn't forget that. And after a while he'll get over it. He may even marry someone else in a year or two."

Edward snorted mirthlessly. "Is that what you mean when you say there'll be no real harm? That he may someday marry?"

"Yes. At least, there'll be no *permanent* harm."

He was silent for a moment. When he spoke, it was in the regretful, weary tone of one who has surrendered. "We shall be tampering with people's lives," he said, stroking his wife's hair gently, "and I don't think anyone can know what permanent harm may come from that."

Tess was much relieved to learn from Julia that Edward had "come round," although Julia admitted frankly that her husband had quite serious reservations. Nevertheless, Tess wanted to celebrate. There was to be a performance of *Cosi Fan Tutte* at the King's Theater, and, knowing how much Edward loved Mozart, she insisted on taking them as her guests. It was difficult to procure seats, for all of the boxes of the theater's five tiers were sold by subscription for the season, but Julia's butler showed himself to be unexpectedly knowledgeable in these matters and managed (with a well-placed bribe) to obtain a box for them for Monday evening. Tess promised that it would be an evening of relaxed pleasure; there was to be no connection at all with, in Edward's words, "the business with Lotherwood."

It was a relief for all three of them to put the Lotherwood business out of their minds for an evening. Tess could be herself, and Edward and Julia would not have to worry about remembering to call her Miss Ashburton. They dressed up in the splendor required for an evening at the opera, they laughed and joked over dinner as if none of their heads had ever contained a serious thought, and they climbed into the carriage in the most festive of moods. The box to which they were shown was well situated—in the second tier just a little left of center—and they took their places with a sense of real exhilaration. Edward had just leaned over to Tess to point out the newly appointed Prime Minister, Lord Liverpool, and his wife sitting just two boxes away, when Julia drew in a gasping breath. "Good God, Tess, they're *here!*" she whispered, hiding her face behind her program.

"Yes," Edward said, "I've just pointed out Lord Liverpool—"

"Not Liverpool," Julia hissed. "*Lotherwood*. With Miss Lovell and other friends. There, just below us to our right."

"Oh, my *word!*" Edward turned to Tess in irritation. "You promised that this would be a quiet evening! Especially for my pleasure, you said! Tess Brownlow, if this is another of your idiotic schemes—"

"No, really it isn't! I swear to you, Edward, I had no idea he would be here," Tess said with sincere chagrin.

Edward glared at her suspiciously. "Is that really the truth?"

"Of course. I'm as dismayed as you. I hate having to meet him by chance. Unless I've planned an encounter and am fully prepared with what to say, I'm quite uncomfortable in his presence. I'm always afraid I shall forget myself and say something to give myself away."

Edward sighed. "Then I suppose we had better leave."

"Oh, Edward, no," Tess demurred, very reluctant to rob him of his promised treat.

"I don't think that will be necessary, my love," Julia pointed out hopefully. "They *are* below us, after all, and the overture is about to begin. Perhaps they won't take notice of us."

Edward shook his head dubiously. "They need only glance over their shoulders and look up. Even if their fascination with the opera keeps their eyes fixed on the stage, they're bound to notice us during the interval."

"During the interval, Edward," Tess declared firmly, "I shall hide myself in the ladies' retiring room. Thank goodness *Cosi* has only one. In the meantime, let us sit back and enjoy the music. I, for one, refuse to have my evening spoiled."

The gaiety and charm of the music soon relaxed Edward's tension, and the first act passed without incident. Before the curtain fell at the intermission, Tess excused herself and hurried down to the retiring room. There she took a chair in a corner almost completely obscured by a screen and watched surreptitiously as hundreds of chattering ladies came and went. She did not emerge until she heard the music start up again. When she did, she found to her relief that the wide staircase was deserted. As she made her way up the stairs, she anticipated the second act with pleasure; now that the interval was over, there was no likelihood that she and the Quimbys would have to endure an encounter with Lotherwood and his party. The only way they could meet now would be in passing when they left the theater, and, in that unlikely event, the only exchange necessary would be a brief greeting and a bow.

As she approached the landing at the first tier, a handsome young man appeared above her at the top of the stairs, making his way down. As he took his first step, he lurched and lost his balance. "Ouppff!" he grunted as he tripped and stumbled down the two steps that separated him from Tess.

It was obvious that he was about to pitch forward and fall headlong down the stairs. Acting completely by instinct, Tess braced herself with one hand on the banister and, with her free arm and shoulder, managed to catch hold of him. The fellow, also acting on instinct, flung one arm round her neck and clutched her about the waist with his other, clinging to her for dear life. But the force of his weight threw her off balance, and the two of them teetered dangerously on the edge of the stair. Only Tess's grip on the banister kept them from toppling over. Finding strength from the fear that she could be dragged down the stairs in this stranger's grip, Tess pushed heavily against his chest, causing him to teeter back in the opposite direction. This eased the force propelling them forward, and she was able to regain her balance.

The whole incident took only a moment, but the moment was long enough to indicate to Tess that the fellow was utterly foxed. His breath reeked. The smell of spirits seemed to exude even from his pores. As soon as they were both firmly on their feet, she tried to push away from him. But the fellow did not let go. Instead, keeping both arms tightly about her so that her arms were pinned against her sides, he leered into her face. "Saved m'life, ma'am," he grinned. "Mus' say I'm might'ly obliged t' you."

"Yes, but I would be obliged to *you*, sir, if you would release me and let me pass," she said, struggling to move her head from its proximity to his.

"In a minute, m' lovely, in a minute. Saved m' life. Wish t' express m' gratitude."

"It's not necessary. Please, sir, let me go! You are making me miss my favorite aria."

He clutched her even tighter. "Pish-tush an' rubbish, ma'am, no one cares 'bout opera. Dull's ditchwater, if y'ask me."

"I am not asking your opinion on opera, you lout!" she muttered, trying with all her strength to push away from him. "I am asking you to *let go of me!*"

"Not yet, m'lovely, not yet." The fellow leered lasciviously at her, causing her chest to constrict in alarm. "Not till I give you a li'l kiss. A reward, y' might say, f' what y' did f' me."

Tess struggled in such desperation to keep her face away from his that she feared they would tumble down the stairs after all. "If you don't release me at once," she said in icy warning, "I shall scream."

But at that moment they heard a step above them, and the drunkard turned his head to look. Before Tess could see what was happening, the fellow's arms dropped from her sides as he seemed to levitate into the air. It took her a moment to realize that someone had lifted him off the ground by grasping him under his arms. "I say!" the boozy fellow squealed, kicking helplessly in the air. "Le' me *down!*"

"I *ought* to let you down!" barked a familiar voice. "Right down the stairs!"

"Lord Lotherwood!" Tess gasped, leaning back against the banister and trying to catch her breath.

His lordship stood the bounder on his feet but kept a tight arm about the fellow's neck. "Are you all right?" he asked Tess.

"Yes, I'm fine. Quite unharmed." But she reddened, suddenly feeling hideously shamed at being discovered—and by him, of all people!—in such humiliating circumstances, and she immediately did what any woman would do in such straits: she glanced down at herself to ascertain the extent of the damage the inebriated idiot had inflicted on her gown. "Only a bit rumpled," she added with an embarrassed little laugh.

He had been studying her carefully for signs of injury, and he'd been struck once again by the effect the sight of her had on his insides. To him she seemed unspeakably lovely at this moment, the dark red velvet of her gown and the embarrassed flush of her cheeks coloring her face with a vivid glow. "You look quite marvelous to me," he couldn't help saying.

"T' me, too," the drunkard agreed.

"Hold your tongue!" Lotherwood snapped, glaring down at the fellow imprisoned in the crook of his arm. "What possessed you, eh? Can't a lady climb the stairs of the King's Theater alone without being attacked?"

"Didn't attack 'er. She saved m' life."

Lotherwood raised his brows. "*Did* she, indeed?"

"That is rather an exaggeration," Tess explained, "although I did prevent him from falling headlong down the stairs."

The fellow nodded. " 'S what I said. Saved m' life."

"And that's how you repay her?" Lotherwood asked. "By trying to maul her?"

"Wasn't tryin' t' maul 'er. Only tryin' t' kiss 'er."

"Oh, is *that* all?" His lordship threw a teasing glance at Tess but spoke to his captive. "I can understand the desire," he said, an amused glint in his eyes, "since I've wanted to kiss her myself. But even I, who am acquainted with the lady, would never have dared to try it in so public a place. And you, I'll wager, haven't even been introduced."

"No, but she saved m' life."

"So you said. Does that mean she has to let you *kiss* her, too?"

The fellow hung his head. "I s'pose . . . I'm a bit lushy."

"Lushy? You're completely cast away! Now, tell the lady how sorry you are, and I'll let you go. And if you have the sense you were born with, you'll take yourself home and put your head under the pump!"

The fellow gave Tess a stumbling apology and made his escape down the stairs. Lotherwood took Tess's arm and escorted her up. At the first tier's turning they had to make their way through a small group of onlookers who had gathered on the landing to watch the to-do. Among them was Lord Kelsey, who'd come out of the box to see what had happened to delay his friend. But Lotherwood was too engrossed in his companion to notice his friend, and Tess, still embarrassed by the humiliating encounter, did not raise her eyes. Tess and her escort continued on their way up to the second tier, and Lord Kelsey quietly returned to the box. But he was troubled for the rest of the evening; he had assured Viola that

Matt was not "taken" with Miss Ashburton, but this glimpse of them together had shaken his confidence. If anyone looked "taken," it was his friend.

Lotherwood escorted Miss Ashburton to the door of her box feeling strangely elated. The two days since he'd last seen her had been difficult; there had been an unpleasant scene with his betrothed. Viola had been badly shaken by seeing him with Miss Ashburton at Lord Elgin's exhibit. "You don't love me," she'd sobbed, "and it will all turn out just as the gypsy predicted!" The girl had wept bitterly and had made him feel like a vile adulterer. He'd had to reassure her that his love for her was as strong as ever, but he knew as he spoke that it was no longer true. Though his words seemed to have appeased her, his conscience pained him, and he'd made a vow to himself that he would put Miss Ashburton out of his life. But this meeting today had not been of his making; therefore, he intended to enjoy it without berating himself with guilt.

When they arrived at her box, Miss Ashburton offered him her hand. "I don't know how to thank you, my lord. You saved me from a most embarrassing contretemps."

Instead of bowing over it, he took her hand and held it. "You should thank Miss Lovell. If she hadn't sent me for a glass of negus, I never should have known you were a few steps below me, struggling with a drunken assailant."

"I would ask you to thank her for me, but I'd prefer that you not mention the incident at all. I found it all rather embarrassing. It's not something I would wish to be the subject of gossip."

"I shall respect your wishes, of course," he assured her, "but I don't see why you should be embarrassed. *You* were not the one inebriated."

"While we are on that subject, my lord, I must compliment you on your handling of the foolish young man. You were appropriately severe, but kind, too."

Lotherwood shrugged. "Oh, well. I've been foxed myself in my time."

At those words Tess felt a chill in her chest. She had, for a while, forgotten that this was the Lotherwood who, wildly drunk, had cracked up a stagecoach and snuffed out a life. "I must get back to my seat," she said, her face stiffening and her hand wriggling from his grasp.

He was again startled by the change in her mood. "Yes, of

course," he said politely, but he was puzzled and irritated. Was this the best reward he could expect for his service to her—a cold dismissal? *The devil take her!* he thought. *I'm weary of trying to understand her mind.* "Good evening, ma'am," he said, making an abrupt bow and striding off.

She stood with her hand on the doorknob, watching him go. *I've angered him again,* she thought with a pang. *If I'm not careful, I'll lose the whole game.*

But after he'd taken a half-dozen steps, he stopped in his tracks, hesitated, and then turned round. "Miss Ashburton?"

Her heart leaped up into her throat. For the second time she'd cut him, and for the second time he was offering her a reprieve. "My lord?" she asked, letting him hear a slight note of eagerness in her voice.

He heard it, and he would have liked very much to wring her neck. Her backing-and-filling was driving him to distraction. He'd promised himself two days ago to cut her from his life. If he had any sense, he would stalk off and never turn back. But with an inner sigh of defeat, he surrendered to the impulse that had made him stop. He had a question to ask, and he was incapable of keeping himself from asking it. "You did say, did you not, that you ride on Wednesdays?"

The corners of her lips curved up in the smallest of smiles. "Yes, I did say that. Wednesdays. Good evening, my lord."

❧ Eighteen ❧

It rained on Wednesday. It poured down buckets, torrents, oceans. Sheets of water fell from a leaden sky and splashed down on roofs, overflowed the drainpipes, and rushed down the streets in streams. It was a day unfit for bird or beast, and only an occasional human, because of some dire necessity, ventured out of doors under the protection of, if not a carriage, at least an umbrella. Lotherwood wondered if he were the only one in all of London who was out in the downpour unprotected.

He sat astride a large chestnut stallion at a turning of the bridle path in Hyde Park where he could see anyone who was approaching from the stables. He'd dismissed his groom, insisting that the fellow take the umbrella back with him to the stable. He knew he was being idiotic to sit out there with the rain drenching his coat and pouring from his hat brim down his back. Miss Sidoney Ashburton wouldn't be coming out on a day like this. Nobody with sense . . . But in case she did, he would be there.

In more ways than one he was a fool to be here. Ever since he'd seen her at the opera, he'd berated himself for being a fool. It was not only because he was betrothed, although that was reason enough; it was not in his character to take that commitment lightly. But it was also clear that something about him was disturbing to Miss Ashburton, and only a fool would permit himself to become involved with a woman who found him abhorrent. There was no question that this entanglement with Miss Ashburton had to end. Throughout the long hours of the two nights since he'd last seen her, he reiterated the vow he'd made to himself to put her out of his life forever. He swore it. Forever. After Wednesday.

He'd looked forward to Wednesday like a schoolboy to a birthday. His desire to look once more into her enchanting eyes was like an ache within him. It would be a last fling, a final taste of youthful irresponsibility before putting on the yoke of middle-aged respectability. He could hardly wait for Wednesday morning to dawn. But when the dawn came, so did the rain. It was almost like a warning that he was transgressing. The blasted rain seemed to him a sort of heavenly rebuke.

After several minutes of waiting—and feeling more foolish than he'd ever felt in his life—he was ready to acknowledge the futility of remaining. She wouldn't be coming. He hadn't really expected it; even if the weather were fine, she would probably not have come. She was playing some sort of deep game with him, a game in which he would be the victim. He was as certain of it as he was sure the gypsy was a fraud. With a shrug that said it was just as well, he turned his horse back in the direction of the stables. It was then he saw her horse approaching.

She, at least, had had the sense to carry an umbrella. She held it over him as they exchanged greetings. "I never dreamed you'd come on such a day," she said with a shy laugh.

He'd never known her to be shy. It warmed him. "Nor I you," he said. "We are a pair of fools." They sat there for a moment, smiling idiotically at each other, neither one quite able to believe that the other had really come.

After a while he lifted a hand to brush a dripping tendril from her forehead. "Why did you ask me to meet you, ma'am? You pointed out to me quite firmly at the exhibit the other day how unsuitable such a meeting would be."

She lowered her eyes. "I know. I don't know why I did it. Perhaps it's because fate is directing me."

"Are you referring to the gypsy's prophecy? No, I can't let you off so easily as that. That excuse won't wash. You once said you had no faith in it. A woman of your intellect must believe that we ourselves, not gypsies, determine our own fates."

"I do believe it. But chance or fate or whatever you wish to call it plays some part, does it not?"

Her mare made a little sidestep, and he leaned forward and steadied the animal. "No, I don't think so. *'The fault, dear Brutus, is not in our stars.' "*

"Shakespeare has the answer to everything, it seems. But, my lord, what about the rain today?" she asked thoughtfully. "Either one of us, or both, could quite sensibly have decided not to come. Might it not be fate that brings us here now?"

"Not in my case. Believe me, my dear, it was a quite conscious decision on my part. In fact," he admitted with a boyish grin, "I could hardly wait for this day to come."

His frankness startled her into a blush. "Truly, my lord?"

"Very truly. Too, too truly."

"Oh." Her voice was very small, not much more than a breath, but her pulse unaccountably began to race. She dropped her eyes from his face. "But if one believed in fate," she said, clinging to the impersonal subject in sudden fear of the intimacy which she could feel impending, "one might take this rain to be a warning that we should *not* have met."

"Yes," he agreed, watching her face closely, "perhaps we shall be punished for ignoring the warning. But must we go on discussing the problem of fate versus self-determination? I think you're trying to deflect the conversation away from my original intention, my dear, which was to find out why you suggested this meeting."

She kept her eyes lowered, but her lips curled in a mischievous smile. "My suggestion that we meet today was . . . well, in truth, it was a wicked impulse. I never should have succumbed to it." The eyes flickered up again. "Shall I be sorry?"

"Not on my account," he said in a voice that was firm and reassuring in spite of the fact that his instinct was again warning him that she was playing with him. "You know how much I've wished for the chance to talk to you."

"Yes, so you said. But why, my lord?"

"I wish I knew. Who can explain what attracts a man to a woman? Perhaps it's that you're like a mystery I'm driven to unravel."

"And when you unravel it, what then?"

Now it was his eyes that fell. For them there was no future in which he could unravel the mystery of her, much less a what-then. But before he was put to the necessity of framing an answer, his horse shied, shedding a spray of water upon them. "Miss Ashburton . . . Sidoney, my dear, this is insane. We can't hold a conversation like this in such a downpour. I have a carriage waiting just beyond the stables. Shall we make for it and get out of the wet?"

They left the horses in the care of the stable grooms and ran for his carriage, a closed phaeton with his crest on the door. He'd driven it over himself, causing both his coachman and his tiger to eye him with reproach when he'd departed, but now he was glad he'd been firm. It would have been awkward to have to dismiss them now.

He opened the door and helped her up. Once settled inside, she took off her wilted riding cap while he dispensed with her umbrella, shook off his hat, and took out his handkerchief to wipe off her face. But when he looked at her with the wetness glistening on her pale skin and the dripping tendrils framing her face, his heart clenched. "I once thought you weren't beautiful," he murmured in amazement.

Her eyes widened, and some wetness that had no relation to the rain trickled down her cheeks. "Oh, *Matt*," she said with a sad sigh.

He'd had no intention of kissing her, but there was simply nothing else he could do. Neither fate nor self-determination had anything to do with it. It was just her nearness, her face tilted up just a little (for she was almost as tall as he), and her eyes looking mistily into his and revealing for the first time the depth of her feeling. He took her in his arms without conscious intent and suddenly found himself kissing her hungrily. He felt her give a little shiver at first . . . a sort of instinctive resistance . . . but almost at once she sagged against him. He tightened his hold on her as if the pressure of his arms would keep her close to him forever, and she, too, seemed to cling to him with the same frenzied desperation. Locks of his hair dripped water, all unnoticed, down her cheeks, while her hands, as if of their own volition, fondled his hair and the sides of his face. He could taste the rain on her mouth, feel the throbbing of her heart against his chest. How could a woman so tall and strong become so soft and pliant in his arms?

No woman he'd ever held had stirred him like this, to his very core. He wanted never to let her go.

Never before had he felt so shaken by an embrace. When he finally released her, they were both trembling. It took him a moment to regain his equilibrium, a moment in which a host of feelings burst on him all at once—guilt, joy, desire, shame, all of them. But he heard a little sob that came from deep within her throat, and when he looked at her, everything else fled from his mind.

She was staring at him with eyes wide with horror. "Oh, my *God*!" she gasped breathlessly.

He recognized that look. He had seen it in a flashing moment during the race. "Good Lord, what *is* it?" he asked in alarm. "What have I done?"

The look remained in her eyes for just a moment more. Then she blinked and, trying to catch her breath, made a dismissive movement of her hand. "No, it's . . . it's nothing . . ." she managed.

"It's not nothing!" he insisted, grasping her by the shoulders as if he would shake an answer from her. "What's amiss?"

She shut her eyes as if in pain. "Nothing, truly. I just didn't expect . . ."

"I know. I didn't expect it, either." He put an arm about her and let her head rest on his shoulder. There was so much he wanted to say to her, but at this moment their feelings seemed beyond words. It was as if they'd known from the first that they would come to this unutterable closeness, and no explanations were necessary. "I've never felt so . . . shattered . . ." he murmured into her wet curls.

"Yes," she said, taking a deep breath. "Yes."

"I am not accustomed to feeling things so deeply. We Corinthians train ourselves to avoid deep feelings."

"I don't think I've felt things deeply, either," she said, a note of surprise in her voice. "Though I was not trained to avoid it."

He stroked the side of her face in thoughtful silence. "But that's not what I saw on your face just now," he said after a while. "What is it, my dear? I wish you'd tell me. Is there something about me that frightens you?"

She shook her head. "I'm ashamed, that's all. Ashamed!

Of both of us. We shouldn't have permitted ourselves to behave so wickedly."

"That is *not* all," he said, deeply chagrined. "But you don't intend to tell me, do you?"

"No," she said, pulling herself away from him. She turned her back to him and stared out at the rain. "If I did," she added in a voice heavy with mockery, "there would be no mystery for you to unravel."

"Ah! Then you admit there is a mystery?"

"I'm very much afraid you'll never know."

He knew from her tone that her answer was final. "What a vixen you are, Sidoney Ashburton," he said, taking hold of her shoulders and forcing her to face him. "A veritable witch. I knew it the moment I clapped eyes on you."

She lowered her head and sighed. "I suppose you rue the day."

"No, but I should."

He tried to lift her chin, but she shook her head. "I think it would be wise if we ended this . . . interview, my lord."

He wanted to object, but he had no right to keep her. He had no right to be here at all. "I'll take you home," he said in gloomy acquiescence.

With a stiffening of his whole body, as if he were preparing himself for a difficult physical endurance contest, he let her go. He let down the front window-panel, picked up the reins, and started the horses. The rain still poured down, the streets were rivers of rushing water, and the sky showed no promise of brightening. The atmosphere could not have been more perfectly suited to his mood. As the horses splashed slowly down the street, he turned back to her, his face taut. "You realize, of course," he said huskily, "that I can't indulge . . . that we won't be meeting again."

"Yes, I know." Her voice was cold and distant.

He winced in pain. He wanted to say something, do something, to recapture one last bit of closeness and warmth. "It will be difficult for me," he said with a quiet but unmistakable regret, "knowing that you're somewhere close by and that I'm not able to—"

"You will survive. Besides, I shan't be close by for very long. I can't remain with Julia indefinitely, you know. I'm merely her guest for the month."

"I see." He was shaken by the realization that the girl was a stranger to him. Despite their moments of intimacy, he still hadn't learned very much about her. "Then will you be going home to your parents?"

She looked down at the hands she'd folded in her lap. "I have no parents. I shall be going to a country home where I've found employment as a governess."

"Good God! I had no idea." He turned to her in deep concern. "Is that the only choice you have for your future?"

"You needn't look so stricken, my lord," she said. "I am quite content. This has been my plan for a long while. And my weeks in London have provided many memories to mull over when my post becomes a bore."

"Where is this country place to which you're going?"

"I'd rather not say."

"See here, my girl, there's entirely too much you'd 'rather not say' to me!"

"Don't flare up at me, my lord! What right have you—?"

His jaw tightened, and he turned away and stared out ahead of him at the horses' heads. "No right. I beg your pardon."

They rode on without speaking until he drew up at the Quimby house. She picked up her soggy riding cap and umbrella and reached for the door handle. "Good-bye, my lord," she said, brittle as glass. "I wish you happy."

But he could not let her go. "Dash it all," he muttered, pulling her roughly to him again, "tell me what it is about me that makes you swing so wildly from warmth to ice! What *is* it?"

Her expression was unreadable. "I have nothing to say, my lord."

"Is there something you want of me? If there is, you have only to ask. There's no need to play games. Just *ask* it."

Her eyes grew scornful. "There is nothing I want of you that you are free to give."

He groaned and pulled her closer, cradling her head in the curve of his shoulder. "Oh, God," he said miserably, "if only that blasted gypsy had pointed you out to me a few weeks earlier."

"Yes, isn't it sad?" She withdrew from his arms and moved to the door. "But there's nothing to be done now, is there?"

There was something in the angle of her head, the strange edge in her voice, the opaque look in her eye that he was beginning to recognize. It was her "game" technique, a certain unnatural, calculating manner that told him she was playing with him. "I wish I understood the mystery of you, ma'am. It is driving me to the brink of distraction."

"Is it? That is something else you will survive, I think." She studied him coolly for a moment, but then her expression softened. "I'm sorry, Matt," she said, her voice low and melancholy. "I shouldn't poison our last meeting with dissension. Since it will be for the last time, perhaps . . ."

"Perhaps. . . ?"

"Perhaps you'd like to kiss me again, in farewell."

Though still convinced he was being used as her pawn in some mysterious game, he could not refuse this last gift. He put his hand gently on her cheek and lifted her face. Slowly, with a tenderness even he did not know he possessed, he kissed her mouth. It was a light kiss, barely touching, but it managed to shake him up again. "I love you, Miss Sidoney Ashburton," he murmured with his lips still on hers. "For what little it's worth, I love you. Mystery or no mystery."

She withdrew from his arms and smiled at him, a smile that was somehow both teasing and sad. "And I love you."

He shook his head. "No," he said flatly, "I don't think you do. You needn't offer me Spanish coin, ma'am. When I first kissed you, I did believe for a moment that I'd touched something real in you. But now, no."

A shadow seemed to cross her face. She turned away abruptly and threw open the carriage door. He made a move to jump down and assist her, but she shook her head. "Don't come round, my lord. I shall manage," she said, and climbed down.

He picked up the reins, but before starting up the horses he turned to take one last look at her. She was standing facing the open carriage door, the rain dripping down her face like tears. "For what little it's worth," she said, meeting his eyes with a look of self-mockery in her own, "I *do* love you. It's so funny! I've been waiting all my life for the Grand Passion. And now, when it finally comes to me, I discover that I feel it for the very *last* man in the world I should have chosen!" With a laugh that was also a sob, she turned and ran through the rain to the house.

❧ *Nineteen* ❧

Viola Lovell was known to be a young lady of rare good nature and sweet disposition, but she was not often described as clever. Sweetness and cleverness are not characteristics that are supposed to go hand in hand. And since cleverness in a woman was not a requisite virtue—and not a virtue *at all* in the minds of many wife-seeking gentlemen—Viola did not bother to prove the evaluation to be mistaken. She knew that she was considered both lovely and amiable, and that was enough.

But despite the innocence of her wide-eyed gaze and the vulnerability in her trusting smile, Viola Lovell was no fool. She knew very well how to add two and two, and in the case of her betrothal, she had added up all the advantages before she'd given her hand. She'd known exactly what she was doing. Her value on the marriage mart was high—she had (1) a respected if not titled family name, (2) her reputed amiable disposition, (3) a pretty face, (4) a softly feminine form, and (5) a complexion that was the envy of every girl she knew. These advantages added up to an impressive total. She'd made the best possible trade for those advantages: Matthew John Lotherwood, the Marquis of Bradbourne. He, on his part, had (1) breeding, (2) titles, (3) a sizable income and a magnificent estate in Essex, (4) virile good looks, and (5) a charm of manner that made him sought after by every female he met. The match had a beautiful mathematical symmetry. It seemed to add up to the most glowing prospects for her future comfort and happiness. Until just a short while ago, she had considered herself to be the luckiest girl alive.

But now her prospects for the future appeared to be seriously flawed. She'd avoided facing the problem squarely for almost a fortnight, unwilling to believe that anything could spoil the neatness of her arithmetic. But signs were accumulating that his lordship was beginning to believe he'd not made the best of bargains in committing himself to her. It was not merely the gypsy's prophecy that had shaken her confidence, although that had certainly been a blow. (She was willing to concede that Matt and Dolph were right in denying that gypsies had magical powers, but even if gypsies weren't supernaturally gifted, they did have, she was convinced, an uncanny ability to read people's characters in their eyes. Lady Wetherfield's gypsy might not be a true seer, but time had proved she undoubtedly knew *something*.)

However, with Dolph's encouragement, she'd put aside her doubts. But a strange event during the night at the opera had added another clue to a rapidly accumulating body of evidence pointing to the fact that Matt no longer wanted her. It was time, she realized, to give the matter some serious attention.

It was not ignorance or innocence that had kept her from facing her problem before this. Viola was not the bubblehead that everyone thought her. She'd taken note of Matt's apparent attraction to the peculiar young woman staying with Julia Quimby almost immediately, and she'd made some scenes and shed some tears. But in her deepest heart, she hadn't been unduly alarmed, because Miss Ashburton did not strike her as a formidable rival. Other than her strikingly odd eyes, Miss Ashburton had little to recommend her. She was (1) much too tall, (2) too strong in chin and nose (and colorless in complexion!) to be considered beautiful, (3) cool and distant in manner, and (4) so far out of the common way that Viola found her almost eccentric. Nor was Viola alone in her assessment; Dolph Kelsey was in complete agreement with that judgment. Thus Viola had easily convinced herself that whatever it was that Matt had seen in Miss Ashburton could not possibly be serious. It didn't add up.

But the night at the opera gave Viola what she believed was the definitive clue to prove that she'd been too complacent. During the intermission a number of well-wishers had invaded their box, and when the members of Matt's party had finally

settled into their seats for the second act, she'd asked Matt to
bring her a glass of negus. He'd teased her about her taste for
that tepid concoction ("Adding hot water and spices to wine,"
he'd quipped, "is like pinning a flower on Dolph's orchid-
hued waistcoat—too many sensations from one source."), but
he'd gone off in perfectly good spirits to do her bidding. When
he didn't return for what seemed an unduly long time, Dolph
went off to look for him. Dolph returned a moment later saying that he couldn't find Matt anywhere, but Viola thought
that he seemed disturbed. When Matt returned shortly after-
ward—and without her drink—she thought the incident quite
strange, but she decided not to question him. It didn't seem
important, and it would have been too awkward to discuss
anything while the opera was in progress anyway.

After the opera, however, when they stood waiting under
the portico of the King's Theater for Matt's coachman to
bring round the carriage, she caught a glimpse of Miss Ashburton and the Quimbys coming down the stairs. She was
about to draw the attention of her party to their presence when
she noticed that Dolph, too, had seen them. Dolph's ears grew
red, and he glanced up at Matt with a look of concern. It was
then that Viola realized that Matt's absence from the box and
his failure to bring back her drink had had some sort of connection with Miss Ashburton. It was clear to her at last that
something was amiss. It was something perhaps not havey-
cavey but serious nonetheless.

She thought about it all that night and the next day. She
remembered all the little warning signs: Matt's interest in Miss
Ashburton at Lady Wetherfield's dinner party, his attentions
to Miss Ashburton on the day of the race, his look of admiration for Miss Ashburton at Lord Elgin's exhibit, and his air of
abstraction when he returned to the box that night at the
opera. In addition, she realized that he'd been, of late, very
different in his manner toward her, his own intended bride.
Instead of becoming closer since their betrothal, his manner
had become more formal and distant. She'd tried her usual
wiles to ease the strain between them, but they had little effect.
She now admitted to herself that she'd been finding herself
more and more uncomfortable in his company. All this surely
added up to serious trouble.

By Tuesday evening she still had not decided what to do.
She supposed she should confide in her mother or father, but

she knew what they would say: "You must do nothing, child. Nothing at all." She could hear her mother's jittery whine: "I *knew* something like this would happen! I *knew* it! It was too good to be true, your snaring Lotherwood! This is all that uppish Lady Wetherfield's doing. She didn't want you for her precious nephew from the first!"

And her father would be no better. "Nothing to worry about, if you hold fast," he'd say, puffing on his pipe. "You're safely betrothed. Banns posted, announcement in *The Times*. As good as wed. Nothing he can do about it now. So hold on fast. Many a woman has to bite her tongue while her husband cavorts about. There's only one woman who wins in the end, and that's the legal wife. So hold on."

That sort of advice from her parents was not what she wanted to hear, so there was no point in seeking it. There was only one person whose presence might be soothing and whose advice might be useful to her, and on Wednesday morning she sent a footman through the rain with a note for him.

The note only contained a simple request that he call at his earliest convenience, but Dolph knew at once what she wanted to talk about. Late that afternoon, as soon as the rain lessened, he presented himself at her door. Viola told her mother, who was at that moment wandering through the hallway looking for a mislaid piece of needlework, that she wished for some private words with Lord Kelsey. Without heeding the look of astonishment that crossed her mother's face, she took Dolph's arm, pulled him into the sitting room and shut the door.

"If you're going to ask me something about Matt's doings at the opera the other night, Vi, you're wasting your breath," Dolph said flatly, putting down his rain-spattered hat. "I don't like tattling."

"There's no need for you to tattle," she said, sinking down on the sofa and folding her hands into a tight, tense knot. "I know he must have met Miss Ashburton. I don't need any details."

"Good. Because I wouldn't blab any even if I knew them, which I don't." He pulled up a straight-backed chair in front of her and perched nervously on the edge of it. "What *do* you want of me, then?"

"Only some advice." Her eyelids lowered pathetically, and her underlip began to quiver. "Oh, Dolph, I'm so confused!"

Dolph shifted on his seat uncomfortably. "Thought you might be. Dashed unpleasant situation."

She clasped and unclasped her hands. "Then you admit that there is a situation. Just what is it, Dolph? Can you tell me that much?"

"I don't really know anything to tell you. It's only a feeling I have."

"Yes, just as I have. It's Miss Ashburton, isn't it? You once said that he couldn't care for her. But now you're not so sure, are you?"

Dolph shook his head unhappily. "Wouldn't have thought it of Matt. True sportsman, Matt is. It isn't like him to play foul."

"Play *foul?*" Her eyes flew up to his face in dismay. "Do you think matters have gone as far as that? That he's actually been . . . *unfaithful?*"

"*No!* Good God, no! I didn't mean . . . !" He reached out and grasped her hands in his. "I *do* beg your pardon! It's only my way of speaking. Confound it, Vi, he's not a *cad!* I only meant that it's foul of him to treat you so. So sweet and good and lovely as you are, you don't deserve . . . ! It's foul of him even to *look* at anyone else."

The feeling in those words undid her. "Oh, *Dolph!*" she cried, the tears spilling over. "It's *you* who's sweet and good. I only w-wish . . ."

"Wish what?" Dolph asked, awkwardly dropping his hold on her hands in order that he might pull out his handkerchief and dab at her eyes.

She let him mop her cheeks for a moment and then shook her head. "I can't tell you!" she cried, pulling the handkerchief from his fingers and weeping into it. "I just c-can't!"

She jumped up and crossed the room to the window. The rain still dribbled down the panes, making the world outside seem utterly dismal. It seemed to her at that moment that the sun would never shine again. With her back to Dolph, she let the tears run freely down her cheeks, but he knew she was still weeping. With a sigh, he stood up and followed her. "You can tell me, Vi. I'd do anything for you, you know. I'll talk to Matt for you. This business with Miss Ashburton can't be serious. I'm sure he wouldn't stay for a moment in her company if he knew it made you unhappy. That's what you wish, isn't it—that I go to see Matt in your behalf?"

"No!" she exclaimed, wheeling about. "That's the last thing in the world I wish!"

"Then what—?"

Bursting into sobs, she threw herself into his arms. "Oh, D-Dolph! What I w-wish is that *you* were my b-betrothed instead of him!"

"Vi!" His jaw dropped down in astonishment. "You can't mean that!"

"Why not?" she demanded with a sudden burst of spirit. "*Why* can't I mean that?"

"Because it's *Matt* we're speaking of. Matt! He's the best! In every way the fellow's better'n me. In riding, in boxing, in—"

"Who cares for that?" she cut in furiously. "You're better than he for *me! You* never speak to me as if I were a spoiled child! *You* never make me feel uncomfortable when I'm with you. *You* never make me feel ashamed to say what I really feel about things. I'd rather have a conversation with you than with him . . . or anyone else, if you want the truth!"

"Good God!" Dolph exclaimed in stupefaction. "You must be addled in your upper works!"

But Viola's upper works were far from addled. She'd done her arithmetic carefully this time. As a prospective husband, Dolph had almost as many advantages as Matt. True, he was not a marquis, but viscount was not a title to be sneezed at; and true, he was not so famous a Corinthian or so outstanding in sports as Matt, but she cared nothing for that. For the rest, Dolph was really a superior choice for her: (1) his income was rumored to be enormous, (2) his taste in attire was not so somber as Matt's, and (3) he was by far easier to control. Perhaps her parents and the rest of the world would think she'd taken a step down, but she'd decided last night that she would rather be married to a viscount who truly desired her than to a marquis who felt trapped.

She turned her sweet, tear-streaked face up to his. "It's not too late for us, is it, Dolph?" she asked softly.

There was hardly a man in the world who could resist such an invitation. To Dolph's credit, he did hesitate for a moment. He was beset with a flood of confused doubts. Was he in love? he wondered. Was he a rotter? Was he being disloyal to a long-admired friend? What was he doing here at all? An hour ago he'd had no intention of getting himself leg-shackled, but at this moment it suddenly seemed a very real possibility. How had he gotten himself in this position?

But that lovely, creamy-skinned, soft-lipped face was tilted up, the eyes moist with yearning, and the urge to kiss her proved to be irresistible. With a sigh of surrender, he took her in his arms. Later, he told himself, they would talk things out. Later they would face Matt and tell him all. Later they would make things straight. But this embrace, these sighs, this pressing together of hands, of lips, of hearts . . . these were for now.

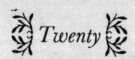

Twenty

It continued to rain all night, not heavily but steadily. Tess knew all about it, because she'd lain awake and listened. The dripping sounds on the eaves and windowpanes seemed a fitting accompaniment to her thoughts. Not that starlight or moonshine would have made any difference; there was no celestial atmosphere that nature could provide that would be bright enough to affect the brooding darkness inside her. The inescapable fact was that Tess was miserable.

She should have been happy, she told herself, for she was on the verge of success in her plot against Lotherwood. After this morning she knew she'd caught him. The dreadful irony of the situation was that she'd caught herself, too.

What she'd said to him was true: she *did* love him. What a shock she'd felt when she realized it! She had no idea how it had happened. She'd concentrated so intently on her plot for revenge—on every step in the carefully mapped route toward his seduction—that she hadn't noticed that she herself was being seduced. It was only when she lay trembling in his arms after he'd kissed her that the awareness burst on her like a sharp blow to the face: she loved him.

Until that moment it had seemed so certain that the game was hers. At every crucial crossroad, when he could have chosen a path away from her, she'd won. Even when she'd played the game badly, like the day at the race or the other night at the opera, he'd succumbed. It had seemed so easy.

Too easy. Why hadn't she seen it before? Lotherwood was too clever (and probably too experienced a lover) to be taken in by a woman playing a game. He was not fooled by pretense. It was her *real* feeling that had taken him in!

But she herself had not recognized the fact that she *had* real feelings. Not until he'd kissed her. Her reactions during that embrace had been utterly beyond her expectations. They had had nothing to do with playing a role. They were too spontaneous, too intense to have anything to do with pretending. They had come from her very depths.

Even now, so many hours later, she was still shaken by the recollection of that experience. She had completely lost her head this morning. Never before had she so wildly abandoned all inner restraint. She'd pressed her body and her lips to his . . . she'd clung and clasped and clutched in a burst of such unbridled passion that she hadn't known where she was or why she was there. But she did remember thinking, during one moment when her mind was still functioning, that this must be what her mother had tried to explain—the intoxicating blending of body and spirit that makes a passion Grand.

How the gods must be laughing at her, she thought. What an ironic twist her so-well-calculated road had taken! Was this the price the gods intended to extract for her hubris in taking it upon herself to inflict revenge? Was she to be punished for giving Lotherwood his punishment?

Tess was so shaken by this discovery that for a short while she actually considered the possibility of abandoning her plan and running home before matters developed any further. If she left things as they were right now, no one would be much affected. Julia and Edward would be relieved, Lotherwood would marry his Viola, and Tess would not have to suffer the torture of torturing the man she loved.

But then she remembered Jeremy. Poor Jeremy, to whom she'd never said a word of love. At last she understood the full extent of what she'd withheld from him. She'd never even *kissed* him properly! He'd died without having experienced even a bit of the Grand Passion. She owed something to his memory. Lotherwood had snuffed out Jeremy's life and had gone on with his own without caring. *We train ourselves not to care deeply*, he'd said. It was only simple justice that Lotherwood be made to pay! And if she was now to share the cost, in the pain of giving him pain, perhaps that, too, was simple justice.

Morning came, bringing with it a decisive frame of mind. *She would proceed as planned.* And, as if the gods were giving her a sign that they agreed, the rain stopped at that moment.

She remained in bed, staring up at the ceiling of her small bedchamber. She heard the sounds of the waking household. She heard Julia and Edward go downstairs. She heard the sound of the door as Edward left the house. She heard the clock strike nine and then ten. And then she fell into a doze.

The clock was striking eleven when Julia tapped on the door. "Tess?" she whispered urgently. "Tess? Are you up?"

"Yes, love, come in," Tess answered in a voice thick with sleep. "I'm sorry I'm such a slugabed. I don't know what made me—"

"Never mind that," Julia hissed, coming in and closing the door carefully and quietly behind her. "You've got to come at once. He's *here!*"

Tess froze in the act of stretching her arms. "*Who's* here?"

"Lotherwood! He seems a bit unstrung. I left him pacing about like a caged lion." She looked about her nervously, as if she suspected the presence of an eavesdropper, before she went on. "Honestly, Tess, I think he's going to make an *offer!* If ever a man had the appearance of a hopeful suitor, it's he!"

Aghast, Tess stared at her cousin for a moment and then leaped out of bed. "He can't be here for that!" she muttered, searching about madly for her robe. "It's too soon. What about Viola? Why, only yesterday, he—!" Her eye fell on her reflection in her dressing-table mirror. "Oh, good God, just look at me! I'm a veritable *fright!*" She dropped down on the bed and put a shaking hand to her forehead. "Tell him to go away. I can't see him looking like this. Tell him to go away and come back later. Tonight. Tomorrow. But not now."

"I can't tell him that," Julia said, pulling her up. "He insisted that I drag you down just as you are. It is urgent, he said. We've already kept him waiting too long." She put Tess's arms into the sleeves of her rose-colored robe and pulled it up on her shoulders. "There, that's presentable enough. Now tie the sash and run a brush over your hair!"

That done, Julia pushed Tess to the top of the stairs.

"That's as far as I go," she whispered. "From this point on, you must make your own way." And before her cousin could object, she flew down the hall and into her bedroom.

Tess stood at the top of the stairs, her heart pounding. She knew very well that she was not properly prepared for this interview, whatever the subject of discussion was to be. She looked dreadful. She had dark circles under her eyes, her hair was unkempt despite the hurried brushing she'd given it, and her robe was a silly, flouncy bit of fluff that was quite out of character for her. Worse, she had not decided just what mood and tone she should adopt for this meeting. She would be at a decided disadvantage this time. It was quite possible that she could lose the game today.

However, the game had to be played. She took a deep breath, stiffened her back, and descended. As she came to the half-landing, she saw him standing below waiting for her. He was dressed in riding breeches and a tweed coat, looking every inch the dashing, worldly Corinthian he was reputed to be. But his hair was boyishly tousled, and his eyes held an unmistakable glint of youthful anticipation. Her pulse began to race at the sight of him. She had an almost irresistible urge to repeat to him the lovely words he'd said to her the day before: *I once thought you weren't beautiful.* But all she did was stare down at him and utter a breathy, "Oh!"

"Good morning," he said, a grin lighting his face. "I see I've roused you from your bed."

Her hand unwittingly flew to her hair, but she immediately brought it down, telling herself angrily that she refused to let him see her embarrassment. "So you have," she said, lifting her chin in an attitude of proud reproof. "It was very rude of you. A true gentleman does not call on a lady before noon." *There*, she thought, *that should give him a set down. The best defense is a strong attack.*

But he showed not a sign of mortification. "You're right, of course," he agreed, "but since I knew that you are on the bridle path on Wednesdays by eight—and in all weather, too —I naturally assumed that you're an early riser."

"On *Wednesdays* I am on the bridle path at eight. On *Thursdays* I sleep until noon," she informed him coldly, raising her chin higher. "One would think, my lord, that by your advanced age you would have learned that ladies are notoriously inconsistent."

His grin widened. "I'm rather glad I haven't learned it, for if I had, I *would* have waited until noon and missed this glimpse of you in your charming disarray. You do look charming, you know. Even at my advanced age I've never encountered a more delectable vision."

It was hard to maintain her pose of chilly *hauteur* when struggling against an urge to laugh. She leaned over the banister and made a face at him. "*Now* who's offering Spanish coin?" she teased.

"I never offer Spanish coin, ma'am. Blunt to a fault I am." He moved closer to the stairway so that he was right below her and lifted up a hand to her. "I hope you don't intend to linger there on the landing for very long. Please take my hand and come down, my dear. At my advanced age, it's hard on my neck to keep looking up this way indefinitely."

Laughing, she slipped her hand into his. He led her down the stairs, the banister making an ever-decreasing barrier between them. "What brings you here, my lord?" she asked as she descended. "Wasn't it only yesterday that we exchanged final farewells?"

"We should have known better," he said, coming round to the foot of the stairs. He dropped her hand, picked her up by the waist and lifted her up over the few remaining steps. "Final farewells can't possibly be exchanged between us."

He held her to him for a moment before he set her on her feet. The brief bodily contact left her breathless. She backed away from him and hurriedly turned round so that he wouldn't see how his touch affected her. "Seriously, my lord, why have you come?" she asked, leading the way to the library.

He followed her in and closed the door behind him. "I came, ma'am, to suggest a fifth category of gentlemanly types for you to consider."

His words made no sense. "What?" she asked, feeling thick-headed and bemused.

Smiling a roguishly secret smile, he led her to the sofa. "You remember, don't you, that I once described four categories of gentlemen for you: the religious, the scholarly, the military, and the athletic? I think we both agreed that the athletic was beneath your consideration for wedlock. And since I certainly cannot claim membership in any of the other three, I've thought of a fifth: the Country Gentleman. He is sturdy, hardworking, reliable, and is responsible for the advantageous use of the land for the prosperity of the nation. Do you think you might consider such a one?''

Sinking down on the sofa, she put a hand to her forehead. "Whatever are you talking about, Matt?"

"I'm speaking of myself, ma'am," he answered, taking a seat beside her with an air of such amused self-satisfaction that she had an urge to box his ears. "I admit that I haven't made a mark in that category thus far, but I'm not without experience. While concentrating all these years on my foolish sporting activities, I've nevertheless managed my Essex estate with enough skill to keep it unencumbered. And now, with you beside me, I'm certain I shall soon make a quite respectable Country Gentleman."

She gaped at him for a moment, wide-eyed. "With *me* beside you?" she gasped.

"Yes, my love, exactly." The teasing look faded from his eyes. "I'm asking you to marry me," he said earnestly, taking both her hands in his. "You see, all of a sudden I find that I'm quite at liberty to do so."

"At . . . *liberty?*"

He nodded. "Since last night. Miss Lovell paid a call on me, in company with my friend, Lord Kelsey. She informed me that she feels she and I do not suit. It seems I've been a most unsatisfactory betrothed. I've been inattentive, insensitive, abstracted, uncaring, and neglectful. While Dolph, on the other hand, has been devoted, sympathetic, affectionate, and kind. So I was given my walking ticket."

"Oh, *Matt!*"

"Don't look so dismayed, my dear. It's a perfect solution to everyone's dilemma. Viola seemed quite smitten with Dolph, and Dolph, bless him, was very content to take my place with her. As for me, I felt as if I'd had a reprieve from a prison sentence! Now there's only you to hear from." He lifted her hands to his lips and kissed them each in turn. "I wanted to rush right over last night to tell you," he added softly, "but it seemed too opportunistic to do so. I decided to wait till this morning. It was the longest night I've ever endured."

"I see," she murmured, gently withdrawing her hands from his clasp.

"You *see?*" His brows lifted in restrained surprise. "Is *that* the best response you can make to my recital of these momentous events?'' He moved a small distance away from her so that he could scrutinize her face. "Good God!" he exclaimed, the lightly mocking tone of his voice at variance with the sudden tightening of his jaw. "I believe I've been a coxcomb again. You're going to *refuse* me!"

She threw him a quick glance. "What makes you think that?"

"Well, my dear, your reaction has been somewhat lacking in maidenly delight."

Her eyes fell. "I'm trying to restrain my maidenly delight."

"Why, ma'am? Why should you restrain it?" He leaned back against the cushions but kept his eyes fixed on her face. "Don't tell me that you feel this is too sudden! Surely Miss Sidoney Ashburton is not the sort to think in such clichés."

"But it *is* too sudden," she murmured, keeping her head resolutely lowered. If only he knew how very sudden his offer was. She was struck with terror at the necessity of giving him an answer. She would have liked to have a little more time. She'd made up her mind last night about what her course of action would be, but this was her very last chance to change it. *We are heading toward a precipice, my love,* she cried inside, *and you are urging us headlong to the edge.* She could still withdraw, still run back home and save them both from the grief her plot would bring. But once she accepted him, there could be no turning back.

"Too sudden? Everything that's happened between us has been too sudden." He leaned forward and pulled her abruptly into his arms. "Look at me, girl. You said yesterday that you loved me, did you not? Was it the truth, or was it part of this game you're playing with me?"

She looked up at him obediently, her eyes brimming with tears. "It was true. It *is* true. I *do* love you, Matt."

"Then, damnation, what is the impediment?" He waited a moment for an answer that didn't come. Then, expelling a long breath as if he were releasing the tension of his frustration, he cradled her head in the curve of his shoulder and stroked her hair. "Sidoney, my love, why won't you speak to me? What is it about me that frightens you so?"

She shook her head and hid her face in his coat, unable to speak. She was poised, terrified, at her life's most significant crossroad, but each path led to a dismal end. Whichever she chose, there was no hope of happiness for her. But if she refused him, she could at least keep *him* from the full brunt of the suffering she'd devised for him. If only he would show one slight sign that he regretted his thoughtless past and the error which had caused Jeremy's death.

She turned her face up to him. "You *can* be frightening sometimes, Matt, don't you know that? You have the reputation of having been very wild."

"I have?" He stared down at her in sincere bewilderment. "Who on earth could have told you that? Lady Quimby? Sir Edward? Whoever it was, he was mistaken."

His earnestness was almost convincing. "Have you never done *anything* you consider wild?" she asked, hoping he would feel impelled to confess his crime. If he showed even the slightest repentence, she would forgive him. She wanted with all her heart to be able to forgive him and to go away.

His brow knit in an intense effort to understand what it was that troubled her. "Is it the race you're thinking of, my dear? I know there was something about it that shook you. If you consider *that* to have been an act of wildness, then I suppose I'm wild. I've raced horses all my life. But I've never hurt anyone."

Never hurt anyone? The words seemed to reverberate in her head. How could he lie to her like that? He claimed to *love* her. Didn't love mean sharing, even one's darkest secrets? She would give him one last chance to confess. She would make her voice warm, enticing him with the offer of complete and sympathetic understanding. *Dear God,* she prayed, *let him tell me the truth.* "Never hurt *anyone?*" she asked gently.

But the softness of her voice and the pleading look in her eye did not mask the intent of the question. "Good God, girl," he demanded furiously, "what do you take me for? I may not have done much good with my life, but there's not a man, woman, or child in this world whose life was made *worse* because of me!"

His words made her heart sink in her chest like a stone. She felt herself stiffen in his arms. She'd failed. *He'd* failed. There was no doubt left in her mind of what her course of action would be. She lowered her head to keep him from reading the feelings that were undoubtedly revealed in her face.

But he didn't miss the look that flared for the briefest moment in her devastating eyes. "Sidoney, *don't!* Why do you look at me so? Dash it all, why won't you ever tell me what you're thinking? What is this game you feel impelled to play with me?''

She had to say something, she realized. She had to go on with her scheme. She had no choice, now that she knew him for the miscreant he was. He appeared to be so open and honest on the outside, with his sportsman's bluntness and his unaffected charm, but they were only coverings that masked a craven, indifferent soul. He was a man who could ruin lives and then forget he'd done it. She didn't know how she'd come to fall in love with such a man, but she couldn't help that now. But she could, and would, punish him for what he'd done to Jeremy, no matter what the cost to herself.

He'd taken her chin in his hand and forced her to look up at him. "Can't you tell me, you ice-eyed witch, just what is going on in that brain of yours?"

"I'm thinking, Matt, that you've been captured by this so-called game. It's the *mystery* of me that's attracted you. You said so yourself, did you not? But I'm not a witch. I'm a quite ordinary girl. If you knew what I was thinking, you might not love me at all.''

"Not love you?" He laughed shortly. "I think it more likely that the sun won't go down!" With both hands he tilted up her face to his and kissed her, gently at first but soon with a fervent desperation. His hands moved from her face to her neck and down her arms. She shivered and flung her arms about him, pressing herself against him with a low, almost gutteral moan. The sound stirred something deep within him, and he lifted his head to stare at her. He didn't understand her, but she inspired feelings in him he didn't dream he was capable of. They were the kinds of feelings that a true Corinthian would scorn, but only because he'd never felt them. "If that was a game," he murmured, trying to catch his breath, "I'm willing to play it all my life."

"No, that was . . . not a game," she said, furious at herself for letting him shake her again.

With an effort he pushed her from him but held her arms in a tight grip. "Then, confound it, say you'll marry me!" The words were harsh, but his expression was touchingly tender. "I shall be the gentlest and most loving of husbands," he pleaded, his voice choked. "I'll never frighten you, I promise.

No one will ever call me wild. Once we're wed, I'll prove to you that there's nothing in me to be afraid of.''

She gave a little sob and flung herself against him. "I'll marry you, Matt,'' she said, burying her face in his shoulder.

She tried not to enjoy his reactions to her words—his breath of relief, the tightening of his arms about her, the touch of his lips on her forehead. She despised him, really. He was a coward, a liar, and a killer, and she was glad she'd just pushed him over the precipice to his destruction! In less than a fortnight he would come crashing down to a terrible emptiness, a terrible loneliness and the terrible pain of living forever with what might have been. Of course, she was hurtling down with him, locked in his arms as she was. She would come crashing to the same disastrous end.

But she did enjoy his reactions . . . she couldn't seem to help herself. *Oh, well,* she thought, *for the moment there's no real harm in it.* For the moment she might just as well enjoy these inexplicable sensations that overwhelmed her when she lay in his arms like this. Soon enough there would be nothing to feel . . . nothing, that is, but regret and pain.

Twenty-one

Matt put forth several good reasons for setting an early date for their wedding, the most logical being a necessity for them to leave London as soon as possible. He explained that it did not behoove a decent gentleman to be seen going about everywhere in the company of a new love when just having broken with an old. It would not be kind to Viola if his behavior encouraged speculation among the gossips of the *ton* that she'd broken with him because he'd found someone else. It was all very well for Viola to be seen with Dolph, of course, but Matt would be a cad to behave in that way. Everything possible had to be done to maintain the fiction that it was the *female* of the pair who broke the troth; the male had to pretend to be the party to be pitied. He had either to appear in society in a lonely state and with a long face, or he had to disappear. And since Matt could not bear to appear anywhere without being in the company of his new beloved, the only answer was to leave London. If they were married, he explained, they could go abroad for a month or two and be constantly together without constraint. By the time they returned, their marriage would have ceased to be a subject for gossip.

Tess was happy to acquiesce. The sooner this business was over, she knew, the better it would be for everyone. She found his companionship too wonderful to bear, and she realized that the longer she enjoyed it, the more difficult the end would be. Therefore it was agreed between them that they would keep their "understanding" secret, that Matt would arrange for a special license, and that a small ceremony would be held in Lady Wetherfield's library with only Lady Wetherfield, the Quimbys, and the bride and groom in attendance. With arrangements thus simplified, the wedding could take place in a week.

It was a week that Tess would never forget. She and Matt rode together every morning at first light, before the bridle path was generally used, either ambling along side by side engrossed in whispered conversation or racing madly down a stretch of path feeling the wind whip at their faces. In the afternoons they strolled down unfashionable streets, poking into out-of-the-way shops and buying each other ridiculous presents like a briarwood pipe for Matt, who never smoked, and an enormous and completely impractical Russian sable muff for her. They took tea and dinner at either Letty Wetherfield's or Julia's, and both their hostesses were kind enough to allow them several hours alone.

Those could have been the best times of all, if Tess had been able to be herself. They sat together, sometimes deliciously entwined, sometimes with Matt stretched out on the rug in front of her chair with his head resting on her knee, while he told her about the estate in Essex—the manor house with its turrets, its hidden passages and its enormous public rooms; and the grounds, with their beautiful gardens, shaded walks, and unspoiled woodlands. Sometimes he spoke seriously about his plans for the modernization of the farms; sometimes jokingly about the sort of pompous Country Gentleman he would someday become. He liked to tease her, too, about her forthcoming role as countess, as hostess of the estate, as housewife, and mother. Because she so often seemed abstracted, he had the impression that she was terribly absent-minded, and he drew amusing word-sketches of the new Marchioness of Bradbourne getting utterly lost in the manor house's miles of corridors and not finding her way back for days.

Tess, on the other hand, could not speak freely. Since she was locked into her role as Sidoney Ashburton, she had to guard her tongue at every moment. Once she forgot herself and almost made a serious faux pas. He had given her an entertaining account of the first time he'd jumped a fence on horseback and had fallen into a shallow brook. He'd broken his ankle and had lain helpless in three inches of bubbling water until he was rescued by the pretty barmaid of the local inn who'd come wandering into his vicinity to keep an assignation with her swain. This reminded Tess of *her* first spill from a horse, and she was halfway into the tale when she remembered that *her* rescuer had been none other than Jeremy! That was a name that Lotherwood was certain to find familiar, and her brain raced about like a crazed rat in a cage to fabricate a fictitious name that would sound convincing. She managed to complete her narration with a minimum of awkwardness, but she resolved never again to indulge in reminiscences.

Another topic that had to be avoided was the wedding trip. Matt had made out an itinerary that would make any girl's heart dance in anticipation: Naples to see the blue grotto, a fortnight each in Rome and Florence, and then an indefinite period to, in Matt's words, "rest in dissolute luxury" amid the breathtaking beauties of Venice. Planning this dreamed-of journey (that she knew they'd never take) caused her too much pain. To silence him on the subject, she told him that she wanted the details of their wedding trip to be a surprise.

It was only when they engaged in the sort of lovers' badinage that all betrothed couples exchange that Tess could permit herself to be natural. It was delightful to participate in such conversation: to identify with absolute precision the very first moment they each knew they were in love; to describe with gurgling laughter each one's very first impression of the other; to recall each early encounter in exact detail and reveal the quips, comments, and retorts each had been tempted to deliver but resisted. For that sort of conversation there was no need for her to inhibit herself, and she enjoyed it to the full.

After each delightful evening Tess found it necessary to remind herself of the reasons she was living this terrible lie. As she lay tossing in her bed, she told herself over and over that he was a coward, a liar, and a murderer. Never once, in all their intimate exchanges, did he indicate by so much as a word or a look that he harbored a horrible, guilty secret. As far as she could tell, he'd put the coaching accident completely out of his mind. It was as if he had no conscience at all. *There's not a man, woman, or child in this world whose life was made worse because of me*; not only had he said those words, but he seemed actually to believe them! It was difficult to remember, when she was with him, that this warm, charming, straight-forward-seeming fellow was in reality a blackguard. Only by constantly repeating those words to herself was she able to strengthen her will to proceed with her plans.

They were to be married on Thursday, one week to the day following their betrothal. On Wednesday, after their morning ride, she permitted him to drive her back to the Quimby house in his carriage, but she informed him on the way that it was to be their last encounter until the wedding. "You must stay away for the rest of the day," she told him. It took all her self control to keep her voice steady, for she knew it was the last time she would ever see him. At this moment all her bags were packed and ready for her return to Todmorden, and a carriage had already been hired to come for her as soon as darkness fell. Julia and Edward were rehearsed in their roles for the evening. By this time tomorrow, Matt would be in mourning, and she would be back home, her London "idyll" over. But there must be nothing dramatic or significant in her farewell to him today. To become overly emotional would be to give the game away.

He was handling the ribbons, as he had done the day of the rainstorm, preferring his own driving—and the privacy it afforded—to the presence of his coachman. "Stay away?" he asked, his eyes on the road. "Whatever for?"

She gave a flippant wave of her hand. "You are not permitted to see the bride till the wedding day," she declared, keeping her voice light.

"But why, my love?" He took his eyes from the horses for a moment to throw her a look of amusement. "You've consistently denied it, but I think that in the secret depths of your mind you're superstitious. Do you honestly think my dropping in for tea will bring bad luck?"

"No, but I shall not tempt fate. Besides, I have too much to do. Julia's dressmaker wants to put the finishing touches to my gown, and I must complete my packing for our trip. And one thing more . . ." She smiled at him with what she hoped was bridelike fondness. "I must pick up a special wedding gift I had made for you."

"Wedding gift? From the bride to the groom? That's a custom I've not heard of before. Is it a family tradition of some sort?"

"Not that I'm aware of. It's my own idea. You'll be giving me a ring tomorrow that I shall wear forever. It seems only fair that I give you something, too.''

"Splendid idea. I accept.'' He pulled back on the reins lightly to slow the horses' pace. "What is it?''

"I think it should be a surprise, don't you?''

"No, I don't. You know you'll receive a ring from me. Why can't I be similarly informed?''

She hesitated. She hadn't intended to tell him about it, but, on consideration, she supposed there would be no harm to her plot if she did. "It's a fob for your watch chain.'' She gave a gurgling little laugh. "I've thought of the most appropriate design for it.''

"Oh?'' Catching the teasing note in her voice, he turned from the horses with eyebrows raised suspiciously. "Appropriate, is it? Let me guess. If it's a fob, it must be a gold piece of some kind. I know. A gold disk with a diamond set in, to represent your diamond of a husband-to-be.''

She tossed her head scornfully. "Conceited jackanapes, aren't you? Diamond indeed! As if I could afford such a thing. I'm not a marchioness yet, you know.''

Unperturbed, he went on. "A gold heart, then. With our initials all intertwined in florid script, surrounded by dozens of curlicues and flourishes.''

"Oh, pooh! I am neither so sentimental nor so commonplace. It's a gold *cock's comb*, if you must know. And well you deserve it!''

He laughed. "Your point, my dear! I never would have guessed, but I can't think of a more appropriate symbol. I shall wear it for all eternity, as a constant reminder to stay humble.''

They drew up at the Quimbys' door. While he concentrated on stopping the horses, she stared intently at his profile. She wanted to remember every detail of his face . . . the strong line of jaw, the narrow, vertical crease that dented his cheek, the dark eyes, the heavy brow, the thick hair that, despite its short-cropped Corinthian style, never looked properly combed. But his attention to the horses was momentary, and as soon as he turned to her, she dropped her eyes.

He climbed down from the carriage and came round to her door. "This is good-bye, then,'' he said cheerfully, assisting her to alight. "Until tomorrow at ten.''

"Yes,'' she said, unable to match his tone. "Until . . . tomorrow.''

He lifted her hand to his lips. "After tomorrow, thank heaven," he said with a rakish glint, "I shall be able to kiss you properly when we say good-bye."

She lowered her head and gulped down the tears that had suddenly gathered in her throat. "No one seems to be about," she suggested, attempting a mischievous smile. "Why don't you kiss me properly right now?"

He was delighted to acquiesce. He pulled her close and lifted her chin. "*Damnation*," he muttered before he could proceed further, "here's comes Julia's blasted butler."

There was nothing to be done. He let her go, bowed over her hand, and returned to his seat in the carriage. She watched numbly as he waved farewell and, without remaining to see the carriage disappear down the street, turned and followed the butler into the house. She handed him her riding crop and walked slowly up the stairs. There was no hurry; her hired coach would not be arriving for hours. She had all day to weep.

With his impending nuptials a secret, Matt could not celebrate his last evening of bachelorhood with the traditional carouse, but he went to White's anyway, hoping to forget his impatience for the morrow by indulging in cards and drink with his cronies. After the usual exchange of pleasantries, however, and two hours of piquet, he'd had enough. He arrived home before eleven, three hours earlier than was his wont, but he was nevertheless surprised to find his man waiting for him. The fellow had standing orders not to stay up for him on the nighs he attended his club. "Why aren't you in bed, Rooks?" he asked, handing him his hat and stick.

"Visitors, my lord." Rooks couldn't hide a look of concern. "Sir Edward and Lady Quimby. I've put them in the drawing room."

A premonition of disaster struck Matt like a body blow. Frowning, he strode across the hall to the drawing room and threw open the doors. "Julia? Edward? What—?"

They had been sitting silently side by side on the sofa, but they both rose at the sight of him. "Ah, here you are, Matt," Edward mumbled, and cast an enigmatic look at his wife. Then he cleared his throat. "We've come on . . . er . . . a most unfortunate . . . that is, I am sorry to . . ." He paused and looked at his wife again in obvious discomfort.

"Good God," Matt exclaimed impatiently, "speak up, man! Something is obviously wrong. Is it Sidoney?"

Edward dropped his eyes. It was Julia who answered. "Yes, Matt," she said in a voice that shook. "I . . . we . . . don't know how to tell you—"

"Has she taken ill? Is that it?"

"There's been an accident," Edward said, keeping his head lowered.

"A terrible accident," Julia amended, taking a step toward him.

Matt felt himself suddenly transplanted into a nightmare—the kind in which one tries to move quickly but everything is slowed down as if the air were made of water. "Please," he muttered hoarsely, "just tell me. How badly is she hurt?"

"She is . . . gone," Julia said.

"Gone?" Matt stared at her in utter disbelief. "You don't mean *dead!*"

"Yes," Edward said flatly. "She's been killed."

No one spoke or moved for a long moment. It was Matt who broke the silence. "This can't be! It's a game, isn't it! This is Miss Sidoney Ashburton's idea of a game!" He took two strides to Julia and grasped her by the arms. "If this is some sort of joke, you can tell her for me it is *not* amusing. In fact I've a good mind to go over there right now, pull her out of bed, and *wring her neck!*"

"It's no game, my dear," Julia said, a tear slipping down her cheek. "I think you'd better hear the whole. It . . . happened about three, I think. She'd walked to Bond Street to pick up a parcel. The jeweler would have sent it round, but she insisted on getting it herself. She wanted to assure herself that the work had been done properly, you see, and . . . and she said she needed some air." Julia slipped out of Matt's slackened hold and sank down on the sofa, burying her face in her handkerchief. "It seems she picked up the parcel and then decided to hire a hack to take her home. There was a collision, and . . . and . . ."

Matt stared numbly down at her. Then he turned to Edward. "Is this *true?*"

Edward turned away. "I'm so sorry, Matt," he said with a sigh.

Matt felt the blood drain from his face. He swayed on his feet. Edward came up and steadied him. "Shall we ring for your man?" he asked gently.

Matt shook his head. "No, it's not necessary. I must . . . I can't seem to *think*. If you'll both excuse me, I'll . . ." With an abstracted, dismissive motion of his hand, he turned to the doorway.

Julia rose and followed him. "They found this parcel in her hand, Matt," she said, holding it out to him. "The one she'd gone to fetch. It was her wedding gift to you. We thought . . . Edward and I . . . that you might like to have it."

Matt stared down at it in horror. The little parcel was wrapped in tissue-thin white paper and tied with a silver ribbon. Tess had, in reality, done it up herself. And as if the dramatic scene she'd so carefully composed were not grim enough, she'd added a final, artistic touch: she'd daubed the white paper with a little smear of blood.

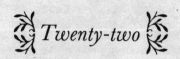

Twenty-two

Todmorden

22 June, 1812

My dear Dr. Pomfrett:

As you can see by the above, I have returned home, but before I settle back into the old routines of my life before London, I am taking this opportunity to write to you. I promised to let you know when the goal I set for myself in regard to the Lotherwood matter had been accomplished; you will be pleased, I think, to learn that it has. Lotherwood has been given his just deserts in a manner and degree completely appropriate to his crime. I was not present when the sentence was meted out, but my accomplices inform me that his suffering was not "hidden in his soul" but quite apparent to the onlookers. I am certain that he will never again deal carelessly with human lives.

I admit, dear doctor, that this experience was extraordinarily difficult and painful for me, but despite all, I am convinced that I was in the right to seek and achieve this retribution. It was only simple justice that Jeremy Beringer and all of you who suffered in that stagecoach accident be avenged. I must believe in that justice, or the thought of what I've done would be unbearable to me.

159

This letter to you is my last task in this affair. Now I intend to put the whole matter behind me and try to find, if not contentment, at least some peace of mind. I hope that now you, too, will be able to do the same.

Yours,

Teresa Brownlow

❧ Twenty-three ❧

Throughout the summer Lady Brownlow watched her daughter with increasing alarm. Something dreadful had evidently occurred to Tess in London, for the girl who'd come home was not the same as the one who'd gone away. She was quiet, introspective, pale, sad of eye, and devoid of the youthful energy that had been so much a part of her before. The girl rose reluctantly from her bed in the morning, pushed herself without enthusiasm through the routine of the days, and took herself up to bed at night with a sigh of hopeless weariness.

Lady Brownlow tried, by both direct and indirect questioning, to find out what had happened, but Tess would not speak of her two-month absence from home. She would only say that her visit to London had gone very well, thank you, Mama; that Julia and Edward had been the very best of hosts; that she had seen London Bridge, the Tower, St. Paul's, and the Elgin marbles; and that she intended never to visit the city again as long as she lived.

One day in late July, when the weather outdoors was too sultry to bear, Lady Brownlow sat with her needlepoint at an open window in the drawing room, wondering where her worrisome daughter was hiding herself. The girl's bedroom faced south, so it was hardly the coolest room in which to spend so humid an afternoon. Determined to find her and drag her down to the relative comfort of this northern exposure, she put aside her needlework and crossed the hallway to the stairs.

Before she mounted them, however, she glanced inside the open door of the downstairs sitting room and saw Tess slumped in an easy chair, her eyes fixed on the portrait of her father that hung over the fireplace. "Goodness, my love, whatever are you thinking of, sitting there like that?" Lady Brownlow asked from the doorway.

Tess barely stirred. "I was wondering about Papa. Tell me, Mama, was he a good magistrate?"

"A good *magistrate*?" She crossed the threshold and stared at her daughter in bewilderment. "I don't know what you mean."

"I mean was he considered to be a good judge of men? When criminals were brought before him, was he kind? Fair? Forgiving?"

"Good heavens, child, how should I know? I was never present at the trials."

"No, I didn't think you were. But you must have some impression. He told you about some of the cases he judged, did he not? And you must have heard others speak of him. Judges have reputations, don't they, of being easy or hard, honest or corrupt, prejudiced or fair?"

Lady Brownlow shook her head, wondering if her daughter was turning queer. But she nevertheless knit her brow and tried to answer the question. "Well, your father was not corrupt—that much I can say with certainty. He never lied; it was not in his nature. And from that I assume that he was also fair. But as to his being *kind*, well, I rather think not. He was quite unbending in his standards for himself, so I presume he did not bend them for others."

"Hard and unforgiving, then," Tess murmured.

Her mother shrugged. "I suppose so. But what difference does it make to you now?"

"No difference, really," Tess said, pulling herself up from her chair. "Except to determine if I am like him. I rather think I am."

"Hard and unforgiving? I would not describe you so, my love," Lady Brownlow said, taking her daughter's arm and strolling to the doorway. "In any case, since you are not a judge of criminals, what does it matter whether you are like him or not?"

Tess paused and looked once more over her shoulder at the haunting portrait. "Not a judge of criminals," she muttered to herself. Then, with a shake of her head like a puppy shaking off raindrops, she turned to her mother with a reassuring smile. "You're right, Mama. It doesn't matter at all. Come, let's go to the drawing room where it's cooler."

After two months of watching this behavior, her fears becoming more worrisome each day that her daughter was descending into an irreversible decline, Lady Brownlow consulted with her friend Lydia Beringer about the problem. Lady Beringer's health had seriously declined since the death of her son—a condition that required frequent bed rest and a style of living much more sedentary than it had been a year ago—but her mind was as sharp as ever. "Take her abroad," she advised the troubled Lady Brownlow. "When I was young, a trip abroad was considered the best cure for girls with broken hearts, broken troths, or broken spirits. I should think travel would be as effective now as then. Close up the house for a couple of months—I shall miss you dreadfully, of course, but it will be worth it if Tess is cured!—and go off to Florence or Lisbon or Geneva. Too bad that the dreadful Bonaparte keeps Paris out of our reach, but there's a whole world of exciting places the British nobility can visit with impunity. Take her abroad, my dear. It will do wonders for her, see if it doesn't."

To Lady Brownlow's surprise, she had no trouble persuading her daughter to agree to the plan. Tess was unenthusiastic but perfectly willing. She had no objection to taking a journey; as much as her mother did, she wanted to shake off the depression that had engulfed her. She had no real confidence in the curative powers of a voyage to a foreign city, but she was willing to try. Any distraction from her misery, even a temporary one, would be welcome.

The only subject of contention was where they might go. For some strange reason, Tess was adamantly opposed to visiting any city in Italy. She would not explain herself but merely declared that Italy was out of the question. "You may choose any other place on the globe," she told her mother, "but not Italy."

It was Lydia Beringer who actually made the final decision: Lisbon. Having done a great deal of travel in the early years of her marriage, when Lord Beringer had been in diplomatic service, she had many helpful hints to pass on to her friends who'd never been abroad before. "When visiting a foreign city," Lydia Beringer told Lady Brownlow, "it is always comforting to have in one's possession the address of a few friends (or friends of friends) on whom one can call. Such acquaintance helps one to become less strange; one learns one's way about, one makes other acquaintance, and before one knows it, one develops a circle in which to . . . well, in which to circulate! And I have a friend in Lisbon who will admirably answer those needs.''

She gave Lady Brownlow the address of a certain Senhora Carlotta da Greja, a London heiress born Charlotte Finch, who'd married a Portuguese merchant and now made her home in a charming villa in the heights of Ajuda, just outside the city. ''Be sure to call on her at once. She will know just where all the visiting English congregate and will help you to find gentlemen companions for Tess.''

But Tess found herself a companion even before she and her mother called on the Senhora. In the entryway of their hotel near the Terreiro do Paco (which the British visitors called Black Horse Square because of the huge equestrian statue at the center) Tess literally bumped into a round-cheeked young student evidently making his Grand Tour. Mr. Barnabas Thomkins, his head buried in a book, blundered into her and knocked her down when she was leaving the hotel on her very first outing. Red-faced and agonized, he helped her to her feet while uttering a profusion of apologies. In the midst of a sentence he gazed into her eyes and fell helplessly in love. From that moment on he took every opportunity to be at her side. He was quick to inform her that he'd taken leave from Cambridge, where he was a student of Romance languages, in order to take his tour. He'd been in Lisbon for almost a month, he said, and his expertise on the ways and byways of the city would be of enormous help to her. He insisted that he would be ''excessively delighted'' to put himself at her disposal as escort and guide. Since he gladly included her mother in his offer, Tess accepted his escort. For the first few days of their stay, the fellow proved indispensible and was almost always in their company.

After a week had passed, Lady Brownlow paid a call on Senhora da Greja, who received her most graciously. The result of the visit was an invitation to accompany the Senhora, in two days' time, on a trip to Cintra. ''It is the most picturesque mountain spot in the world, my dear,'' the senhora told her. ''There is a Portuguese proverb that says 'To see the

whole world and leave out Cintra is to travel blindfolded.' "
But the invitation was not merely for sightseeing; it included a
stop at the Beckford Palace, an estate that an eccentric and
wealthy Englishman named William Beckford had built two
decades before. "It is an astonishing sight," the senhora explained. "Pure white stone wrought in the Moorish style, with
a surrounding park of plants, giant ferns, and flora from all
over the world! There will be a fete, and every well-connected
Briton in Lisbon will be there."

Lady Brownlow returned to the hotel in a state of high excitement. When she told Tess and Barnabas Thomkins about
it over dinner in the hotel's dining salon, the young man
agreed that a visit to Cintra and the English palace would indeed be desirable. "I was going to arrange an invitation for
you myself," he said.

"Oh? Are *you* going?" Lady Brownlow asked with a touch
of dismay.

"Yes, I've been invited," the boy said. "The Beckfords are
acquaintances of the Marquis of Anglesey, who is somehow
related to my father."

If this explanation was incomprehensible to Tess, it was not
to her mother, for Kate Brownlow was well aware of the efficacy of good connections. But Barnabas Thomkins's good
connections notwithstanding, Lady Brownlow was not happy
at the prospect of having him as escort. After dinner, when
Tess excused herself and went up to bed, Lady Brownlow requested that the boy remain for a few moments at the table
with her. "Now, Barnaby," she said with blunt fondness (for
intimacy comes quickly to compatriots who make friends on
foreign soil), "I don't want you to take this amiss, but I don't
wish you to hang about Tess too closely at the Beckford
Palace. It is essential that she become acquainted with some
other, more eligible young gentlemen, and they won't approach her if you are always in the way."

"I *say*, Lady B.," the boy objected, "you can't be serious.
I'm as eligible as anyone else, ain't I?"

"You're an absolute dear, and Tess and I both adore you.
But she doesn't consider you a proper suitor, and you know it.
You're *years* too young for her."

"*Years?* I'm twenty-two!"

"Bosh! You're not half over twenty, if I have eyes in my
head. And though Tess is only twenty-four, she is years older

in experience. To her you are the little brother she never had."

Barnaby, pouting, propped his chin on his hands. "Yes, she seems to treat me so. But I've been hoping that in time—"

"In time, my boy, you will forget this infatuation as if it had never been."

"Infatuation!" He lifted his head, his round cheeks quivering in offense. "How can you call it infatuation? You can't know what I feel."

"But I do, Barnaby, I do," she said, reaching across the table and patting his hand soothingly. "I know that you will feel love for many and many a girl before you settle down. You have many such adventures before you. But Tess . . ." She paused, sighed, and began to fiddle with a teaspoon.

"What about Tess?" Barnaby prompted, leaning forward interestedly.

"She's suffered a great deal, you see," Lady Brownlow admitted. "She was to be wed, but on the eve of the wedding her betrothed was killed." She fixed a pair of pleading eyes on the young man's face. "She has not yet recovered from the blow, though it's been almost a year. If you truly cared for her, Barnaby, you would help me to help her."

Barnaby looked down glumly at the teacup still before him on the table. "So that's it. I wondered why she so often seems to be somewhere else in her mind. Very well, Lady B., I won't stand in her way. I'll even introduce her to one or two chaps with whom I'm acquainted." He rose and came round the table to help Lady Brownlow from her chair. "But if it ever should come to pass that Tess takes a fancy to *me*," he added, his usual optimism reasserting itself, "I hope that *you* won't stand in *my* way!"

They rode to Cintra in Senhora da Greja's open carriage. It was a fascinating ride through rugged, mountainous roads. Tess had brought along her copy of *Childe Harold's Pilgrimage* in order to read aloud the stanzas describing Cintra, but the lively senhora was already familiar with them and enchanted everyone by declaiming them aloud. When the high peaks ("the horrid crags, by toppling convent crowned," Byron had written) came into view, Tess found herself speechless at the awesome sight. The Beckford Palace was bound to be an anticlimax, she thought.

But of course it was not. It was like a magical oasis in the midst of Cintra's rugged mountain mass. The white stone of the building gleamed orange in the late afternoon sun, and the lawns, spread like carpet on the surrounding mountainside, were as lushly green and perfect as any in England. The reception was well under way when they arrived, the guests all gathered on the south slope, wandering about with their glasses of Amontillado on the graveled walks and among the wonderful trees and shrubbery that edged the lawns. Senhora Charlotte, as Barnaby called her, immediately bore Lady Brownlow away to meet their hostess. "Don't forget your promise," Lady Brownlow muttered to Barnaby before she was swept away.

"What promise, Barnaby?" Tess asked him curiously.

Barnaby frowned disgustedly. "I promised I would stay out of your way so that some other fellows might have a chance with you."

"Oh?" Tess laughed and patted his arm comfortingly. "Well, there's no need to take a pet. No 'other fellows' seem to be crowding about me to elbow you out."

"Yes, but they will, as soon as I introduce you to a few of them. Not that I see very many acquaintances here today whom your mother would consider eligible. There's Trevithick, mooning over there by himself near that grove of palms. He's all right, if you like moody Cornishmen. And there's Rob Westall, the fellow in the Hussar boots, talking to Lord and Lady Horleigh. He's going to be an earl, but he ain't much older than I. Oh, *there's* someone who might interest you. He drinks, but there's no telling what the influence of a good woman might do for him." He walked a few steps down the path and waved to someone in a group of ten or twelve people some distance away. "Lotherwood! I say, *Lotherwood!*" he shouted. "Over here!"

❧ Twenty-four ❧

Tess's heart stopped beating. She felt her knees turn to water and the blood drain from her face. "Barnaby, *don't*—!" Terror-stricken, she looked about her for a place to hide, but the world was spinning about in a dizzying pace, and she couldn't see where to go. If only she could sink into the ground, evaporate in a fog, or just die.

"What?" Barnaby had turned back and was looking at her strangely.

"Please! You mustn't *let* him . . . he mustn't *see* me!"

"But why not?" He glanced over his shoulder. "It's too late, anyway. He's heard me. Can't you see him coming this way?"

She looked round again, more desperately, for a place to hide, but she seemed unable to move. The only thing capable of motion was her mind. *He mustn't find me here!* her mind screamed. She had to find a hiding place . . . but where? And what if he'd already *seen* her! In absolute dread she covered her face with her hands, and, peeping through her fingers, lifted her eyes to Barnaby's face and followed the direction of his gaze.

There was a man making his way through the milling guests toward them, but it was nobody she'd ever seen before. She took her hands from her face as her pulse began to pump again. "That's . . . that's not Lotherwood," she breathed as the world slowly steadied itself.

"Ah, but it is," the strange gentleman said, coming up to them. He took a swig from the glass he carried before studying her with interest. "I'm a little squiffy, but I'm not drunk enough to forget my own name."

Tess's obvious agitation had unnerved Barnaby. He had to perform the introductions, but he did it with distinct unease. "Miss Brownlow, may I . . . er . . . present Lord Guy Lotherwood?"

"*Guy? Guy Lotherwood?*" She stared up into his face. This Lotherwood had thick black hair and broad shoulders, but there was no other resemblance that she could see. He was younger than Matt, one or two inches shorter, and more than a stone heavier. His features were handsome, but they were already somewhat coarsened by drink, the nose in particular. It was swollen and covered with the small red lines that come from heavy indulgence in alcohol.

"You are surprised, ma'am," he was saying. "I take it you are acquainted with my brother."

Tess stared at him in wonder. "If your brother is Matthew Lotherwood, the Marquis of Bradbourne, I *am* somewhat acquainted with him."

"Ah, yes," Guy Lotherwood said bitterly, taking another swallow of his drink, "but you find no family resemblance. Is that what so surprises you?"

"What surprises me, my lord, is that you exist at all. No one in his circle every mentioned to me that he had a brother!"

"It doesn't surprise me, however. You see, my dear, I am the proverbial black sheep. Quite unmentionable in family circles."

Tess was dizzy with these revelations. "I'm afraid," she said, putting a hand to her forehead, "that I must sit down. Is there somewhere we might go, Lord Guy, where we can talk?"

"I say, Tess," Barnaby cut in, "let *me* take you to a quiet spot. Guy, here, ain't in the best condition to keep a lady company. Said himself he was squiffy."

"Squiffy, old man, but not drenched. I'll take her to the grove of palms over there. You can trust her with me, I assure you," Guy Lotherwood said, waving the boy off and taking Tess's arm.

"Tess—!" Barnaby objected.

"It's all right, Barnaby," Tess said, abstracted but trying to smile at him reassuringly. "There's something I wish to ask his lordship that is of most urgent interest to me. There's no need to worry about me. If I don't return to your side in half an hour, you may come and fetch me."

She leaned heavily on Guy Lotherwood's arm as he led her down the path, her mind whirling with the possibilities this man's identity suggested . . . possibilities that terrified her to think about. There were things this man could tell her that might affect her very life.

He brought her to the palm grove, but in the cool circle of trees there was only one seat—a carved marble bench on which the gloomy Cornishman whom Barnaby had pointed out before was brooding. The Cornishman looked up at the sound of their footsteps, glared at them for intruding, and rose. Before either of them could apologize and back away, the fellow marched past them through the trees and out of earshot. "That was obliging of the fellow, I must say," Lotherwood said, laughing as he led her to the bench. "Do sit down, ma'am. May I go to find a drink for you? You look as though you could do with one."

"No, thank you, my lord. It shocked me to learn your name, but I shall soon recover. Please sit down. There is a great deal I wish to ask about you."

Guy Lotherwood raised one eyebrow curiously. "I can't imagine what about me should interest you, ma'am. I'm nothing more than what you see . . . the proverbial second son, the proverbial black sheep, the proverbial *persona non grata*." He took a seat beside her and sipped at his drink. "But I am quite at your disposal. What is it that you so urgently wish to know?"

Tess drew in a trembling breath. "A number of things, I'm afraid. I hope you won't think me idly curious. I have good reasons for taking this interest in you."

"I can tell from the excessive pallor of your cheeks, my dear, that your curiosity is more than idle. Fire away, then."

"You are Lotherwood's younger brother, I take it. Isn't it unusual that he never mentioned you in the two months I knew him?"

"I *told* you, Miss . . . Miss Brownlow, is it? . . . that I'm the black sheep. No family likes to refer to its black sheep."

"But what makes you the black sheep, my lord? Did you . . ." she paused and bit her lip nervously ". . . did you do something . . . d-dreadful?"

"I did several dreadful things," he said, draining his glass. Then he looked directly at her and smiled bitterly. "They were so dreadful he banished me."

"*Banished* you? *Matt* did?"

" 'Matt,' is it?" He raised his brows in a manner that reminded her of his brother. "You must have known my brother well."

She stared at him for a moment and then, with a little shiver, dropped her eyes. "Perhaps not well enough," she murmured, half to herself. It was another moment before she looked up again. "What do you mean, banished?"

"You know the word. *Banished. Exiled.* I am given a generous livelihood in return for having pledged my word never to set foot on English soil."

"I see. Would it disturb you very much to tell me what dreadful things you did to cause this banishment?"

He shrugged. "Again, I don't know why this should interest you, ma'am, but I suppose there's no harm in telling you. I cracked up three vehicles with devil-may-care driving. Destroyed two horses. Made any number of drunken scenes. Wounded a scoundrel in a duel. I should say for my brother that through all of this he stood by me, picked me up, dusted me off, set me on my feet, and saved me from punishment and disgrace. But then I did one thing more."

Tess felt her fingers begin to shake. "One thing m-more?"

He stared at the empty glass in his hand. "One thing that pushed him past his endurance. The last straw." He gave a mirthless laugh and threw his empty glass crashing against the nearest tree.

The sound of shattering glass coincided with a little cry that came from deep in Tess's throat. The look on Guy Lotherwood's face when he'd thrown the glass had cut her like a knife. It was the look Dr. Pomfrett had once described as "suffering in one's soul."

He turned back to face her, but his eyes did not see her. They were looking at some vision from his past he could not erase. "Do you want to know what that last straw was?" he asked. "I—"

Tess put out a hand as if to ward off what was coming. Two silent tears rolled down her face. "You wrecked a stage-coach," she said quietly, "and a man was killed."

He blinked as his eyes returned to the present and focused

slowly, bewilderedly, on hers. "Confound it, who *are* you? How did you—?"

There was no anger in the voice that cut him off. Only an unutterable sadness. "Jeremy Beringer was my betrothed."

"Oh, God!" Guy Lotherwood muttered, shutting his eyes in anguish. "Oh, God."

They sat there unmoving for a long while. Then he got to his feet and paced back and forth among the trees. When next he looked at her, he was startled by her appearance. Her face was as white as chalk, her hands were clenched in her lap, and her strange eyes were staring straight ahead of her with an expression of utter shock. It was as if the death of her betrothed had just occurred instead of having happened almost a year before. The look in her eyes undid him. That he could have been responsible for it was more than he could bear. In an agony of guilt he ran up to her, fell to his knees on the ground before her, and grasped her hand. "Forgive me," he whispered in despair. "Forgive me! I never meant . . . ! I would give my life if I could only . . ."

She looked down at him and laid a hand on his cheek. "No, no. There's no need," she said in a low, hoarse voice. "I haven't asked you all these questions to berate you. You have my forgiveness, for what it's worth."

"For what it's *worth?* If only I could *tell* you what it's worth!" He lowered his head until his forehead rested on her hand. "For all these months I've wished . . . ! Perhaps now it will be possible, someday, to forgive myself."

"I hope someday you will, my lord. If you do, you will be more fortunate than I."

There was a crack in her voice as she spoke that brought his head up. "What do you mean? What have *you* to forgive yourself for?"

She shook her head, withdrew her hand from his, and rose. "I think," she said, starting to walk away, "it is something worse."

"Something worse?" He got to his feet and stumbled after her.

"Oh, my God, it's *true!*" she said, looking back at him with an expression he would not ever forget. It was as if the truth she'd just discovered was the darkest truth one could learn. "It's something much worse than you've ever done!"

Twenty-five

Matt's summer passed in a fog of grief that was unrelieved by the solace society usually provides for those who suffer loss. Because there had not been any familial or legal connection between him and the deceased Miss Ashburton, society did not offer the usual mourning rituals: no wreath was hung on his door, no clergyman called with words of comfort, no stream of visitors came to express condolences, no friends gathered to share his grief. Because he'd had to keep his wedding intentions secret, very few of his circle even knew that Miss Ashburton existed. Sometimes he himself didn't believe she existed; his only tangible proofs of her presence in his life were the special wedding license, which had never been signed, and a little gold watch fob shaped like a cock's comb.

His aunt Letty knew she existed, of course, as did Julia and Edward Quimby. Letty tried to offer what comfort she could, but Julia and Edward seemed ill-at-ease in his company after the night they broke the news to him, and after a while he avoided them. Most of the others in his circle of friends had never even met Sidoney. Dolph and Viola, the two who had, were involved in preparations for their nuptials, and though they took brief notice of Miss Ashburton's sudden absence from the scene, they simply assumed that Matt had lost interest in her and that she'd gone back to wherever it was she'd come from. (It occurred to Viola, in a sleepless hour late one night, that she'd perhaps been hasty in severing her betrothal to Matt, but she put the thought aside. As her old nurse used to say: better to be a lesser man's first choice than a greater one's second.)

Matt did not regret that most of his friends knew nothing of his tragedy; he simply didn't believe that their sympathy, if they *had* known, would have been any real comfort to him. The blow of her death had left him reeling as nothing that had happened in his life had done before, and he soon realized that, if he was to regain his equilibrium, he'd have to do it for himself.

Letty did not neglect him, but sometimes he wished that she would. She visited him with devoted regularity, but her attitude toward his grief was not particularly soothing. "It was such a brief acquaintance," she'd point out repeatedly. "Too short to leave a lasting wound. You'll get over it. By fall, we shall find a new prospect for you. I've been thinking that perhaps it's time you began to think seriously about Miss—"

"I know . . . I know." He'd cut her off each time with a wry smile. "Miss Sturtevant. Cut line, Letty. I've no interest in new prospects."

For a while he continued to follow his usual daily routine. He dressed, he rode in the park, he met with friends, he boxed at Cribb's Parlor, he spent evenings at one or the other of his clubs. He even attended a ball or two and stood up with Dolph at the Lovell-Kelsey wedding. But the activities which had in former years seemed exciting and fulfilling were now empty and meaningless, and one by one he dropped them. His friends remarked from time to time that Lotherwood was turning mopish, but since sporting types were not inclined to be analytical, they did not pursue the matter.

More and more he preferred his own company. He spent hours each day walking through the London streets, letting his feet take what direction they would. His eyes did not notice much of what passed before him. His thoughts roamed where they willed, while the fingers of his right hand played with the little fob he'd hung on his watch chain. He spent much time thinking about that fob, for he'd discovered that Sidoney had had a few words engraved in tiny letters on the back: *I love you anyway.* The words now seemed to him an enigmatic message from the grave—a message that was, somehow, rather important to decipher. What exactly had she meant?

The *I love you* was clear enough, but what did she mean by *anyway?*

As the summer passed and the winds brought in the cool smell of fall, he continued to tramp the city streets. The sharp pain of shock had eased, leaving him with a dull ache in his chest that was even more depressing than the earlier, more stinging grief, for it bore with it the heaviness of permanence. But he'd begun to think about his future, which was a sign of the curative—though limited—powers of time. He decided that London held nothing more for him and that the only hope of a new life lay in Essex. On his estate in the south he would make himself heal. He would become the Country Gentleman he'd always planned to be. The prospect was the only brightness in what had become a grim, gray world. He did a great deal of planning during those long rambles, but even then his mind still occasionally gnawed, like a dog at a bone, on the question of the words on the watch-fob: *I love you anyway.* What had she meant by them?

The most obvious explanation was that she meant she loved him in spite of his being a coxcomb. It was a perfectly logical interpretation for a sentence of four very simple words, but somehow it didn't satisfy him. There was just enough ambiguity in that fourth word to keep him puzzling; it's indefiniteness had the same aura of mystery that was part of his memory of the girl herself. Sidoney had always been troubled by something in him, some serious flaw he himself did not recognize. He'd hoped that their marriage would sooner or later bring the secret to light, but now, of course, it was too late. Was this little message another indication that she had serious reservations about his character? Did she mean she loved him in spite of *that?*

He couldn't answer, nor could he guess that an answer would soon be found. And it was about to be found right there on the city streets.

It happened on a crisp day in late October. He had wandered east from Oxford Street, along High Holborn, across Gray's Lane and into Grevil Street. The streets were noisy and crowded with pedestrians and vehicles of all descriptions, for the Clerkenwell section of London was a far cry from the prosperous elegance of the West End. Today, however, there seemed to be greater confusion than usual, and he was forced out of his abstraction by an unusual burst of noise emanating from round the corner on Leather Lane. He walked round and discovered that a farm wagon, heavily laden with potatoes, had lost a wheel and tilted over. Some of the sacks of produce had slipped over the wagon's side and were now fair game for looting. While the farmer struggled with three of the looters, others came running over from all directions, tearing open the sacks or even lifting whole sacks on their shoulders and making off with them. Matt, feeling quite ripe for a good fight, waded into the throng in support of the farmer, throwing his highly praised right hook at any target that looked promising.

The force of his fist, combined with the din of the farmer's outraged shouts, were just beginning to take effect when a particularly enthusiastic pillager conceived the idea of using the loose potatoes as a weapon. He picked up a few of the hardest he could find and began to heave them about wildly. One of them struck Matt's forehead, right above his left eye. It felled him at once.

He toppled back and lay stretched out on the cobbles unmoving. A woman screamed. The noise and looting stopped at once, and the miscreants immediately ran round the corner to the busier Grevil Street and melted into the passing crowd. Only the farmer and the man who'd thrown the missile remained, staring down at the fallen pugilist with worried frowns. "I'm bum-squabbled," the potato-tosser muttered. " 'E looks t' be a *nob*."

"Aye. That's trouble for 'ee. An' serves ye right, I say."

"Is 'e dead, do y' think?"

"Nay, I sh'dna think so." He knelt down and listened at Matt's chest. "E's breathin'."

"Praise be. I din't mean 'im no 'arm, y'know. There's a doctor roun' on Brooke. Will ye gi' me a hand to take 'im there?"

"Be 'ee daft? There wouldn't be a sack remainin' t' take t' market when I came back!" the farmer declared.

"There wouldn' be a sack remainin' *now*, if 'e hadn' took yer part." He rubbed his stubbled chin speculatively. "Seems t' me a nob like this un 'd be 'appy t' pay ye fer yer trouble. More'n ye'd get fer *double* that load."

It was a convincing argument. The farmer lifted Matt under the arms, the looter took his legs, and they awkwardly dragged him back down Grevil to Brooke Street, to a neat, two-story edifice with a brass plaque near the door reading JOSIAH POM-FRETT, PHYSICIAN AND SURGEON.

Matt's first conscious thought was to wonder where the dreadful, stinging odor was coming from. He opened his eyes to find a stranger with wild gray hair and thick white eyebrows bending over him and holding a vial of spirits of ammonia under his nose. "Uch! Take it away," Matt muttered.

"Ah, that's better," the stranger said cheerfully and helped him to sit up. "Now, just sit still for a bit. I want to look you over."

Matt found himself in a bare, neat surgery, sitting on an examining table. His forehead throbbed badly, but he seemed otherwise in good condition. "How did I get here?" he asked the stranger, who'd turned aside to replace the spirits. "Are you a doctor?"

"I'm Dr. Pomfrett," the man said, returning to the table. "You were brought here from the Grevil Street corner by two loobies, one of whom admitted to throwing a potato at your noggin." As he spoke he lifted Matt's upper eyelids, one at a time, and peered into his eyes. "The scoundrel was full of apologies, of course. Said he didn't mean you harm. The other one seemed to want you to buy his load of potatoes." He ran his fingers skillfully over Matt's skull, feeling for signs of injury. "Since I gather that you'd sustained this injury by going to his assistance—and quite heroically, too, from the sound of it—I read them both the riot act and sent them on their way. There, now, let's get you on your feet and see how steady you are."

"Thank you, Doctor, for dealing with those louts," Matt said, rising carefully and putting a hand to his aching head. "I'll think twice, next time, before I let myself be drawn into a street-corner mill."

Dr. Pomfrett made him walk back and forth and then sat him down on the table again. "I don't think you've sustained a concussion," he said, turning to his shelves and taking down a bottle, "but you will have to be watched for a day or so. I'll give you some laudanum for the pain, which I'm afraid will be considerable tonight, but you should send for your own physician right away and let him examine you."

"I have no physician, Dr. Pomfrett. And you seem to me to

be quite competent. I'd be grateful if you yourself would provide whatever future examinations or treatment might be necessary."

The doctor paused in the act of pouring the drug from a large bottle to a small one and looked up at Matt quizzically. "I? Are you sure? I'm not the sort of doctor to attract your set, you know. I haven't a single member of the nobility on my list of patients."

"Well, you have one now," Matt said, smiling. He slid down from the table and offered his hand. "I am Mathew Lotherwood, Marquis of Bradbourne."

Dr. Pomfrett, in the act of putting out his hand, froze. "Lotherwood?" He blinked up into the taller man's face in confusion. "You can't be!"

Matt studied him curiously. "Oh? Why can't I?"

"Because I . . . I've met Lord Lotherwood. I remember him well. He was . . . stockier than you, a bit younger, features somewhat . . . coarser—"

Matt's expression hardened. "I think, sir, that you must be speaking of my brother."

"*Brother?*" The doctor's whole face seemed to go slack. His hands went about the business of closing the bottles of laudanum, but his eyes did not leave Lotherwood's. "I have never heard mention of a brother!" he said, placing the bottles down on the table like an automaton.

"Probably not, since he resides abroad." Matt's response was cool and aloof. "I'm afraid I don't see why the subject is of concern to you."

"Abroad? He resides *abroad?*" He came round to Matt's side of the table, rubbing his forehead nervously. "Has he been abroad for very long?"

Matt stiffened, bracing himself for who-knew-what sort of tale of his brother's involvement in yet another scrape, although it did not seem possible after the remorse he'd showed the last time. "I don't think I care to answer these questions, Doctor, unless you give me sufficient reason why I should do so."

"You *must* tell me!" the doctor insisted, a note of desperation in his voice. "Has he been away for more than a year?"

"No, something less than a year, I believe."

Dr. Pomfrett sank down on a stool. "It was *he*, then, and

not you!'' He buried his head in his hands. "Oh, my God, what have I done?''

Matt wondered if the potato blow had affected his ability to think. "I don't understand, Doctor. *What* have you done?''

The doctor couldn't bring himself to meet his eyes. "I think I've done you a great disservice,'' he said miserably.

"How can that be? We've never met until today. You haven't done me a disservice by *treating* me this afternoon, have you?''

Dr. Pomfrett shook his head. "How can I explain? I never thought . . . ! You see, he called him Lotherwood that night. Simply Lotherwood. He did not give a Christian name.'' He looked up at Matt with an expression of anguish. "How could I have guessed he was a younger brother without hearing the Christian name?''

"What night was that, Doctor?'' Matt asked, a glimmer of light dawning at the back of his brain. "The night of the stagecoach accident?''

"Yes, yes! No one *ever* spoke of a younger brother. How could I have guessed?''

Matt tried to cut through what seemed to him mere babbling. "*You* were on the coach that night?''

"Yes, I was. And the boy . . . the one who died . . . he recognized your brother when he climbed up on the box. *Lotherwood* is all he said. And I assumed . . . *assumed* . . . !'' He dropped his head in his hands. "How could I? I am a man of science. I am trained *never* to assume!''

"But I see no reason for this agitation,'' Matt pointed out calmly, although his mind was racing about trying to understand the doctor's ramblings. "You assumed it was I who drove the coach, and now you learn it was my brother. Does it make so great a difference to you which Lotherwood it was?''

"Not to me,'' the doctor answered, looking up. "To *you!*''

"To me? I don't understand.''

The doctor's eyes fell. "I think you have lately endured something which brought you considerable suffering, is that not so?''

"What *is* this?'' Matt demanded, a pulse beginning to throb in his temple. "What are you trying to tell me?''

"Simply that when she came to ask . . .'' He wrung his hands in abject shame. ". . . *I told her it was you!*''

Matt's heart lurched in his chest. "She?"

"Miss Brownlow."

"Miss Brownlow?" Matt's whole body tensed itself as if waiting for a blow. But the blow had actually struck him already, in the explosion of understanding that had suddenly broken upon his brain. It was not coherent; he would have to sit down and think over what had actually happened, step by painful step. But in the essentials, he *knew*. Nevertheless, he had to ask one last question. He had to *know* he knew. The words came out slowly, each with its own breath. "I . . . don't . . . know . . . any . . . Miss . . . Brownlow."

The doctor looked at him sadly. "Are you sure? I can describe her to you. She is tall, quite tall, with dark hair cut in a short, curly fashion, and—"

Matt had backed away as the doctor spoke until he was stopped by the wall. With a sound that was not a sob or a groan but something between the two, he turned and let his bruised forehead fall against it. "You don't have to tell me," he said, clenching his fists. "She had . . . *has* . . . ice-blue eyes."

Twenty-six

Soon after her meeting with Guy Lotherwood, Tess insisted on returning home. She was too miserable to endure traveling. She could not put on a bright morning face and accompany her mother through castles and cloisters, for every beautiful church, every frescoed tower, every magnificent mosaic and painting seemed especially designed to break her heart. Lady Brownlow, recognizing the increased unhappiness in her daughter's face, agreed that she would be better off at home. Lydia Beringer may have been right about travel being curative for some, but in Tess's case, it seemed to have made her worse.

They came home in late October to a chill, damp English autumn. Tess immediately retired to the hermitlike existence she'd indulged in before they left, seeing no one outside the household except for occasional visits to Lady Beringer, speaking only when absolutely necessary, moving about the house with a morose listlessness, and, when the long days were finally over, crying herself to sleep. Her mother, who sometimes listened outside Tess's door to the forlorn sobs, often wept herself, wondering what had brought such misery to her daughter and how it would all end.

One afternoon of a crisp fall day, Tess returned from a long walk to find her mother waiting for her right inside the front door. "Thank goodness you're back," Lady Brownlow said in a worried whisper. "You have a caller."

"A caller? Who—?"

"Sssh! Do you want him to hear you? He's right back there in the drawing room. He seemed too grand for the sitting room, so I put him in the drawing room and closed the doors."

"But, Mama, why did you find it necessary to close the doors, for goodness sake? Whoever it is will think you very inhospitable."

"I wanted to *warn* you. If I'd have left the doors open, he'd have seen you as soon as you came in."

"Warn me? Of what?"

Lady Brownlow wrinkled her brow. "I don't know, exactly. It's just a feeling. The way he asked for you . . . it made me jittery."

"Jittery? Why? Did he ask for me in some special sort of way?"

"I can't explain. It's just that he sounded so . . . so forbidding! 'Is this the residence of Miss Brownlow? Miss *Tess* Brownlow?' From his tone he might have been an exciseman looking for a smuggler, except that there's no exciseman in all of England with so exquisite a coat."

"What is this exquisite-coated fellow's name, Mama?"

"He wouldn't give it . . . not to Mercliff or to me. And there's something else that's strange. Mercliff told me that when he informed the gentleman that you were not at home, he ordered Mercliff to have his carriage taken round to the stable. Mercliff thinks he didn't want you to see it at the door. There was a crest on the side, you see, and Mercliff suspects that your caller feared you would recognize it and not see him."

"A crest? That *is* strange. What crest is there in the surrounding fifty miles that Mercliff wouldn't recognize?"

"Oh, my dear, this gentleman isn't from these parts. Didn't I tell you at once? He's from London."

"*London?*" Tess gasped, turning pale. "Good God, it can't be—! *He* couldn't have learned—!"

"Tess? What *is* it? Who—?"

But one of the double doors of the drawing room opened at that moment, and the London gentleman in the exquisite coat stood framed in the doorway. "Good afternoon," he said, his eyes on Tess. "Miss Brownlow, I presume?"

"*Matt!*" Her hand fluttered to her breast and clenched. "Oh, God!"

"Tess!" Lady Brownlow exclaimed. "Do you *know* this gentleman?"

"Yes, Miss Brownlow," the gentleman said. "Answer your mother. Do you know this gentleman?"

Tess's breath came in short, painful gasps. "Please, Matt . . ."

He turned to Lady Brownlow. "It seems she knows me," he said dryly. "In that case, may I have your permission, ma'am, to have a brief interview with your daughter in private?"

Lady Brownlow looked from his rigid face to her daughter's agonized one. "No, you may not," she declared firmly. "In view of my daughter's obvious distress, I think it better for you to say what you have to say before me."

"No, Mama, it's all right," Tess said, her voice shaking. "I will see Lord Lotherwood alone."

"You will do no such thing," her mother insisted. "See here, Tess, I don't know what this is all about or who this Lord Lotherwood is, but you are a young lady of proper upbringing, and I will not permit you to closet yourself in a room with this stranger unprotected."

"Lord Lotherwood is not a stranger to me." Tess stiffened her shoulders, walked to the drawing room and opened the second door. "Come in, my lord."

"Tess!" her mother cried as Matt gave her a brief bow, walked past Tess, and went inside. Lady Brownlow stormed across the hall. "Step aside, Tess Brownlow, and let me in."

"Go upstairs, Mama," Tess said with a quiet authority that brought her mother up short.

Lady Brownlow's show of matronly consequence wilted. There was something in Tess's expression that told her this meeting was something momentous in her daughter's life. "Tess," she pleaded, "why won't you let me—?"

"I will come up to you later, Mama." With that, she closed the doors.

Tess stood for a moment with her back to the room, trying to dredge up the courage to turn round. But he did not wait for her courage to come. "So you do have a family after all," he remarked. "It seems that everything you ever said to me was a lie."

"Almost everything," she admitted, facing him. It was her first close look at him in months. "Oh, my *dear*," she exclaimed, her arms going out toward him in an involuntary gesture, "how gaunt you are!"

"I haven't come to discuss my appearance, ma'am," he said curtly. "I just came to ascertain with my own eyes that the woman I idiotically took to be the deceased Sidoney Ashburton was really the living Tess Brownlow."

She took a step toward him, twisting her fingers behind her back. "How did you—?"

"I came upon a Dr. Pomfrett, quite by accident. When he heard my name, he was quite overcome. He realized at once that he'd sent you to the wrong man."

"Oh. I see," she said in a small voice.

He raised his brows. "You don't seem surprised to learn that you wreaked your monstrous vengeance on the wrong man."

"Well, you see, I'd learned it already. I met your brother, quite by accident. In Lisbon."

"Did you indeed?" He gave a sneering, contemptuous laugh. "I shudder to think of what must have occurred. What did you do to *him*, Miss Brownlow, when you learned the truth? Push him off one of Portugal's high crags?"

"Please, Matt, *don't!*" she begged, dropping down on one of the sofas and burying her face in her hands. "I know I did a t-terrible thing to you. I am s-so very sorry—"

"*Sorry?* How good of you!" He strode across the room to her and pulled her to her feet. "So you're sorry, are you?" The words whipped out at her, little knives cutting into the marrow of her bones. "Do you have any idea of what you put me through? Can you imagine what it was like for me these past months, trying to keep myself from visualizing you crushed and bleeding under the wreckage of a carriage? Reeling from the suddenness of it? Trying to make myself accept the finality of your absence from the world? Do you think your *sorrys* are an adequate atonement?"

His grip on her arms was bruising, but she didn't feel it. Anguished tears fell from her eyes. "Oh, Matt!" she moaned.

"Oh, the tears are splendid," he jeered acidly. "You always were convincing with tears. But I'm afraid your uncannily successful scheme worked so well that it hardened me." He threw her back upon the sofa and turned away. "I'm quite impervious to them now."

"What can I do, Matt?" she pleaded softly. "I would do anything—"

"Do you really think there's something you can *do?*" He went to the window and stared out at the leaves blowing about in the wind. "Can you erase the last six months and bring us back to the day before I laid eyes on you? Witch though you are, that is beyond your powers."

She tried to stem the flow of tears with shaking fingers. "I made a d-dreadful mistake, I know that. B-But I believed you to be guilty of a heinous crime—"

"That's just it, ma'am," he said, wheeling round. "That's just the point that I think you *still* fail to understand. Even if I *had* been guilty, any civilized purveyor of justice would have given me the right to *face my accuser.* Good Lord, woman, why did you never *ask* me?"

"I d-don't know! I wanted . . I waited for you to c-confess."

"No, ma'am. That's not good enough! Knowing me as you did, did it never occur to you that *just possibly* I might have had nothing to confess?"

"No, it n-never did," she said miserably. "The evidence seemed—"

"But the evidence was misleading, wasn't it? In the end it proved to be utterly wrong. The fact that evidence can sometimes be misleading is the reason why, in any enlightened court of law, the accused is given the right to speak before he is sentenced. *Before*, ma'am! Only a tyrant, a barbarian, or a supreme egotist would believe he knew all the answers before he asked the questions!" He turned back to the window and waited until the fury that had churned up into his throat receded. "You must have had yourself a grand time playing all the roles—Tess Brownlow as judge, jury, even *hangman!*"

"I kn-know you're right," she said, trying to swallow her sobs. "I *was* b-barbaric."

"The fact that you agree with me, my dear, doesn't change a thing." The words were said with an air of finality, and after he said them he strode to a table beside the sofa on which he'd placed his hat, gloves, and stick. "Knowing that anything we might say would be pointless, I hadn't intended to discuss the matter like this. I didn't drive all the way from London for recriminations, explanations, or apologies; they are all equally repellant to me. I only came to see Tess Brownlow with my own eyes." He placed his hat firmly on his head. "Well, I've seen her. That makes an end of it."

She watched as he pulled on his gloves with calm deliberation. She tried urgently to find something to say to melt the rigid coldness of his expression. There had to be something! He'd loved her once. He had been angry with her before, and she'd managed to win him back. Was it possible, even now, for her to do it again? But there was nothing she could think of to say that would in any way lessen the enormity of what she'd done. "I suppose you hate me now," she mumbled in helpless, childish desperation.

"You surely don't expect an answer to so ridiculous a question, do you?" he said, starting for the doors. "Good day, Miss Brownlow."

"Matt?" She jumped up and blocked his path. "Please! Is there no way for us to . . . to even *speak* to each other any more?"

Coldly, he placed his cane under one arm, put both hands on her waist, and lifted her out of his way. "No way in the world, my dear," he said, proceeding to the door. "I could never trust anything you'd say to me now. Now that I realize you lied about your name, your family, your past, your future, your feelings, your hopes, your intentions—about everything, in fact—it is not possible for me to believe you again."

"I didn't lie about *everything*, Matt. I *do* love you, you know."

"I don't know anything of the sort, though you've said it convincingly enough in the past. Even engraved it on the watch fob, didn't you? A masterly touch, that." With an abrupt twist of his wrist, he snapped the little cock's comb from his watch chain. With three quick steps he returned to her side, lifted her hand, and wrapped her fingers about the fob. "Here. It's yours. If what it says on this fob *is* true," he added with an unexpected softness, "it's a strange sort of love. I couldn't have done to someone I loved what you did to me."

The truth of those words was the greatest blow. Wincing with the pain of it, she had to lean against the back of the sofa to keep from reeling. When she regained her balance, she held the gold piece out to him. "I would rather that *you* kept it," she said. "Please!"

He wouldn't even glance at it but turned and strode to the door. With his hand on the doorknob, he paused. "I suppose, in a way, you should be complimented. Everything turned out exactly as you planned. I was completely duped." He shook his head as if everything was still incomprehensible to him. "I've never encountered anyone so adept at concocting falsehoods. If it weren't my aunt Letty who'd hired that blasted gypsy, I'd even be inclined to believe you bribed— Good God!" He turned and regarded her with an almost admiring revulsion. "Not that too! You *didn't—!*

Somehow, though her cheeks were wet, her lips were trembling, and her heart ached in her chest, she lifted her chin and said proudly, "Yes, I did! But I am not a liar. Not usually. I thought . . . I believed . . . that the end justified the means. I was very wrong. But you needn't insult me by assuming that I would lie to you now."

"Well, it hardly matters at this point, does it?" He threw open the doors and stepped into the hall. "I'll say good-bye again, Miss Tess Brownlow," he said, taking one last look at her. Then he smiled a wry, ironic smile. "So your name is Tess. *Tess,* of all names! So unpretentiously English. It suits you. How could I have been so stupid as to swallow a name as patently false as Sidoney? Of all the ways you made a fool of me, ma'am, it now strikes me that making me call you Sidoney was probably the most mortifying."

❧ Twenty-seven ❧

When the sound of Matt's carriage could no longer be heard, Tess retreated from the window, sank down upon the sofa, and waited for misery to overwhelm her. But it did not come. At first she didn't understand herself. He had left her forever, and with words as final and unforgiving as any could be. Why was she not awash in tears?

It took a several minutes of rueful contemplation before she discovered the single-worded answer: truth. What she was feeling was the blessed *relief* of knowing the truth and knowing that Matt knew it, too. The truth was indeed wonderful; only in its light could she see how dismal and grim living a lie had been. Some words that John Milton had once written sang in her spirit like a hymn: *Daylight and Truth meet us with a clear dawn.*

Relief flooded over her with the restorative powers of a fresh breeze. A short while ago she'd thought that her life would be forever devoid of hope. When she'd seen him standing in the library doorway, she'd been overwhelmed by shame. Revealed as a liar, a schemer, and a fraud, guilty of the cruelest misjudgment, she felt that her life had sunk to its nadir. But that low point had passed. In this new light of truth, both she *and* Matt could now begin to find a way out of the morass she'd created.

It was amazing how good it felt to know that he'd learned her true identity. Even if he hated her, at least he knew her now as she really was. No longer would she have to hide in shame. No longer would she have to carry in her heart the painful guilt that had weighed her down since her interview with his brother Guy; for Matt, freed by truth as she had been, would no longer be mourning the death of the imaginary Miss Ashburton. He was hurt and very angry, yes, but he was no longer crushed.

Tess's spirit, like a healthy bird kept too long in a dark, covered cage, flew up into the bright air of hope on wildly flapping wings. Someday, she told herself, she would see Matt again and make him love her. If he had once loved Sidoney, he was bound to love Tess, for in normal circumstances Tess was really an open, honest, loving girl. Sidoney had been calculating, dishonest, and manipulative, but time would prove to him that Tess was not. Someday she would find a way to make up to him for all the pain she'd caused. There had to be a way! She was determined to find it.

It was a letter from Julia that set her inventive mind working again. *We had a visit from Lotherwood,* Julia wrote, *in which he took us severely to task for our part in the deception. I must say, Tess, that he brought me several times to tears. I tried to defend Edward, but my dear husband would not let me. He told Matt that he was without defense; women were emotional creatures, he said, and one expected them to jump to idiotic conclusions, but he, a male, should have known better. I was hard-pressed to know how to defend him on the one hand and berate him for his insults to womankind on the other! In the end, however, Edward's abject regret for what we'd done impressed itself on Matt, and he forgave us. And oh, my dear, what a relief it is to feel like a truthful person again! If ever the occasion arises in which you find it necessary to concoct another scheme, you may be sure that neither Edward nor I (much as we love you) will aid or abet you in any way.*

Later that week we dined with Lady Wetherfield, the Kelseys, and the Fenwicks at Matt's table. (None of them are privy to the truth about you, by the way. I suppose Matt does not feel it necessary for them to know.) Matt took the occasion to announce that he is closing his townhouse and taking up permanent residence at Bradbourne Park, his estate in Essex. He seemed quite enthusiastic about the prospect of facing his duties as landowner and turning himself into what he calls a Country Gentleman. Dolph Kelsey spoke for all of us when he raised his glass and said that the extent of our sorrow at his departure is equal in degree to the fervency with which we wish him happy.

The letter was interesting to Tess in all its particulars, but the item that stimulated her instinct for invention was the news that Matt was leaving London. His Essex estate was huge, she knew, and on its vast acreage all sorts of opportunities might be found that her imagination could shape to her advantage. Her very first thought was that, in a newly opened household, someone (even someone inexperienced in the ways of the working classes) might find employment. And employment at Bradbourne Park might be the very means she was looking for! She held the letter aloft and danced about her bedroom in girlish excitement. Perhaps she had a future after all! At least, at this moment, there seemed to be the prospect of a clear dawn.

The manor house at Bradbourne Park, impressive though it was from the outside (its wide "panoramic" lines achieved by three long rows of windows and two flights of balustraded steps which led to a portico whose pillars and triangular pediment were acknowledged in architectural circles to be among the finest in England), showed the neglect of absentee ownership within. Of the one hundred rooms under its roof, half of them had not been used for a generation. But beyond ordering that all the rooms be closed but for a mere handful he needed for daily use, Matt took little interest in the interior of the house. His concerns were exterior: to learn the best ways to breed cattle, to help his farmers make use of new ideas and new machinery, to bring about some much-needed improvements to the homes of his tenants and to the outbuildings on his own lands. To assist him he hired an able Scot, Alistair MacCollum, as his bailiff, and it was with MacCollum that he spent his time. The management of the inside of the manor house he left to Rooks, whom he had brought with him from London, and to Mrs. Tice, the housekeeper who had run the household since the day his mother had come there as a bride.

Despite the fact that his lordship was using only fifteen rooms, his presence in the manor necessitated a sizable increase in the household staff: a cook and two kitchen maids, a baker, an additional scullery girl, a new upstairs maid, a general housemaid, and two footmen. Beyond giving his permission to Rooks and Mrs. Tice to hire whomever they needed, Lord Lotherwood did not take notice of the staff who attended his comfort. He had been bred to expect all household details to be taken care of without any effort on his part. He paid generous salaries and said "please" and "thank you" at all the right times. In return he expected tasty meals to be served, hot, whenever it pleased him to eat; to have his bed made daily and warmed before he retired, to have his clothes washed and pressed and waiting for him in their proper drawers or cupboards; to have fires burning in the grates of every room he deigned to enter; and to have everything he touched, leaned on, or sat upon clean and free from dust. *How* all this was done interested him not at all.

What interested him at this time of his life was the estate. He had much to do and much to learn. The enterprise which most demanded his attention was the expansion of the stables, which required the services of what seemed to him a small army of architects, stone cutters, masons, carpenters, and assorted other craftsmen and workers. This project, added to the duties he'd already taken upon himself of improving the farms and the tenants' homes, kept him busy all day and half the night. The problems of the household staff had no place on his mind.

It was surprising, therefore, when the name of one staff member seemed to come to his attention more than any other. Annie, the upstairs maid. The first time it came to his notice was a chilly night in November, when Rooks was pulling off his boots at bedtime. He noticed a bowl of bright red flowers on the table near his bed. "Where did those come from?" he asked curiously.

"From the greenhouse, my lord," Rooks explained. "If nobody picks the blooms, they only die on the vine, so we thought we might just as well use them to brighten your lordship's bedroom."

"That was most kind of you, Rooks," Matt said pleasantly. "Thank you."

"No need to thank me, my lord. It was the new maid thought of it. Annie's her name."

"Then thank this Annie for me, will you?" his lordship said, and thought no more about it.

The next time it was MacCollum who mentioned the name. Matt received a note from a Mrs. Whittle thanking him—in words of misspelled but sincere gratitude—for having fixed her dangerously crumbling doorstep. "What's this?" he asked his bailiff. "I don't know anything about fixing a doorstep."

"Dan Whittle's one o' the cottagers, m'lord. Seems yer upstairs maid . . . Annie's her name . . . paid 'em a call on her half-day, and she brought the matter t' my attention. I asked ye if I might send o'er one 'o the masons t' mend it, if ye recall, an' ye agreed."

"Well, I don't recall, but I'm glad it was done. Give this Annie my thanks, MacCollum."

Then there was the night Rooks served him a portion of some sort of poultry in a greenish sauce that he found most delicious. "What is this I'm eating, Rooks?" he asked.

"Couldn't say, my lord. I'll ask Mrs. Tice."

Mrs. Tice bustled in, beaming. "Do you really like it, my lord? Cook will be in transports. It's hazel hen in a puree of celery. Our Annie gave her the recipe."

His lordship raised his eyebrows. "Annie? The upstairs maid I've been hearing about?"

"Yes, my lord. A treasure, she is. Worth her weight, that one."

"Well, give the cook my compliments, Mrs. Tice. And Annie, too."

The very next morning Mrs. Tice sang the girl's praises to him again. On the way down to breakfast he passed the housekeeper hurrying along the corridor with an armload of linens. The woman was humming to herself happily until she caught sight of him. " 'Morning, your lordship," she said, dropping a curtsy.

"Good morning, Mrs. Tice. You're wearing a very cheerful face today."

"And so would you be if you'd seen your linen cupboards made over. Y'see, my lord, over the years everything got so confused like, I didn't know how I would ever make 'em straight. But now they're as neat and orderly as they could be. I tell you, your lordship, it's a joy the way she's set the arrangement to rights."

"She? Your Annie, I suppose."

"Oh, yes, my lord. She's a—"

"I know," he said wryly, making his escape. "A treasure."

It occurred to him as he ate his breakfast that he didn't know the name of anyone else on the household staff except Rooks and the housekeeper. The first footman, who was always on attendance at the door, might possibly have the name of Charles, but he wasn't even sure of that. But he could not avoid knowing Annie's name. This Annie was certainly making her presence felt in this house.

But the most impressive encomium the new maid received was from MacCollum a few days later. The two men were at the desk in Matt's study, a dim room on the second floor that faced north and was chilly even with a roaring fire. They were bending over the plans for the extension of the stables, discussing the direction the expansion should take. A wing on the east end of the present stable building, going northward, would make the most desirable design, but it involved destroying a lovely summerhouse that Matt's grandfather had built for his bride eighty years before. The summerhouse was made of stone, with graceful, fluted columns and a round base, and Matt had often played in it as a boy. "It's a shame to have to knock it down," he said with a sigh, "but it's the best thing for the stables."

"Y'know, m' lord," the Scotsman mused, "I was speakin' o' this verra problem in the kitchen today . . . takin' a wee bite o' luncheon, y'see . . . and yer maid Annie asked why we couldna just *move* the thing."

"Move it?"

"Aye. Lock, stock, an' barrel. 'Twould be a bit o' labor, mind, takin' the stones apart, but it could be done."

"It's a deucedly good idea," Matt said, studying the plans. "I don't suppose this Annie suggested a place where we might put it, did she?"

"Aye, she did that!" MacCollum laughed. "She said she spied a pretty promontory on the far side o' the lake. With a goodly bit o' shrubbery about the base, she said, it would make a fair scene, 'specially from a distance where one could see it reflected in the water."

Matt shook his head in admiration as he rolled up the plans. "This Annie appears to be quite the treasure Mrs. Tice says she is. We'll take a look at her promontory tomorrow, shall we, MacCollum?"

"Aye, we'll do that. 'Twouldna surprise me t' find she's picked the perfect spot."

They stowed the plans away on the bookshelves behind the desk and strolled to the door. "One of these days, I must take a look at this Annie, too," his lordship remarked with a grin. "If this house has a treasure, I ought to see it for myself."

❧ Twenty-eight ❧

They did not go to see the promontory after all, for a deep snow fell in the night and kept everyone imprisoned indoors the next day. With nothing better to do, Matt decided to tackle the account books, a task he'd been long avoiding. To his surprise he became completely engrossed, and even after hours had gone by he didn't look up from his labors. Day turned into evening. The wind picked up in the north and howled at the windows. And although the footman or Rooks came tiptoeing in every hour to replenish the fire, Matt had to blow on his fingers or hold them over his lamp to keep them warm. At dinnertime, Mrs. Tice stalked in and delivered a scold. "No need to do a year's work in one day, is there, my lord? It feels like the North Pole in here, it does. Why not come away and have a good, hot dinner. Cook's made some wonderful filets of veal and a pearled barley soup that'll warm you right through—"

"I don't want to stop right now, Mrs. Tice," his lordship said, not even looking up from his work. "Just bring me a bowl of that barley soup to drink right here, if you don't mind. And tell Rooks I could use a warm blanket to put over my shoulders. I'll be fine."

He went to bed very late, his fingers and toes almost numb. But his bedroom was cozy, his sheets had been warmed with hot bricks, and he went promptly to sleep. The next morning he was wakened by a streak of snow-bright sunlight which had crept in through an opening in the draperies and spilled across his face. When Rooks came in to help him dress, the butler looked as cheerful as the day. "We've a surprise for you this morning, my lord," he said with very unbutlerish glee. "I can't wait to show it to you."

As soon as his lordship was dressed, Rooks led him down to the second floor. "This way, my lord, just past the yellow saloon. Look!" And he threw open the door of a room that had been closed for years.

Matt gaped. The room had been newly painted an eggshell white and sported shiny new draperies of flowered chintz. There was a mulberry-and-cream-colored Persian rug on the floor that Matt remembered vaguely as having come from one of the long-unused bedrooms, and a velvet-covered wing chair near the window. His desk had been moved from his study and stood, gleaming with new polish, near a large fireplace over which a George Stubbs painting of two nuzzling horses (a work that had long been a particular favorite of his) was hung. His bookshelves, too, had been moved in, cleaned, polished and their contents replaced. "What *is* this, Rooks?" he asked, bemused.

"It's your new study, my lord," Rooks said with satisfaction. "We've moved you."

"But, good heavens, man, *why?*"

"Why, my lord? Because we all agreed that, if you were going to spend half the night at your accounts, you shouldn't do it in the coldest room in the house."

"But I don't mind the cold. I don't understand this, Rooks. Most of these things were in the other room just a few hours ago. How could you have moved everything in so short a time?"

"We did it after you retired, my lord. Mrs. Tice, Charles, Annie, Ben from the stables, and myself. We wanted to do it all at once so that you wouldn't guess what we were planning. To surprise you, you see."

"Well, you certainly succeeded. I'm dumbfounded." He walked about the room examining the details. "It was very thoughtful of you."

"But you don't seem very pleased, your lordship," the butler said, crestfallen. "Don't you like the room?"

"Oh, yes. It's a pleasant room. But I'm accustomed to my old study, I'm afraid."

The butler nodded knowingly. "Annie *said* you might not be pleased. 'Gentlemen can be very set in their ways when it comes to their workplaces,' she said."

Matt frowned. "Was this *Annie's* idea?" he asked.

A note of disapproval in his voice made Rooks shift his weight uncomfortably from one foot to another. "I suppose it was, my lord. Mrs. Tice and I were remarking, in the servant's hall, about you spending so much time in that drafty room, you see, and Annie wondered why you didn't change it, what with so many empty rooms to choose from. So one idea led to another, and we made the plans. There's still the wallpaper to be hung in the panels and another chair—" He glanced up at his lordship askance. "We'll put things back as they were, my lord, if you're displeased."

"No, it's a sensible change. I'm quite grateful, really. But I would like to have been consulted first. I know you all meant well, Rooks, but it seems to me that this Annie of yours has been taking a great deal on herself. Send her to me at once, will you? I'd like a few words with her."

Rooks bowed in acquiesence but bit his lip. At the door he paused. "Your lordship," he ventured, "you won't be too harsh with her, will you? She didn't mean any—"

Matt was already rearranging some of the books on the shelves. "You don't think I'll put her in chains, do you?" he said, turning and waving the butler off. "Just fetch her, and don't trouble yourself—" He stopped speaking, having noticed something gleaming on the rug. "Wait a minute, Rooks!" he said in a completely different voice. "What's *that?*"

"What, my lord?"

His lordship had turned white to the lips. "This!" he demanded, picking up a little gold piece and holding it out to the butler.

"Oh, that's nothing, my lord. Just a trinket. I think it's meant to be a cock's comb. It belongs to Annie. I've seen her wearing it on a chain round her neck. She must have dropped it. I'll take it to her."

"No, thank you," his lordship said between clenched teeth. "I'll take it to her myself." His eyes were blazing, and an angry muscle twitched in his cheek. He strode past the astonished butler and out the door. Then he swung about. "Where can I find her, Rooks?"

Rooks was both startled and disturbed by his lordship's sudden change of mood. He was not unfamiliar with his lordship's character, having been his butler and valet for more than fifteen years, and he recognized restrained fury when he saw it. For some reason quite beyond Rooks's understanding, Lord Lotherwood was about to vent the full force of his spleen on poor Annie. "Right *now*, my lord?" he asked, temporizing.

"Yes, right now!" his lordship barked.

"Doing up your bedroom, I surmise, my lord. This time of day is customarily—"

But his lordship had already taken off down the corridor. Rooks ran after him. "Do you wish me to accompany you, my lord?"

"I wish, dash it," his lordship muttered, wheeling round, "that you'd go about your business. I don't want to see you again this morning! Do I make myself clear?"

"Yes, my lord." Rooks watched as his lordship disappeared up the stairs. *Poor Annie*, he said to himself with a sigh and, shaking his head in bafflement at the peculiar ways of the nobility, went down to the servants' hall.

Matt threw open the door of his room with a crash. The draperies had been opened, and the room was flooded with white sunlight. Almost silhouetted by the brightness was an aproned, mobcapped female whom no tricks of light could disguise. Caught in the act of shaking out his comforter, she jumped and uttered a frightened little scream.

He surveyed her icily for a moment while his eyes adjusted to the glare. Even in her neat black housemaid's dress with its starched white collar and apron, and that silly cap covering her dark curls, there was something imposing about her. He wondered how that special quality had been overlooked by his household staff. He supposed it was her talent for dissembling that made them accept her so easily as one of their own. "So you're Annie this time, eh?" he said with devastating contempt. "Can't you *ever* use your own name?"

Tess, clutching the comforter to her chest, dropped a curtsy. "G-Good morning, your l-lordship," she stammered.

He leaned on the doorjamb and folded his arms. "What sort of game are you playing this time?"

"Nothing harmful, I promise you," she said, giving him a tremulous little smile.

"You aren't so foolish as to believe I would take your word, are you? What are you doing here, ma'am?"

She took a step toward him, the comforter dragging on the floor. "Please believe me, Matt," she begged softly. "I only wanted to do something to . . . to make amends."

"Good God, woman, do you think that hiring out as a housemaid and making my bed is making *amends?*"

She shrugged helplessly. "It was all I could think of. Besides," she added proudly, "I do more than your bed, my lord. Have you seen your new study?"

"Yes, I've seen it. Did you really think it could make a difference? I don't want your services, ma'am," he flared. "I don't want your good works." He strode across the room to her, pulled the comforter from her grasp, and threw it on the bed. "I don't want you in my bedroom, I don't want you in my house, I don't want you anywhere in my vicinity!"

The bitter anger in his voice seemed to have no effect on her. She kept her eyes fixed on his face. "But you needn't know I'm in your vicinity. I've been here a month, yet you didn't know until today that I was anywhere about."

"Only because I'm an idiot. With all the talk I'd been hearing about Annie, I should have *guessed.*"

She smiled. "You would not have guessed. You are only here now because you found the fob."

That startled him. "Are you saying you left it there on *purpose?*"

Her eyes searched his face questioningly. "It was an impulse. I was so proud of having done up your new study. Oh, dear. I've made a mistake, I think. It was too soon . . ."

"Everything you *do* is a mistake! Don't you see it even yet? You make everything into some sort of . . . charade! A watch fob becomes a symbolic talisman, a racer becomes a murderer, a spoiled girl becomes a housemaid. You change identities as easily as I change my coat! What on earth is *real* to you? Tell me, ma'am, do you think all of *life* is a game?"

She had anticipated having some difficulty with him, but she hadn't expected his bitterness to be so lasting. If this *was* a game, she was playing it badly. Alarmed, she put a hand lightly on his arm. "I know that coming here as a housemaid is, in a sense, playing a game. But I didn't know how else to do something tangible to make up for what I'd done. I shouldn't have revealed myself today. It was indulgent of me. Can you pretend that today didn't happen? Let me stay, Matt. I'll never bring myself to your notice again. Let me try, by working here, to do something useful for you.''

He brushed her hand away. "Don't be a fool," he said, turning away. "I want nothing to do with your pretendings." He went to the window and squinted into the sunlight. "Go to your room and pack your things. I'll have my carriage made ready to take you back to Todmorden. The snow is melting. You'll be able to leave as soon as the roads are passable."

She didn't move. "It isn't a game to *me*, you know. Coming here and serving in your household made my life bearable again. It made me feel a little less . . . blameworthy. If you send me away, it will be like a prison sentence to me."

"And what do you think it would be to me if you stay?" He whirled on her furiously. "Do you seriously think I could bear living here knowing you were somewhere in the house?"

For the first time her eyes wavered. "Oh, Lord!" she muttered, dismayed. "Do you hate me as much as that?"

He shut his eyes for a moment, as if he wanted to blot out the sight of her. "My feelings for you are quite beside the point," he said, trying to behave sensibly in what seemed to him an utterly implausible situation. "The point is, ma'am, that you are playing a role again . . . a role you obviously can't continue to play indefinitely. Go home, and for once in your life, try to live it as yourself."

"How can I, without you?" she murmured sadly. "Loving you as I do."

For some reason that innocent remark infuriated him. It seemed to him to be too facile, too lacking in sincerity. It sounded like Sidoney, toying with him again. "Stop it!" he said between clenched teeth. "I don't want to hear those words from you again!"

"*Matt*," she cried in chagrin, "why won't you *believe* me?"

"I believed you once and paid for it dearly." He held the gold watch fob out to her. "Here, ma'am, take your bauble and go. It will be better for us both to make an end of this."

Her eyes searched his face for any sign of vacillation, but there was none. She took the fob from him and walked slowly to the door, defeated. The grim days, like all those she'd suffered through before, were about to envelop her again. She had no choice but to follow his orders and leave. *But, dash it all*, she thought suddenly, *I am not a housemaid! I don't have to depart like a meek little mouse!* Taking a deep breath, she drew herself to her full height and wheeled about. "Very well, Matthew Lotherwood, I shall go. We'll make an end of it. I shall play no more roles. But before I go, you will listen to me speak my true mind for once! I know I've lied, I've dissembled, I've treated you with the cruelest injustice. But I've never, *never* lied about the words on this 'bauble.' It says I loved you even when I thought you a liar and a murderer. It says that, whatever you were, I loved you *anyway*." She was making an earnest effort to speak calmly, but her voice began to shake and a tear slipped down her cheek. She dashed it away angrily with the back of a hand. "You are my Grand Passion, whether you choose to b-believe it or not! If you think I would come here as a *servant*, to rise in the morning before five—which I assure you I'd never done in my *life* before!—to wash in a tiny bowl of ice-cold water, to wear this ugly black bombazine monstrosity, to scrub floors and empty chamberpots and do all manner of lowly things if it were not for love of you, then you haven't the brains you were born with!"

He stared at her, overcome. Standing there in the doorway, tall and proud, she looked as magnificent as she'd looked the day at the Elgin marbles, in spite of the incongruity of her apron and mobcap. He didn't know what to make of her or his own feelings. He was essentially an uncomplicated man, he believed. He'd spent his life in sporting pursuits where every contest was very clear. The goals were marked, the opponents recognizable, the results conclusive. But these matters of love were much more confusing. In his mind he and this girl had had a match in which he'd been the loser. She had not played fair, of course, but he'd taken his loss like a gentleman. Was she here for a rematch? Could love be played like a boxing match, in which the opponents return for another go? But even if it were, he didn't dare step into the ring with her after the beating he'd taken. Oh, no, not he!

She turned on her heel and marched out the door with her chin in the air. In that second, like a momentary flash, he knew that he *had* to enter the ring again. There was no hope for any happiness in his life if he didn't. The truth was that no matter what name she called herself or what she did to him, he would love her *anyway!*

He took a stumbling step toward the door. "*Tess,*" he muttered hoarsely, "Tess!"

She heard him. He'd never called her by her own name in that way before. Hesitantly, not trusting the shiver of joy that had bubbled up in her veins at the sound of his voice, she glanced over her shoulder at him. That one look was all she needed. "Oh, Matt!" she sobbed in relief as she flew across the room to him and flung herself into his arms.

They kissed until his knees grew weak, and then he sank on the bed, drew her on his lap, and kissed her again. It was a long while before they could speak. It was she who finally broke the silence. "I told Mama this might happen," she said with a sigh, "but I didn't really believe it."

"Your mother must be a queer sort of parent, to permit you to leave home to become a housemaid," he remarked.

"She *didn't* permit it. Even when I told her I would wed you or no one. I had to steal out of the house in the dark of night. You know, of course," she added plaintively while nevertheless snuggling contentedly in his arms, "that we can never be wed."

"Oh?" He took off her mobcap and, nestling her head on his shoulder, placed his lips on her hair. "Why not?"

"How can we? How could we explain it to the world? How could you present me to Lady Wetherfield or the Fenwicks or your friend Dolph? What could you say: 'I'd like you to meet my wife, the deceased Miss Ashburton'? Or, 'This is my wife, the Sidoney Ashburton that was'? It's quite impossible."

"Is it?" he murmured, blissfully entranced by the charm of a tendril that had curled around her ear.

"Unless we can concoct a plausible explanation. Sidoney could have had a *twin*, perhaps, or—"

"Not on your life!" he declared, lifting his head sharply. "We shall be wed quite properly with our true names, and when the time comes for me to present you to the world, you will tell the *truth!*"

"The truth?" she exclaimed, appalled. "Matt, no! I promise I shall always tell the truth to *you*—always!—but, my love, it would be quite awkward to have to—"

"Awkward or not, you will face everyone squarely and admit *everything*. There has to be *some* punishment for your heinous crimes. If you ask me, you are getting off much too lightly." But he softened these stern pronouncements by kissing her again.

"Lord Lotherwood!" came a shriek from the doorway. The lovers lifted their heads to find a scandalized Mrs. Tice gaping at them. "I can't believe my *eyes!*" she gasped in horror. "That *my* Lord Lotherwood would ever be found fondling a housemaid is something I never thought to live to see! *Fondling* a *housemaid!* It's the most shocking sight these old eyes of mine have ever *seen!* Have you no *shame?*"

Matt looked down at the girl in his arms with a barely disguised gleam. "Well, ma'am, are you just going to sit here gloating while my reputation as a gentleman is torn to shreds? You're the one with the remarkable talent for scheming and concocting tales, are you not? Well, then, let's see you concoct something to get me out of *this!*"

A STIRRING PAGEANTRY OF *HISTORICAL ROMANCE*

Shana Carrol

___ 0-515-08249-X Rebels in Love $3.95

Roberta Gellis

___ 0-515-07529-9 Fire Song $3.95
___ 0-515-08600-2 A Tapestry of Dreams $3.95

Jill Gregory

___ 0-515-07100-5 The Wayward Heart $3.50
___ 0-515-08710-6 My True and Tender Love $3.95
___ 0-515-08585-5 Moonlit Obsession $6.95
                    (A Jove Trade Paperback)
___ 0-515-08389-5 Promise Me The Dawn $3.95

Mary Pershall

___ 0-425-09171-6 A Shield of Roses $3.95
___ 0-425-09079-5 A Triumph of Roses $3.95

Francine Rivers

___ 0-515-08181-7 Sycamore Hill $3.50
___ 0-515-06823-3 This Golden Valley $3.50

Pamela Belle

___ 0-425-08268-7 The Moon in the Water $3.95
___ 0-425-07367-X The Chains of Fate $6.95
                    (A Berkley Trade Paperback)

Shannon Drake

___ 0-515-08637-1 Blue Heaven, Black Night $7.50
                    (A Jove Trade Paperback)
